ATTIC LETTERS
Secrets of Love and War

Laurie Gifford Adams

ATTIC LETTERS

SECRETS OF LOVE AND WAR

LAURIE GIFFORD ADAMS

WINDSWEPT PUBLISHING

Attic Letters: Secrets of Love and War

Copyright © 2019, Laurie Gifford Adams

First Edition

ISBN: 978-0-9904647-4-7 (print version)

This is a work of fiction. All of the characters, names, incidents, organizations, and dialogue in this novel are either the products of the author's imagination or are used fictitiously. Because of the dynamic nature of the Internet, any Web addresses or links contained in this book may have changed since publication and may no longer be valid. The views expressed in this work are solely those of the author and do not necessarily reflect the views of the publisher, and the publisher hereby disclaims any responsibility for them.

Windswept Publishing

Stanley, New York 14561

windsweptpublishing@gmail.com

Printed in the United States of America

Windswept Publishing

06/18/2019

Cover Design and Interior format by Kris Norris

CHAPTER ONE

November 1994

The rosary beads Maggie Coughlin clenched were hot from an hour of unrelenting use. If there was hell on earth, then surely, she was dancing at the gates. Despite being in the presence of God, the devil was grappling for her soul.

The decisions she and Timothy had made decades ago had seemed right. Now, the truth slithered around her conscience like a venomous snake with fangs exposed and ready to strike.

She didn't move from the pew four rows from the front, nor did she turn her head to watch the last parishioners leave Mass. She stared straight ahead at the crucifix hanging between the two stained glass windows above the altar.

Guilt clawed her conscience, making her stomach

raw. For decades she'd lived with the fear that this day would come.

The slight shuffle of Father Prior's feet gave away his approach. Out of the corner of her eye, Maggie saw him stop at the end of the pew in front of her, genuflect as much as his seventy-year-old knees would allow, then move into the wooden seat. He slid across until he was slightly to the left in front of her. For a moment, he closed his eyes and lowered his chin. Then with a barely audible, "Amen", he made the sign of the cross.

"You are troubled, Margaret." He was one of the few people who called her by her given name. Her husband's brother, Father Michael, was another. Father Prior had been his protégé.

"Aye, deeply troubled, Father." The truth was, she hadn't been this frightened since she was a young lass stepping on the boat with her parents to emigrate from Ireland. She dropped her gaze to the back of his skullcap. Fine white hair peeked out from around the edges.

"I made a bad decision, Father, and now I fear it will cost me my son."

The priest tipped his head slightly, and in his quiet tenor voice asked, "Do you need confession?"

Maggie pursed her lips. She had no doubt her confession would be face-to-face with Daniel when he finished reading the letters. "No, I've done my penance for my actions, Father."

"Then what do you wish of me?" the priest asked.

Maggie leaned slightly forward and whispered, "I need the box and envelope Father Michael left with you."

The priest stiffened. "Daniel knows?" His voice was a hoarse whisper.

"He will soon. The truth should have come out sooner, but I was always afraid I would lose him."

"God gave you the child, Margaret. It was His will. You must not question but go on faith."

Tears gathered in her eyes. The *child* was now almost fifty.

Her heart ached. Daniel was the only child she and Timothy had been blessed with. If this had all been God's will, then was it His will now to take her son away?

Maggie closed her eyes to retreat into prayer. She heard Father Prior slide across the pew then walk up the aisle. The rhythmic padding of his soft-soled shoes was nearly drowned out by the blood swooshing in her ears.

"Please, Lord," she whispered, "tell me that I am doing the right thing." Tears stung her eyes, and she sighed with resignation. "Thy will be done, even if it means I lose my son."

Her eyes were still closed when she heard Father Prior return a few minutes later. Maggie finished her prayer, crossed herself, then kissed the rosary beads twined in her arthritic fingers. She was doing this for Daniel.

When she opened her eyes, Father Prior stood at the end of the pew holding a very large dark cherry-colored wooden box.

"The envelope is in the box," he said.

Maggie swallowed the lump in her throat and nodded, her heart pounding. For years she'd imagined what the box looked like and fantasized about its contents. But it wasn't for her to open. Giving Daniel the letters would be difficult, but giving him this box and envelope had the potential to drive him away forever. If what he learned saved the relationship with his own son, she had to believe that was God's will, too.

∽ઠૐ

Daniel didn't believe in ghosts or haunted houses. But one thing was certain; the crate his mother had insisted he drag out of her attic and take to his house did haunt him. He'd tossed and turned since getting into bed, unable to clear his mind of the urgency in his mother's voice as he'd left her house earlier. Now, the scene played out in his mind for the umpteenth time.

"Ye need the healin' that's in those letters," she'd said, the slight lilt of her Irish accent still discernible. And as she shooed him out her door, she made him promise on the Bible that he'd read every one of the dozens of letters she'd bundled. "What could possibly be so important in a bunch of old letters, Ma?"

The gray box was bulky, and it banged against his thigh as he lugged it down the concrete front steps. If she hadn't been so insistent that he read the letters inside it, it would still be sitting in her attic, right where she said it had been for almost fifty years.

"What ye'll read may hold the answers ta the troubles between ye and yer boy." She followed him down the sidewalk to his car, her spryness still a source of amazement. Her three mile walk every day kept her in better shape than anyone else in the family.

"You've read them?" he asked

She nodded. "Every last one of 'em. Some I wrote."

He set the crate on the back seat of his blue, late model Buick and slammed the door.

"Then why don't you just save me the trouble and tell me what they say? You know how crazy it is right now with Christmas just around the corner."

She tucked her wrinkled hands in the pockets of her flowered bib apron and shook her head.

"No, Danny Boy, I'm not goin' ta tell ye what's in there because the message is more powerful first hand. And it's exactly what ye need now. There shouldn't be trouble in the family at Christmas."

She stepped forward and reached up to lay her warm, time-worn hand against his cheek. Her hand smelled like fresh baked bread, the same homey essence from his childhood.

"I sorted through 'em," she continued. "The most important for ye to read are the ones with the red braided string around them. Someday, maybe ye'll want ta read all of them in the crate, but for now, listen to me. What those letters have ta say to ye is somethin' ye'll need ta work through on yer own."

"Maybe I'll read them with Liz and —"

"No!" His mother grasped his forearm and squeezed. Her gray eyebrows pulled together to reflect what looked like anxiety. A shard of panic sliced through his chest.

"Ma, I've never kept important things from Liz."

"In the end, I know ye won't be keepin' anythin' from her." She shivered against the cold mid-December air and slipped her hands back into her apron pockets. "Ye'll tell her in due time, but not 'til ye've read all this for yerself. And if there's anything ye don't understand, ye ask me." She peered around him to look through the car window at the crate. "If I'm not missin' me guess, the letters will heal the trouble between ye and yer boy and change yer life. Ye just have ta trust me on this one, boy."

Boy. He was approaching fifty, and she still referred to him as boy. But he loved her dearly for her wonderful mothering. He'd grown up as the center of his parents' universe. And when he'd married and had kids, his parents' universe expanded. With his father now gone, Daniel had grown even closer to her.

He pecked her on the cheek. "Get back inside before you get pneumonia, Ma."

"Ye promise me, Danny."

He made the sign of the cross. "God is my witness," he reassured her. "Now get back in the house."

She had complied but waited with the front door open to wave goodbye with a worn dish towel she'd produced from her apron pocket.

When he'd returned home, he'd lugged the crate into the house, more aware of the weight than when he'd first picked it up. He knew the crate wasn't heavier than when he'd placed it on his back seat, but it banged against his thigh and pulled on his shoulders as if it were weighing him down. He'd left it in the den, vowing to himself that he wouldn't be pressured to read them. But, the truth was, even though the crate was out of sight, the question of its contents had weighed on his mind all night.

Now, hours later, here he was, sitting on the edge of his bed wide awake well before dawn, his mind churning. He rested his elbows on his knees and laid his head in his hands. Since Liam had announced his engagement to Mora over the weekly family dinner a few weeks before, he'd hardly slept. Something had to give.

The clock in the hall downstairs chimed. Daniel

rolled his forehead against his rough palms and squinted toward the digital clock on the nightstand on his side of the bed. Four-thirty! At this rate, he'd be worthless at work in the morning. He wouldn't want to be one of the passengers on his train. And the trains were full these days with the heavy traffic of post-Thanksgiving shoppers headed to and from Manhattan.

He glanced over his shoulder at Liz. She was snuggled into her plush pillow, her lips buried into one of the deep creases. In the light cast from the street lamp, he could just barely make out the faint shadow her eyelashes created against her cheek. Lord but she was beautiful.

At least with her eyes closed he couldn't see the bridled irritation in their green depths. In their nearly thirty-year marriage there'd hardly been a cross word between them, and now, her silent accusation was palpable. This was the first time in over a week that she'd slept facing him. It had been the longest week of his life. He wanted things right in his family as much as his mother and wife did.

And all this because of Liam. Why couldn't the boy see how difficult his marriage to Mora, a Jewish girl, might be once they had children? They were so blindly in love that they couldn't fathom that at some point they'd have to decide what to teach their children. He worried that Liam would abandon his own faith for himself and the children. He wasn't prejudiced or anti-Semitic he'd told Liam when the discussion became heated, just realistic and practical.

Forcing his fingers through the thinning hair at his temples, he gave up the fight. He wasn't going to get a decent night's sleep until he at least looked at those letters from the attic. With another glance at Liz, he knew the truth was he wouldn't rest until he and Liam had made peace. They hadn't spoken since that Sunday dinner. He'd seen Liam cruise by the house in his patrol car, but there'd been silence otherwise. Liz had talked to Liam, tried to ease the estrangement, but Liam vowed that with or without his father's blessing, he and Mora would marry.

An image of the crate and the echo of his mother's insistent words filled his mind. He couldn't imagine how those letters could help, but he didn't have a better solution.

He rose gingerly from the bed to minimize the groaning of the springs. When the floorboards creaked under the carpet, he froze in mid-stride. He held his breath, listening for her soft exhalations. Finally satisfied, he continued around the end of the bed. After retrieving his reading glasses from the top of the dresser, he stepped into the hall, softly closing the door behind him.

It wasn't until then that he realized his lungs were ready to burst. He'd been holding his breath for fear even breathing would wake his wife. A faint wash from the nightlight in the bathroom illuminated the hallway. He walked past his youngest son's room. Brendan, a junior at Keuka College in the Finger Lakes, would be home for the holidays soon.

He thought again of Liam. He was first born, smart as hell, and stubborn as a mule. He'd graduated from NYU with a pre-law degree but opted to take the test to become a police officer. And for the last two years he'd patrolled the 94th Precinct. It was the same station where Daniel's uncle, John Patrick Coughlin, had been a policeman until he enlisted in the Army in World War II.

Daniel heard the bedsprings in his room creak. He cocked his head to listen for telltale movement, hoping Liz had just turned over. A few seconds later, she stepped into the doorway. She leaned her head against the doorjamb and squinted against the night light.

"Danny, what are you doing? Are you okay?" Her voice was raspy with sleep. Between that and her thin, satiny pink nightgown, she made a sexy picture, but he pushed the amorous thought aside. The problem with Liam had chilled any ideas in that direction.

"Yeah, fine," he answered. "Just going to get something to drink."

She rubbed a fist against her eyes as an unstifled yawn made her beautiful pink lips form an O. The yawn ended on a sigh, and she started to turn toward the bedroom then stopped. Frowning, she asked, "Why do you have your reading glasses to get a drink?"

He glanced down at the wire-rimmed glasses dangling between his fingers. "I'm having trouble sleeping. I might look at those letters Ma gave me. Go back to bed, Honey. I'm sorry I woke you."

Apparently satisfied, she turned and shuffled back into the bedroom. He drew in a deep breath and let it out slowly. He missed lying next to Liz and holding her as she slept cradled against his shoulder. He missed feeling her feathery breath warm his bare skin. But they'd argued more than once over his stubbornness in this situation. According to his mother, he now had the means to repair this rift.

The crate. Could it really hold the answer that would

put an end to all this tension and anger? Although he knew Liz was curious, she'd been respectful of his mother's wishes for him to read the letters alone, first.

He'd never known his mother to be wrong. He could only pray this was the case again.

On his way through the kitchen he slipped his glasses on top of his head, grabbed a glass of milk from the refrigerator, and a clawed hammer from under the sink. He carried both to the den, drinking three quarters of the milk before he reached the door.

He flicked on the light switch just inside the door and stared at the crate. His heart thudded. The cool milk residue clung to his upper lip, and after backhanding it, he glanced at his trembling hand. Suddenly irritated, he crossed the carpeted floor and set the glass on the tidy desk. What the hell was he afraid of? An old wooden box?

No, he was afraid he couldn't fix what he'd broken.

"Okay, Ma," he mumbled as he knelt in front of the crate, "I pray to God you're right about this."

A rectangular piece of yellowed paper was taped over on the gray lid. On the paper was John Patrick Coughlin's name, but the address was for Daniel's parents' home in Bay Ridge. Taking a bolstering breath, he forced the clawed side of the hammer under the edge of the lid.

Since his mother had opened it recently, the nails easily backed out of the dried wood. Despite that, halfway through the prying, the top splintered in the middle and one portion fell away. He set aside the hammer and removed both pieces of the lid, resting them against the light stand.

Inside was worn, dark brown, canvas oil cloth folded

over onto itself. The pungent, musty odor of old paper and oil assaulted him. An unexplainable ominous feeling gripped his core. He wrung his fingers, aware of how cold they were. He shook out his hands then reached to open the cloth. It was so brittle that it ripped when he pulled back the folds. When it kept folding back onto itself, he put his whole arms in, holding one side back with his elbow. An omen. A warning, he feared, that whatever was inside might not be easy on him.

The crate was jammed with envelopes tanned by age and the effects of the oil. Laid on top were three bundles of probably a couple dozen letters each, tied with red braided cords. Below those, the rest were unbound, neatly arranged in stacks that lined the crate walls.

Several photographs slipped out and scattered among the letters. The brittle corners curled in. He picked up a few of them. The first one was of a woman, whom he guessed to be in her early twenties, with the Eiffel Tower behind her. Her wavy dark hair hung to her shoulders. He flipped the photo, but there was nothing written on the back. Turning it over to look again, he caught himself nodding appreciatively. Whoever this was, she was a pretty woman. There were holes in the four corners as if this picture had been tacked up.

Another picture was of a group of three army buddies, two of them shoulder to shoulder standing in front of a large building with the red medical cross on the roof. None of the men looked familiar. On the back of that one was November 1944, Liege - Hub, Artie and Joe. Daniel smiled at the obvious camaraderie. They looked young and cocky. Immortal.

Sadness radiated through his chest. Was his uncle the

only one of the group of friends who didn't return home from the war?

Two other pictures showed the same woman again, one with her surrounded by several young children, and the last one with an infant tucked against her slim hip. He brushed at a tiny, jagged crack in the image between the woman and child. The fragile paper ripped a little more, seemingly separating the two. There was no information on any of those photos, so he set them back in the crate, hoping some later clue would help him identify her.

He pulled out the three bound stacks of letters. The top envelope with a cancellation date of January 26, 1944 was addressed to his uncle, John Patrick, with an APO address. He pushed the braided string toward the edge of the stack of letters to flip them up and see the other dates. It appeared his mother had arranged these letters chronologically.

Mixed in between were letters dated from January 1944 through the end of December 1945. He'd been an ace in history in high school, particularly when it came to the highlights of World War II. He knew from these dates that his uncle's stint in the army medical corps had taken him through the time periods of the D-Day Invasion of Normandy, Hitler's death and the surrender of Japan. As far as Daniel knew, his uncle had never been involved in combat, but still, he'd died during his service time in Europe. The circumstances had always been murky, and Daniel always felt the subject wasn't one to be broached.

He retrieved one of the letters from farther down in the first stack and held it close to the lamp. It was addressed to Annie Goodman in Paris, France. He studied the name, trying to recall its significance. There wasn't even an inkling of recognition. Shaking his head, he laid the letter back on its pile and picked up a telegram addressed to his grandparents. It was dated October 1945. He started to open it, then stopped. There was no doubt concerning its content, and he assumed that would be the last correspondence to read.

He grabbed a stack of letters so thick he could hardly get his hand around them. After gulping down the remaining milk, he used his bare foot to push the crate closer to the black leather recliner near the window and settled into the chair's soft seat.

Finally, forcing himself to shake his anxiety, he slipped the corded tie from the letters.

The first few told of Uncle John's journey from Brooklyn to Rockford, Illinois where he underwent training to become an army medic. The next set of letters jumped to Fort Dix in New Jersey, chronicling the time before he shipped out to Europe. These were mostly short missives describing some of the other soldiers, duties and living conditions.

Daniel parted the opening at the top of the next envelope and slipped the letter from the square sleeve. The tanned crispness of the paper released more of the musty smell of age. Nostalgia permeated his senses, and he settled back into the chair to allow the story in the letters to take him to another time. Another life.

And, he prayed he'd find the answers he needed to heal his family.

CHAPTER TWO

20 Apr 1944
0330 hrs

Dear Maggie,
Yes, it really is the middle of the night and I'm using a small candle for light. I hope I don't set the blankets on fire, but I needed to get this off my chest. You may be my sister-in-law but to me you're like the sister I never had. My brother is a lucky man! I hope you know how much I appreciate your letters.

I'm sorry it's been so long since I wrote. But I couldn't. You see I hit a rough patch. I was glad I got home before we ship out to Europe but in some ways, I guess it was the worst visit of my life.

When Patty took me to the bus station she kissed me good-bye. A FINAL good-bye. She said while I was at medic training she realized that she couldn't marry me. It made her nervous that I was going to war, but more than that she said she knows she can't marry a policeman. I told her I would give it up for her if that's what she really wanted. But that was just her way of justifying what she told me next.

She fell in love with somebody else while I was away. I suspect it might be someone with money because nice things are important to her. They are going to be married and live in New Jersey. I think probably it's someone she knew before.

I know Patty was never your favorite person and maybe now I know why. You could sense something about her that I couldn't. Maybe I was shallow. Maybe I never looked past her pretty face and nice figure. Maybe I never really knew her. Maybe I didn't give her enough of what she needed. Maybe I didn't love her enough. I know those are a lot of "maybes", but I must have done something wrong. I wrote to her every day while I was away, and she wrote back too.

Every time a new letter came I put it in my shirt pocket and carried it with me so I could read it whenever I wanted. Then when a new one came I put the old one with the rest in my duffel and kept the new one. I keep rereading all of her letters looking for a hint of what I did wrong.

It hurts, Maggie girl. Maybe I'm just not meant to have what you and Timothy have. I want a wife. I want children. And I thought Patty did, too. So, I guess the first casualty of this war for me was the love of my life. After she left me at the station I wondered if I could go on. Crazy thoughts I know, but I felt like I couldn't face this war without her to come back to.

I'll write Mama and Pop a letter after this to let them know in case they see her. Rejection really rips the spirit out. Maybe now that I've told somebody tomorrow will be a better day.

Thank you for listening.

With love from your brother-in-law,

John Patrick (J.P.)

May 4

Dearest John Patrick,

My heart breaks for you. I am truly sorry about Patty. It is her loss not yours. No, I never trusted her with someone as special as you and I will not say I told you so. She has a pretty face but a black heart. There is someone out there for you, J.P., I just know there is. The kind of love you give to people is the kind to be treasured not taken for granted.

She was a taker not a giver. Maybe now you can see how everything was for her. She did not deserve to be with someone who was so giving and put everyone else first. You did not do anything wrong dear man. There is no one who loves more blindly than you.

Maybe you do not want advice, but I am going to give it to you. Throw those letters away. Reading them will give you nothing but heartache. You will find someone else because anyone who is not blind can see the kind of person you are. Your future wife and children will be the luckiest people in the world.

I will not say any more on this subject. Only look forward.

Timothy called me from his base yesterday. For now his unit is going to stay in the states. I am so happy. This means sometimes he will be able to come home.

Every day is still so ordinary for me. I just finished taking in the laundry. It is sitting next to me in the basket and it smells crisp and clean. Sometimes it is hard to just do the everyday things knowing that soldiers are dying in this godawful war. We hear the reports on the radio and I buy a newspaper every day but it still does not seem real. Doing these ordinary chores helps me believe that one day everything will be back to normal. You and Timothy will be home safe and sound.

The flowers are in full bloom so I guess it is true that summer is coming. I think I might take a job. Without Timothy's pay our savings are dwindling. What he gets from the army is not enough. But this country has been good to us so we are not wanting to complain. I may take a waitress job at O'Shea's Pub. I already talked to Kevin and he said he could use the extra help.

I will post this today so maybe you will get it before you ship out. We miss you and Timothy so.

Take care of yourself and let go of that love you had for Patty. There is someone more deserving waiting for you.

Your favorite sister-in-law,
Maggie

16 May 1944
2000 hrs

Dear Maggie,

I only have a few minutes, but I wanted you to know I took your advice. I burned every damn letter from Patty. We ship out tomorrow and I needed this part of my life to be behind me. I watched the smoke curl up from the paper and it felt good. You're right. I don't need her. I'm sure I will love her for a long time because I can't just turn love off like that. But I know she's out of my life.

In some ways I'm anxious to get to Europe. It feels useless

to get this training to just sit here in Jersey. I won't be sorry to get over there and have the war end though.

I have to crawl into the bunk. Thanks for being such a good "sister".

With love,
John Patrick

5 June 1944
1915 hrs

Hello Maggie,

Well girlie, it's hard to believe that I made it across the Atlantic. Out of Fort Dix we went up to the city and took the Queen Elizabeth across to Wales then England. Holy Mary did I get sick. For five days I hung over Lizzy's rails. The guys joked about the green skin looking like it belonged on this good Irishman. It made me wonder if my mother and father got that sick when they came to America. How about you, girlie? You were old enough to remember when you came from the great Emerald Isle. Were you as green as the grass yourself?

It didn't help that the damn Germans were out there in the ocean hoping to sink us. I thank God that good old Elizabeth was so fast or the U-boats probably would have caught up to us.

It's not bad over here in England. I thought everything would be bombed, but it's not like that where we are. I heard Buckingham Palace got hit but our news isn't always right.

The civilians are taking good care of us and all of our troops. We made friends with many and they invite us into their homes to have tea and cakes, and sometimes even whole meals. I've buddied up with a guy named Hubbard from Connecticut. We call him Hub. He and I have become friendly with the Bradford family. They have two daughters, Christine and Margaret. I think Hub is particularly taken with Margaret. Christine is shyer, but we have taken some walks. A couple of nights ago we took the girls dancing. They play American music here so it makes me feel like I'm home.

Does Timothy write to you or did he forget he was married when he got in the service? For all the kidding I do I think he knows how lucky he is to have you. I could only be so lucky to find someone like you to love me. You're such a doll.

I'll be glad when this war is over and we can get on with our lives. I miss my family. I'm not going to lie. I miss Patty. It's hard to know she's not there for me anymore. We planned to get married, you know. As soon as I got out of this damned war. I still get that ache in my gut when I think about her. I almost wrote her a letter the other day.

I'm better off talking about what's happening here because thoughts of home are getting me down. Our first job is to set up a hospital. I've seen lots of wounded men who have come here from the front. They are being shipped back to the States. Lots of them aren't even whole any more. As soon as we stepped off that boat in England and saw some of the troops that were being shipped back injured I knew I'd never take life for granted again. War is hell Maggie girl.

I guess it's time to get some shut eye. Thank you for writing to me. I get letters from Mama once in a while, but I think it's hard for her to write to her son in a war. She tells me that she's wearing out her Rosary beads. I thought she did that when we were all younger and raising hell. I guess it's up to you to keep my morale up. I'm counting on you.

I'm sure you know by now if you see black marks through

parts of my letters it's from the censors. Most of what we write doesn't matter even about our location because we aren't in combat. We're just here picking up the pieces afterward. Being a medic wasn't what I had in mind when I signed up with Uncle Sam, but I guess you take what you get. After seeing some of those guys who were on the front line I guess I got lucky being put in the medical division. Sometimes I'd like to be up front where I feel like I'm making a difference though.

God bless you girlie. Keep us all in your prayers.

Love to you, gal,
J.P.

P.S. If you don't mind, could you read parts of my letters to Mama and Pops? You know which parts not to tell them.

17 July 1944
1730 hrs

Hey gal,

Or as they say in France - Bonjour. I'm sure you were worried when you didn't hear from me for so long. We've been moving a lot. We never did get to operate the hospital we set up in England because of D-Day. We were moved out right away and sent down here to France to help with the wounded that came through. The guys did a helluva job chasing the Krauts out. I may be Irish at heart, but I've never been prouder to say I am an American.

We landed at Omaha Beach in Normandy. I guess since D-Day everybody knows where Normandy is. We were living in tents. This makes me laugh. When Timothy, Michael, and I were young, we made tents out of sheets and thought it was great fun to sleep in the back yard. One time it rained and we thought getting soaked was a big adventure. Fun is the farthest from our reality now. What I wouldn't give for a soft bed in a warm, dry house.

Our assignment has been to treat and ship out the wounded. I'm getting so good at this doctoring stuff I just might give up being a policeman and become a doctor when I get back to Bay Ridge. Wouldn't that be something? It would show everyone what us Irish can do.

I got some letters from my mother. It sounds like she's worried about Pop's health even though she didn't really come out and say that. I think she probably doesn't want to worry me. Last time I was home I noticed Pops seemed to tire easily. How do you think he's doing? You'd let me know if something bad was wrong, wouldn't you? It's times like this that make it hard to be away from home.

Bay Ridge. Lord but I miss that place! I wonder if there are any guys left there to hang out at the Y? This war sure cut into those numbers.

I got five or six letters all at once when I got here to France and things settled down a little. I got two from some high school girls from Mississippi who wrote letters to cheer up soldiers. It is nice of them to remember us. We're only in one place for a few days, setting up field hospitals then we move on. It's hard when the news takes so long to get to me.

Things are getting dicier now that we're in France and closer to the front lines. One of the guys in my unit was killed by a grenade last week. Each night when I go to sleep I pray to God that I'll be alive to say my prayers the next night. Light a candle at church for us okay? The guys at the front can especially use your prayers. Don't tell Mama but sometimes I *have trouble believing there's a God when I see everything that has happened here.*

I know I keep saying it but you're awful swell for writing to me. Timothy is a lucky bloke.

God bless you and keep you. My love to all.
J.P.

30 Aug 1944
1530 hrs

Dear Maggie,

What a surprise! We moved again! (Of course I'm not really surprised. We don't stay anywhere for long.) We're in Paris. Thank the good Lord we're now out of tents.

When I get back home I'm sure I'll have lots of stories to tell you about Hub. I swear the guy is trying to get kicked out of the army — if that's even possible during the war. He's always in some kind of trouble. Nothing terrible, just prankster type trouble. He's got a good heart, though, and his sense of humor keeps us all laughing when it seems like there's nothing good in the world. He's a good friend.

My unit moved in and took over the hospital the Krauts had set up here for their soldiers. The cowards left all their wounded men behind. We're taking care of them, but they're in bad shape. It smells because there is so much infection and gangrene. The Germans used stuff like crepe paper instead of bandages and it's put their guys in rough shape. Now I know where the term sawbones for a doctor comes from. Most of these guys are getting arms and legs amputated because the Germans didn't take good care of them. And lots of them don't even live long enough to make it worth it.

At least we're set up in a hospital here and not out in some field, but the hours are brutal because there's so much to do. If we're lucky we might catch 4 – 5 hours of sleep, and that's not even all at once.

It's a whole different feel here. I'm sure it's because of how long the Parisians lived under the fear of the Germans here, but people seem happy. It's sure good for us guys. Around here, even if you weren't part of the invading troops who liberated the city, if you're wearing an American uniform then the locals love you.

We're ten blocks away from the Eiffel Tower. Who would have thought I'd be looking at that every day? Life is kind of normal when we're not working on wounded soldiers. We get to be like the civilians, and the locals tell us the city is coming back to life thanks to the liberation. Sometimes it's hard to believe we're really in the middle of a war. I thought Paris would be destroyed but things aren't too bad. There were some bombing raids, but the people here feel they got lucky.

The residents are resilient and are determined to make life normal again. There are many open-air cafes. That's where I am right now. I'm writing you a letter from a cafe on a street in Paris. Can you believe it? The indoor cafes have music at night. American music is popular here. French food isn't like what I'm used to but it's still better than army rations.

I go to a nearby park a lot and just sit and think about home. The walk from here to there is about the same as the one from our house to the avenue. The park is called Esplanades des Invalides. I had to ask somebody how to say it and I can't for the life of me tell you what it means. It reminds me of being with my pals in Shore Park. It gives me time to *think about how things used to be, so I don't mind the walk. We had some great times there in the summer, didn't we, gal? I remember that's where you and Timothy met.*

A few days ago, when I was sitting here in the park, my police training came in handy. A French soldier was harassing a young woman who takes care of a dozen tykes from the nearby Catholic orphanage. She didn't look scared, but I couldn't let him get away with treating a lady that way. I won't go into details, but I will say he might have some extra wrinkles in his uniform shirt.

After that, I made it a point to watch out for her whenever I was in the park. I came to her rescue another day when one of the wee ones went up a tree when she turned her back. He fell out and might have broken his arm. I helped her tend to him and then helped get all of the children back to the orphanage.

I come back to this bench every day since then so I can see her. Now she's used to seeing me waiting and she smiles and waves. I don't even know her name, but I do know she has beautiful wavy brunette hair and the softest brown eyes I have ever seen on a woman. Since the day I first saw her, I haven't been able to get her off my mind.

I guess I sound like a school boy the way I'm talking, but you're a swell friend and I know I can tell you anything. I'm kicking myself for not getting her name. I think it would make it easier to go talk to her. I miss having a gal to spend time with. There are lots of (pardon the term) prostitutes here but that's not the kind of woman I want. I've been looking for a woman like you and maybe this gal is the one.

Tell Mama I will write soon. I miss all of you. Keep us in your prayers and God bless you all.

With love,
J.P.

Daniel carefully refolded the letter and slid it back into the envelope. The friendship between his mother and her brother-in-law was enviable. His mother had always been the rock in the family; that safe port where everyone was welcome and could go for help or advice. To know that even as a young woman she'd been the same way strengthened his admiration.

And this uncle of his. It was clear from John Patrick's letters that he was a gentle soul. Before entering the war, he'd been a Brooklyn police officer, walking the neighborhood when community policing was the norm rather than the exception. His photograph hung in the lobby at the police station, a hero never forgotten. Daniel felt cheated that he hadn't had the chance to know him. He was a man of honor. It was his legend that had prompted Liam to become a police officer himself.

Yes, the blood of the Coughlins ran thick and true through all of them.

Leaning over the crate, he picked up the picture of the woman again. Was she the one his uncle met in the park? He pushed aside some letters to retrieve the other picture of the woman with the children around her. Yes, probably the same woman. She was smiling, but Daniel sensed a sadness in her eyes.

The clock chimed. Glancing up, Daniel saw that it was 5:30. He hadn't missed a day of work in the last six years, but today would be different. Besides knowing that he'd be exhausted and a danger on the rails, he was compelled to continue with the letters. He enjoyed the historical aspect, but so far, he couldn't understand his mother's persistence, but there were still dozens of letters in the stacks she'd parsed out and hundreds more in the crate.

He reached over to the desk and removed the cordless phone from its base. After reporting his intended absence, he looked back at the crate. He'd read maybe thirty letters so far. Most were filled with accounts of day-to-day life in Bay Ridge for his mother and in the army for his uncle.

Now his trepidation about reading the letters was replaced by curiosity. Each one filled in a piece of the family history that he knew nothing about. Knowing that his mother believed this connected back to him made it even more compelling.

October 4

Dearest brother-in-law,

I received your latest letters. I don't understand why sometimes we do not get any for weeks then we get three or four that were written weeks apart.

Your friend Hub sounds like a character the way he gets in trouble. It sounds like he is a good friend though. I am glad you have him. Did you tell me he is from Connecticut? Maybe you two can stay friends after the war.

Timothy was home on leave again this past weekend. We

feel fortunate that he is stationed close enough to us that he can visit. We have fun making up for lost time. I guess I should not say things like that to his brother but we do hope to make you an uncle someday. He would like to wait but I want to have a part of him to hug and hold while he is away just to remind me of him.

You asked me to keep you updated on your father. He is trying to take care of the house but he gets tired easily. Your mama is being strong but I know it is hard on her with two of her boys in the war. She is especially worried about you since you are already over there. She goes to Mass twice every day. We are all praying for this war to be over.

This week we finally were able to go to the dinner at the Irishmen's Club. We realized how much news we had not heard. Louis Higgins was killed in the Philippines. George Stevens was shot on Okinawa - that is somewhere in Japan or some such place - but finally the army got him back home. He will never be able to use his left arm again. They say his mind is not right either. Maddie O'Connor's brother was killed on an island in the Pacific. He had been dead two months before the family received a telegram. So much sadness this war has brought to our world.

I pray every day that Timothy will not be shipped overseas and that you will come home safely. It is so hard being here waiting and worrying. Please be safe, dear brother. And I do love you like a brother and a very special friend.

This letter is so long and I am sorry to give you bad news when you have so much over there already. Until now I have kept it from you, but hiding it will not change the facts.

I want to hear all about your angel in the park. Do not be shy. You have not even told me her name. I think you probably just made up that story to see if I would get jealous. Well I am

*not. What would you do if you fell in love with her? I guess
you would have to bring her back to America with you.*

   You are in our prayers.

With love,
Maggie

❧❦

Daniel stared at his mother's last paragraph. There was
no doubt his uncle was enamored by the woman in the
park. Was this only another one of those whirlwind war-
time flings that so many G.I.s had as an escape from
reality?

   Now, there was even more that he hoped to garner
from the letters. For the first time, he was getting to know
his mysterious uncle.

CHAPTER THREE

Mid-September1944

"Mes enfants, s'il vous plaît, restez dans la queue et tenez ton prochain par la main. Nous ne voulons pas que quiconque se sépare."

John listened to the young woman calling out to the children, mesmerized by the romantic sound of the French language. A dozen children straggled behind her across the park grass, their hands grasping a thick rope. He had no idea what she'd said, but all seemed to follow her directive except for a dark-haired boy who darted away.

"Benjamin, il faut rester dans la queue les autres enfants; si non, il faut rentrer a l'ecole!" she called while checking the rest of her flock. The little boy returned, but not until he'd picked up a stick with three protruding twigs.

John felt the corners of his mouth tug up into a smile.

As a young child, he'd been like the mischievous little boy.

"*Laisse ça, s'il vous plaît.*" The woman, clearly exasperated, jabbed her finger toward the ground. The little boy reluctantly dropped the stick, then as soon as she turned to attend to the other children, he retrieved it again.

"Bof!" she exclaimed, pressing her hands against her ears and looking toward the heavens in apparent search of divine intervention.

Captivated by her, by the scene of her with the children, John smiled as he sat on the park bench. His half-eaten croissant sandwich laid on the napkin on his thigh, all but forgotten as soon as he spotted her and the children crossing the busy street.

He'd grown used to the ritual this teacher had established with the children. They came from the Catholic Orphanage three blocks away. And, whenever he could, he made sure he was in the park at the same time. Except for the day when he'd helped with the little boy who'd fallen from the tree, he'd kept his distance. That had only served to fuel his fantasies.

Each night he'd lie in his bunk, fingers laced behind his head, and imagine her at the school. He pictured her leading the children in prayer before their meals. An image of her kneeling with them during Mass, teaching them the proper etiquette, reminded him of his own mother teaching him these rituals.

And he'd close his eyes and fantasize about what it would be like to hold her curvy body against his. Stroke the soft skin of her cheek. Nuzzle her neck. Kiss those lips that looked like they could make any man forget the ugliness of the world around him. And, he, in turn, would show her what it was like to be loved the way a woman should be loved.

As foolish as it was, he realized as he lay awake in the middle of the night, he'd fallen in love with a stranger. He attributed this fascination to a need to fill the emptiness Patty had left in his heart.

But he loved the woman's patience. She laughed at the children bouncing around her during play time, each taking a turn tugging at her calf-length skirt. She whirled and feigned an attempt to catch them. Peals of high-pitched laughter filled the tranquil park. Their game always ended with someone getting caught by her and swept up into an overzealous hug. The children squealed even louder with delight and raised their arms to seek her attention. If she wasn't already, some day she'd make a wonderful mother.

Today the young woman led the students across the grass, then under a stand of trees. One little girl twirled in a circle, her arms stretched out until she fell, overcome by dizziness. The teacher helped her to her feet and brushed the grass and dirt from the little girl's yellow jumper. After a moment, the child rejoined the line of students, and the teacher propped her hands on her hips. She shook her head and, even from this distance, John could see her shoulders lift and fall from a long sigh.

As if sensing his attention, she glanced in his direction. He lifted his hand and waved, pleased when she gave him a little wave back before returning to the front of the group. She'd started acknowledging him on other days, too, sometimes calling hello to him. Some days she called in French and other days in English. This spurt of attention only fueled his desire to meet her.

Finally, she managed to lead the children to a small clearing and produced a brown ball from a cloth bag slung over her shoulder.

"*Formez un cercle, s'il vous plait,*" she said after setting the ball in the grass.

The children moved into a wide circle, then turned their backs to the middle. The teacher went along the circle and patted each child on the head as she gave out what he recognized as a number in French. When finished, she called out a number and the children turned toward the center of the circle. One child ran in, grabbed the ball from the middle and started singing a song while the others moved in a circle around him. The woman stepped back and allowed the children to continue the game without intervention.

Lord, but she was beautiful.

The opportunity to speak to her was too tempting to pass up. He rose from the bench and followed the cinder path toward her, tossing his half-eaten sandwich into a can along the way. He wiped the back of his hand across his mouth, desperately wanting this first official meeting to be perfect.

His heart banged against his rib cage, feeling like the bass percussion section of a marching band trapped in his chest. Twenty feet from her his palms started to sweat.

The sun shone through the leaves on the trees, and the fragmented rays washed over the woman in a surreal cascade of light. Sleek strands of her dark hair were lit from above as if she were being blessed by God. John swallowed hard, realizing how much he wanted to reach out and feel the silky waves. Instead, he shoved his hands into his khaki-colored uniform pants and stopped a little behind her.

"Bonjour," he greeted, knowing full well from their brief encounter when the boy fell from the tree that she spoke impeccable, although accented, English.

Apparently startled, she whirled toward him. Her brown eyes widened with apprehension, but when she saw it was him, she pressed a hand to her heart and smiled. The sunlight captured the sparkle in her eye, a mind-numbing silent welcome to him.

"Bonjour. Comment allez-vous?"

John grimaced, suddenly feeling inadequate. "I'm afraid my mastery of the French language is limited to hello, thank you, please, can I have a beer, how much does that cost, and good bye."

"Oh." Her hand slid from her chest and dropped to her side, but in that moment, he noticed she wore no wedding band. Were wedding bands customary in France? When he glanced back toward her face, she said, "I asked how are you?"

"Right, uh, fine, thank you. And you?" Heat crept up his neck. This wasn't the conversation he'd imagined when he daydreamed about finally meeting her.

"I am well, thank you." She glanced toward the children, then back at him. Ever vigilant.

He withdrew one hand from his pocket and indicated the children. "I was wondering how the little boy is."

She tipped her head and smiled. "Benjamin?"

Shrugging, he said, "Is Benjamin the little boy who fell out of the tree? Is he all right?" He glanced into the group, not sure that he would recognize the child now that two weeks had passed. There was no one with a cast.

"His arm was only badly bruised." She pointed to the little boy who had not stayed in line when entering the park. "He is fine now." She laughed lightly, almost musically. "He is a very curious little boy."

"Yes, I suspected from watching." John pretended to be interested in the children, but when she was distracted by the shouts from their game, he stared at her.

What he wouldn't give for the time to get to know her.

"Michel," she said, "*vous devez être doux.*" Without turning her attention from the children, she said, "The boys. They can be so rough when they play. I always must remind them to be gentle."

"Benjamin, too?" he asked, suppressing a knowing grin.

Her cheeks lifted, pushing her eyes into a soft squint when she smiled. "Especially Benjamin. But I adore him just the same."

"I'm sure you do," was the only response he could think of. He's a lucky little boy, John thought. She was gentle with all of them, and from what he could see, she genuinely cared for each. Since first spotting her with them in the park, he'd seen her hug and comfort them over and over.

Sometimes she gathered them around her under a tree and read books that she produced from the muslin cloth bag she always carried. Their cherubic faces turned up toward her, intent on listening to every word. He was never close enough to hear the story, not that he would have understood it in French anyway, but she always had their full attention. And his.

It was a guilty pleasure to study her this close. She had fine features. The bridge of her nose curved ever so slightly in the middle. Her rosy lips were moist and soft looking. Her hair, tucked behind her ear, curved around the contour like a little "C". It fell just to her shoulders where the waves made it look like it could spring back up. Her skin was creamy white with small splotches of pink on the crest of her cheek. A porcelain doll. That's what she reminded him of.

He was still absorbed in studying her when she looked back.

"My name is John," he stammered, hoping to relieve some of the embarrassment he felt at being caught in his rudeness. "John Coughlin."

Stretching a delicate hand toward him, she smiled. "It is nice to meet you, John Coughlin."

The way she said his name, *Zhaun Coughleen*, prickled the hairs on the back of his neck. She made it sound special. Romantic. Just as everything about her seemed romantic.

He accepted her handshake, relishing the feel of her soft skin against his rough palm.

"It's my pleasure to meet you —" He tilted his head, hoping to prompt her to share her name, but either she didn't pick up on his cue or she purposely chose to keep her identity to herself.

She removed her hand from his gentle grasp and nodded toward his uniform. "Are you a doctor for the American army?"

"A doctor?" He glanced down, wondering what she saw that made her think that. "No."

"Ah, but you had the knowledge to assist me with Benjamin when he fell from the tree."

"Oh, that. I'm part of a medical unit. I was happy to help." He smiled. "And, obviously my diagnosis was wrong, since I thought his arm was broken."

"Better to be cautious," she said. "I am sorry I could not properly thank you. I was lucky that you were in the park that day."

No, I was the lucky one, because I got to meet you, he wanted to say, but knew it sounded too forward. Instead he said, "You are very welcome, mademoiselle."

She smiled at his clumsy attempt at French.

One of the girls broke from the circle of children and ran to wrap her arms around the woman's legs. She cried into the front of her teacher's blue pleated skirt. The woman leaned over to embrace the child, pushing her hands under the girls' braids. She spoke to the child in French, and through tiny sobs, the little girl responded.

"Shhh, shhh," the woman said, her voice soothing. She knelt and rubbed the girl's back until the child calmed.

The woman lifted her gaze to John.

"The ball hit Sarah in the stomach and took her breath away," she explained. She returned her attention to the little girl, speaking quietly. Eventually the girl's sobs subsided, and after a kiss on the top of her head from her teacher, she returned to the circle.

"You're very good with the children," John said. "Do you have any of your own?"

The compliment was genuine, but the second question was a shameful attempt to get personal information. Before he let his heart trip another beat for her, he had to know if he stood any chance with her.

"No, I do not have children. I am not married. But hopefully someday."

There was an involuntary tug in his chest that extended the full length of his torso until it ended in his groin. Have mine, is what he thought but would never say. From what he'd witnessed, his children would be fortunate to have her for their mother.

But the thought was crazy. She didn't even share her name, so what made him think they'd ever be together?

The game she'd organized deteriorated quickly, and before he had a chance to ask her anything more, the children recaptured her full attention. One little boy tugged at her cloth bag and seemed to beg her for something.

She took hold of the boy's hand at the same time she looked up at John.

"Excuse me, sir. I must attend to the children. It was very nice to meet you."

Sir? Was that her way of letting him know that they were, after all, strangers?

Clapping her hands, she gave an instruction, and the children followed her to a nearby tree. She settled herself against the trunk, and the children dropped to the ground around her, several of them vying for positions which would put them in the closest proximity to her. Finally, with the girl in the yellow dress tucked under one arm and a little boy leaning against her on the other side, she searched through her bag and pulled out two picture books. The children chattered their approval, then if it was possible, sidled even closer to her.

John felt a pang of jealousy, wishing he could be that close to her. What did she smell like? How comforting it would be to feel the heat of her body.

Instead, he picked a safe spot several feet away.

"Would you mind if I stayed and listened to the stories, too?"

She tipped her head and gave him a skeptical smile. "But they are not in English. Do you speak other languages?"

Shaking his head, he smiled. "No, but I'll look at the pictures when you show them. Is that all right?" He would have died on the spot if she'd refused him.

"*S'il vous plaît.* Please," she said, nodding toward the ground.

He lay on the grass, laced his fingers behind his head, and rolled his face so he could stare at her. Her true beauty wasn't on the surface, it was inside. And he'd never seen another woman so beautiful.

She read more than the first two books she'd pulled from her bag. By the time she was done, the little boy who'd been leaning against her arm had fallen asleep. When she started to wake him, John jumped to his feet.

"Don't wake him," he whispered.

"But we need to return to the school."

"I'll carry him."

"No, I cannot ask you —"

"Please," he said, already next to her and placing a hand on her shoulder to keep her from getting up. "*S'il vous plaît*? I'd be happy to do it."

His attempt at another French phrase apparently amused her. "*Merci.* That would be appreciated."

To lift the child, he needed to brush against her. The

brief contact was chaste through their long sleeves, but his skin tingled anyway. She wore a light flowery scent. Clean. Fresh. Very feminine. A flutter of awareness startled him, but just as quickly he reined it in, refocusing his attention on the boy. He reached under the child's arms and lifted him against his chest. After arranging the boy's head so he wasn't smothered against his neck, John straightened.

"He will be too heavy to carry for blocks," the woman protested again, getting up. Without looking away from him, she dusted a bit of grass and dirt from her skirt.

John smiled, feeling a paternal stirring toward the sleeping boy. He imagined this child being his and hers. Lord but she could send his imagination racing.

"He's just a wee one. It's no problem, unless of course, we stand here all day arguing about it."

"*Merci*," she said again, gracing him with an appreciative smile. "You are a very kind man."

"It's easy to be kind to someone who is so kind to others, particularly the children."

There was a flash of an indefinable emotion in her dark eyes that caught him off guard.

"These children have no one else." Her voice rose, and tears wavered on her lids. "They have lost their families, their homes, everything, to Hitler's hatred. Someone must protect and love them. I am doing nothing extraordinary."

"But they're fortunate to have you," John said quietly, hoping to diffuse the surprising tension. Guilt replaced the carnal awareness of moments before. He considered apologizing but, then, what would he be apologizing for?

Hitler's atrocities? His own bungled attempt to compliment her?

She drew herself up squarely as if to bolster her stance, took a long rope from her muslin bag, and instructed the children to hold onto it. There was an edginess to her command. He worried that instead of creating the opportunity to open a door to friendship that he had inadvertently slammed one shut. He drew in a stuttered sigh. Only time would tell.

Leading the line, this complex woman with whom he'd blindly become enamored, crossed the park.

At a busy intersection, John dropped back to bring up the rear to ensure the children's safe crossing.

"Are you sure you want to do this?" she called from up ahead.

I'd do anything to make your life better, he wanted to respond. Instead, he lifted his hand and waved her on, hoping a light-hearted response would bring them back to their original comfort. "I'll take him all the way. Lead on, mademoiselle."

Three blocks later they reached the brick building next to a convent which housed the orphanage. She halted the children at the base of the stairs and met John halfway along the line.

"*Merci, Zhaun,*" she said, shifting the limp child into her arms. She staggered a little under the new weight.

John reached out to steady her, his hand on her elbow. They both froze, their gazes locked. Had the jolt of electricity he'd felt jumped from him to her?

For a moment, in his mind, they were alone, the Eiffel Tower looming as a backdrop behind them. Had they been alone, he was sure he would have cupped her chin in his palm and used that opportunity to kiss her. But a whining child broke the spell, and the woman stepped back first.

"It was kind of you to do this for me."

He nodded, retreating a safe step back, as well. "I'm sorry if I upset you in the park."

"No. You did nothing wrong. I must apologize for my rudeness." She rubbed her hand in a circle on the child's back. He'd always admired women who were naturally maternal.

"No apology necessary." There was an awkward silence that seemed to make all of Paris grind to a halt. He scuffed the heel of his shoe against the bottom step. "Thanks for letting me share the time with the children. I enjoyed talking with you."

"And I, you. *Au revoir, Monsieur Coughleen.*" The teacher turned and began the procession up the stairs into the building.

Panic gripped him. The realization seemed foolish, but he'd spent more than an hour with her and the children, yet she was still a tantalizing mystery. He couldn't leave her without the most important bit of information.

"*Mademoiselle*, may I ask your name?" he called after her.

She turned toward him, the dark archway of the orphanage silhouetting the gentle curves of her body. "Anna Goodman," she called, then turned to continue on her way.

"Anna Goodman," he repeated softly. Pretty. It fit her.

He was absorbed in mentally repeating her name

when from just inside the doorway he heard her voice. "*Zhaun*?"

"Yes?" He couldn't believe how hearing her say his name turned the blood in his veins to liquid fire.

"My friends call me Annie."

A captivating smile meant solely for him brightened her face, and his knees weakened. Could he really leave her on these steps?

"So, if that's what your *friends* call you, then what should *I* call you?" The world spun around him while anxiety ebbed through his body. Drawing in a single breath was a struggle. Her answer would determine whether their paths would intentionally cross again.

Her lips curved up and she tipped her head coquettishly. "Annie," she said. "Call me Annie."

His concern melted like the fragile crust of ice on a spring flower warmed by a sun ray. She was his ray of sun, a welcome break in the gray clouds that hung over him day after day in the army hospital. Suddenly, everything around him was a profusion of brightness and hope. He whispered her name to himself just to test it, and the sound was wonderful. Bursting with a desire to dash up the steps and kiss her, he forced himself to take measured steps backward along the sidewalk.

"I'll see you again —" he hesitated, then added, "Annie." If he had his way, he'd never have to walk away from her. At least now he had an unspoken promise of more time together.

She nodded and wagged her fingers in a low wave, inhibited by the slumbering child. "*Au revoir, Zhaun.*" And then she was swallowed up by the cold brick building, taking a chunk of John's heart with her.

CHAPTER FOUR

05 Oct 1944
2200 hrs

Dear Maggie,

I'm sorry that I haven't written in a while, but Heaven descended upon me. I know this is what you have been waiting for. Yes, I finally got the name of my angel. Her name is Annie Goodman.

I've been delinquent on my duties as a good brother-in-law and son to you and Mama and Pops, but I've been spending my time with Annie. I heard rumors that we might be moving out of Paris, so every minute I can get with her is precious.

We've had several picnics in the park. It seems the right place to go since that's where we met. She is a wonderful cook and baker, so we have fresh bread and cookies. It reminds me of being home.

Other favorite places for us to go are to the Eiffel Tower and the Seine River. It's been like this every chance we can be together. Sometimes we just walk and sometimes we go to a nightclub to dance. I like to do that because then I have an excuse to hold her close. She's a swell dancer. The other guys are jealous and want to dance with her, too, but I keep her to myself. There are other women there for them to dance with. They don't need my girl.

You probably want to know about Annie. She's from a German town near the French border. She was in Paris with her grandmother and going to college when the Nazis invaded France.

I don't know what you hear or know back in the States, but here we're all convinced that Hitler is the devil himself. He doesn't hate only the Jewish people. He orders his soldiers to kill gypsies, Poles, old people, sick people, homosexuals and more. Even babies! What kind of a monster kills babies? I don't like war, but I'm proud to say I'm here to help get rid of Hitler's evil.

I'm sorry if this part is depressing. There's just so much hate that sometimes it really gets you down. I thank God every day that I met Annie. She helps me see the good in such an ugly world.

Meeting Annie is one of the few good things that will come out of this war, I think.

I just got the letter from you about the fire at Coney Island back in August. Wow! It's lucky it wasn't worse. That place has had more fires over the years.

Keep sending those letters, girlie. I appreciate every one of them. My love to all and God bless.

Love,
John

❧❧

Daniel smiled and tucked away the letter, then followed that with two more that described other dates with Annie. Paris was the perfect backdrop for the romantic story that was building in his head.

The letters detailed John Patrick and Annie's time together having coffee and croissants in cafés, dancing in nightclubs to American songs like *Boogie Woogie Bugle Boy* by the Andrews Sisters and jazz music, which, as John Patrick had pointed out in one of the letters, was acceptable under Hitler's regime. He described the resurgence of swing music, which had been outlawed by racist Hitler. They were all details from history that Daniel had learned years before but reading about them from his uncle's experiences made them real.

He pulled the next letter from the envelope and unfolded the yellowed paper. The letters told such a vivid story that while reading he felt like he was with his mother in her life in Brooklyn and with his uncle in Europe.

October 18

Dear J.P.,

I hope this letter finds you well and safe. The headlines in the newspaper are still frightening to us. I thought it was good news that Paris was liberated but there are still so many stories of the Nazis and Russians trying to get more power in other countries. I worry for you because I know you are surrounded by this evil.

I don't try to write letters at night because we keep our lights so dim for the blackouts. Even though the windows are covered I worry that an air raid warden will knock on our door and tell us our lights can be seen. Do you remember little Tommy Murphy from down the street? He has become an air raid warden and he is taking his job very seriously. I guess it is better for us all to do our part and keep our adopted country safe.

There was a report in the newspaper that said the blackouts are causing more car accidents and there are more deaths than usual. The street lights are turned off and the car lights are very dim. Most people try to stay off the roads at night because it has become so dangerous.

There was a scrap metal drive recently. We were able to donate an old bed frame that was in the attic. We do not have much left to add to the effort but we know it is needed to provide the troops with equipment.

We have been getting ready for winter here. I hate to see the warm weather end. We are very careful with our ration stamps. You probably will not believe this but I gave up coffee so I could save those ration stamps toward things we need more like heating oil. They are hard times we are living through but I know this is all important for the war effort so I do my duty here.

This week was a good week because we did not hear of anyone we knew getting killed in the war. I wish every week could be like that. I am getting more anxious because I know soon Timothy will have to leave. I keep praying the war will end first. I am sure you pray the same thing.

How is your Annie? I am so happy you are able to have fun there too. She sounds like a lovely woman. I can not wait to meet her someday. I think you are both lucky to have met.

I have to make supper so I will close. Please stay out of harms way. I will write again soon.

With love,
Maggie

2 Nov 1944
1045 hrs

Dear Maggie,

I don't know how I got so lucky to get a sister-in-law like you. I don't think I tell you enough how much I appreciate your letters. It's good for me to hear what's happening there and how the war is affecting my loved ones.

I only have a few minutes to write to you because I am going to pick up Annie soon. With each passing day, I fall more in love with her. She is the kindest, smartest, most generous woman I have ever known. (Besides you, of course. Haha!) I know the time is going to come when I have to leave her, but I try not to think about that, and instead just try to spend as much time with her as I can.

The wounded guys who come through our hospital keep us up-to-date on what's happening on the front lines. I only triage the patients, but that's when they're really talking because they just want to unload their minds of what they've been through. My brother the priest would be very useful here as someone who can listen to them and give them encouragement. We don't have time to do much other than figure out who needs the most help and ship them to the right place.

It's been warm here lately like summer is back. It was really hot when we first got to Paris, so I don't want that

*again, but this is more like Brooklyn summer weather. I'm sure
it will change soon.*

*Sorry to cut this short, but I don't want to be late. I have
something I want to do before I pick up Annie. Take care of
yourself. Thank you again for writing to me, too.*

With love,
J.P.

✧⌒✦

The problem wasn't finding flowers. There were vendors'
carts all over the Parisian streets. The problem was
finding a bouquet of flowers that were worthy of being a
gift to Annie. John moved from one to the other,
determined to find just the right one. They'd spent
enough time together since the day they'd exchanged
names, that he was ready to take their romance to the
next level.

He nearly passed one cart. Its big wooden wheels
were cracked and worn, the small green and cream
canopy tattered at the edges. But he skidded to a halt
when a rose by itself on a shelf caught his attention. It
was a spectacular yellow rose resting on a sparse bed of
greens, its petals just beginning to curl open. Small beads
were draped across the stem and the late afternoon sun
glinted off them.

He'd been looking for a bouquet of flowers, but upon
seeing this rose he realized that's why he'd been having
so much trouble deciding. What he felt for Annie was
more simply stated than a "bunch" of flowers. She was

elegant, poised and bright, like that single yellow rose that was apart from the others.

A small, round woman sat on a three-legged stool beside the cart, her nose buried in an old edition of a newspaper. The headlines were in French, but Hitler's name stood out in one of them.

"Excuse me," he said.

The woman slapped the paper shut, seeming to be startled. "*Oui, Monsieur?*"

"Is that rose for sale?" He hoped the vendor spoke English.

She pointed to the object of his attention. "This beauty?"

"Yes, uh, *oui*," he answered.

Her eyes suddenly sparkled. "*Oui, Monsieur.* You have American dollars?"

The precious American dollar. He'd learned how much the Europeans valued American money.

"*Oui.* How much will it be?"

She studied him for a moment. "Two dollars."

"Two dollars!" He looked back at the flower, aggravated by the woman's greed.

She snatched the rose and deftly wrapped it in a piece of white tissue. "Two dollars for most, but for the American soldier, one dollar and you get just the rose." Tying a ribbon around the paper to hold it, she looked back up at him and added, "*Oui?*"

"What a deal," he mumbled as he slipped his wallet from the pocket of his trousers. Most of his money was sent home for his parents to use for medicines for his father. He was sure they would approve of this extravagance.

The old lady took the dollar he extended and handed him the flower. "She is a beautiful woman?" The dollar was stuffed into a plentiful space in her cleavage. Probably the safest place on her.

"Very." He grasped the flower just below the ribbon. "*Merci*."

"Ah, *l'amour* ," she crooned, patting her pudgy fingers against her heart. "And you are a handsome soldier."

"Thank you," he responded.

He hustled away, eager to see Annie. Although his plan was simple, his heart soared just knowing they would be alone without the children from the orphanage.

On their previous dates, he had met her at the convent, where he always felt he was under the scrutiny of the nuns. But today she had invited him to pick her up at her apartment, so he walked the four blocks to the address she had given him.

The street was lined with buildings three and four stories high. He knew from what she'd explained that her apartment was in the basement with a narrow cement staircase leading down to it. He followed a cobblestone walkway to the side of the brick building and found only two basement entrances. As she had described, the first had a gray door with peeling paint. The window casing had no covering.

The next entrance was hers, and it led to the basement level. There were print curtains hanging in the window, prudently drawn to avoid peeping Toms. The same fabric covered the three small square windows at the top of the door.

Putting the rose behind his back, he descended the ten steps. He knocked twice, then moved back to wait.

There were three small pots of flowers outside her door. In one was the red flower he recognized as a geranium with the fragrance he'd detested all his life. The other two plants, which he couldn't identify, were of the same type of flower with delicate pink and lavender petals. Other than the geraniums, the only thing he could smell was cookies baking.

Finally, the door opened a crack, and he could see a part of her cheek and one eye as she peered out. Just as quickly the door closed. He heard a chain sliding across metal, then she pulled the door open. When he sucked in a deep breath, all the air slammed into his lungs at once.

Her hair was pulled back and fastened neatly in a twist. Unlike the dark, conservative clothing she wore during the day when she was caring for the orphans, the pale peach dress she wore now accented her smooth, feminine curves.

"*Bonjour, Zhaun.*"

He swallowed hard against the lump in his throat. "*Mademoiselle.* You look absolutely ravishing."

She tilted her head and gave him a tentative smile. "Ravishing?"

"Stunning." Her expression didn't change. "Extraordinarily beautiful." He bowed slightly, then pulled the flower from behind his back. "I wish now that I'd brought you a whole garden of roses."

"Oh, *Zhaun.*" She took it and peeled back a corner of the paper to sniff the bouquet. Her eyes misted over. "It is beautiful. You are so sweet." She stretched up on her toes to kiss his cheek. "Thank you. It has been so long since —" She broke off and whirled away, wiping at her eyes as she retreated into her apartment. "I need to put this in water and get the picnic basket. I will be right back."

She disappeared into the dimly lit room. Since she hadn't invited him in, he stayed on her stoop. When she returned a few minutes later, she appeared composed once again. A wicker basket hung from her hands.

"All set?" he asked, taking the basket from her.

"*Oui,* my friend." She moved through the doorway past him, and he closed the door behind her.

"Friend? Is that all we are after all these weeks?"

She looked up at him, and he swore her eyes sparkled as her lips curved into a gentle smile. "Oh, no. You are my first *American* friend."

"Well, then let your *American* friend carry that," he said, putting the same emphasis on the word American as he took the basket from her.

They ascended the stairs side by side, his footsteps scuffing and hers barely audible. "Can friends fall in love?" he asked.

She slipped her hand under his elbow and smiled up at him. "I believe it is how all lovers must first begin. "

At the top of the stairs, he halted. "I like how that sounds."

"What?"

"Lovers."

Her cheeks reddened almost instantly, and a surge of panic cut through him. "Have I embarrassed you?" She dipped her head. He set down the picnic basket and turned to her, lifting her chin with the tips of his fingers, but she left her eyes downcast.

"Annie, look at me." Slowly, she lifted her eyes. "I know it will sound crazy, but I've fallen in love with you. I want to be with you as much as I can while my unit is still in Paris."

She didn't respond, forcing him to continue. He bent his knees slightly, enough to lower himself so their eyes were at the same level. "I'd like to be more than friends, Sweetheart."

A tiny smile returned to her lips. "I would like that, too, *Zhaun Coughleen*."

For a moment he stared into her eyes, wanting more than anything to scoop her up and kiss her until her lips were puckered, but he restrained himself. Barely.

"Well, Annie Goodman, I'm going to tell the world that you're *my* girl. Is that all right?"

She smiled, stretched up on her toes, and kissed him. "I *am* your girl while you are in Paris, *Zhaun*."

He feigned indignation. "Only while I'm in Paris?"

She shrugged. "We can only promise the present."

He stared at her for a moment, not sure what that meant. He tucked her hand back under his elbow and retrieved the picnic basket.

"I'll accept that — for now. So, before I embarrass either one of us with a never-ending kiss on those irresistible lips, why don't we head for the park? I don't want to lose a moment of our time together."

November 17

Dear John Patrick,

   I am so happy when the mail comes and we receive a letter

from you. I know it is scary for you over there but it is also scary for us here. Every time there is a knock on the door we hold our breath hoping it is not a telegram from the government.

By your last letter I know you are happy. At least when you are with Annie. I am glad you are able to spend so much time together and get to know each other. She sounds very special.

I try to keep my mind from worrying about Timothy and you. I miss tending to my little Victory garden. Like President Roosevelt said, we must all do our part for the war effort. Every time I took a vegetable from it I imagined you and Timothy having one more piece of food on your plate.

Your father is doing good right now. The doctor gave him a new medicine and I think it is making him much stronger.

This past weekend I was missing Timothy terribly so I decided to go to some of our favorite places. My first stop was by the water. Even though it was cold, I even took a picnic lunch and imagined the times Timothy and I were there together. It made me both happy and sad.

Charlie Duggan arrived home a few days ago. He had been in the Philippines and got a fever. He was so sick he almost died. He is slowly getting better but he is very weak. I took his wife Mindy some soup for him. She has been so busy taking care of him since he came home that she is very tired. Even though it wears her out, I think she is just glad to have him home and I know their little girls are happy.

I have only been working at O'Shea's Pub from 11 o'clock in the morning until just after the rush at 6 o'clock so I can come home to give your mother relief from taking care of your father. Each time I put money in the bank I know we are a *little closer to buying the house we want when Timothy comes home.*

I am hoping Timothy will be able to come home soon. I miss him so. It gets lonely. I am so glad you now have Annie. I look forward to meeting the woman who has made my friend so happy when he is far away from home.

Take care of yourself and keep out of harm's way. We are sending a small package to Timothy and one to you. I tell you not to ruin the surprise but so you will know to look for it. It is not much but you must have something for Christmas.

We want all of you home safe.

Love,
Maggie

01 Dec 1944
0830 hrs.

Dear Maggie,

Hello my friend. I'm looking out at snow coming down and thinking of home. Snow always makes me think of the holidays. I'm sure the war won't end before Christmas, so I guess there's no celebrating this year.

I had a funny thing happen last night. Annie and I were down by the Eiffel Tower and who walks by but Tom McCooe. At first, I thought I was seeing things, but sure enough he was walking there with a couple of other guys from his outfit. He was part of the corps that liberated Paris last month. Boy did he have some stories to tell. I can't imagine being on the front lines like they are and talking about it so matter of factly. I guess you have to get used to it. If you see his wife or family tell them he's doing fine.

I've spent all of my free time with Annie. I've been going to Mass at the church next to the convent just so I can see her afterward. She never is at Mass when I'm there, but that's probably just as well since I'd be thinking about her rather than focusing on Mass.

I can't imagine life without her now. I don't know how long we're going to be here, but I've heard some rumors that we may be shipping out soon. I don't know where we'll be going, but I'm afraid it's out of France. I don't like to think about leaving her. I've decided that I'm going to ask her to come to the States with me after the war is over. Do you think I'm crazy? I know it's soon, but I want her to know that she'd have a home there.

This war has taught me how to appreciate every moment. You have to live for the day because you might not have a tomorrow. I see more bodies going out of here than I care to think about.

I know it's crazy, but we get a lot of our news from the newspapers just like you. I've been following the campaign in the Pacific. It sounds like we're giving those Japs hell. I'm hoping we'll kick their arses good for what they did at Pearl Harbor. Everyone here knows someone who died in the attack.

I guess I should end this. Keep me posted on Timothy.

Give my love to all and God bless.

With love,
J.P.

❧❦

"Are you available?" John Patrick asked the coachman standing next to the horse-drawn carriage. He hoped the man spoke English.

"*Oui*," he responded, opening the small door to the back seat and sweeping his hand to indicate to John Patrick and Annie to get in.

John Patrick looked at Annie. Tiny, wet snowflakes floated around her, some settling onto her hair and eyelashes, making her look even more adorable.

"Would you like to take a ride through the city?" he asked.

The answer, and his reward, was the excitement dancing in her eyes. "Oh, yes, please."

He handed the driver the payment for a one-hour ride, then took hold of Annie's hand to assist her up the steps into the open carriage. She wiped the few flakes of snow away, then scooted across the worn, velvet seat. John took his place next to her, pressing his hip close to hers.

The coachman pulled a wool blanket from under the wooden seat and handed it to John Patrick.

"This will keep you warm against the cold," the man said. He slammed the narrow door, then climbed onto the driver's bench.

John Patrick held it up and looked at Annie. "Would you like to use it?"

She snuggled closer to him. "Let's both sit under it," she said.

He spread the blanket across their laps, then nodded to indicate they were settled when the driver glanced back at them. The man tipped his hat, then clucked for the horse to step away from the curb.

As the carriage gently swayed, Annie cuddled against John's side. The clip-clop of the horse's hooves echoed off the nearby buildings. Cars buzzing past had no effect on the animal.

"Oh, *Zhaun,* this is so wonderful You make me feel so special."

He draped his arm across her shoulders and wedged her against his side. "*You* are wonderful," he said, kissing her cheek, "and you deserve to feel special."

She smiled and laid her head against his shoulder. "And you make me feel so safe."

John Patrick leaned back and lifted her chin with his fingers, so she had to look into his eyes. Her long lashes curled up, framing her brown eyes. Give him enough time, and he could get lost in them — forget the rest of the world existed. More snowflakes danced down from the sky to land on her rosy cheeks.

"Annie Goodman, I would give my life for you in a heartbeat. I'll always keep you safe or die trying."

"Of that I have no doubt," she whispered, her voice more sultry than he'd ever heard it. The earlier snowflakes melted on her skin leaving tiny drops of moisture in their place. Her eyes drifted closed as she lifted her lips to his.

His heart skipped a beat as he slanted his head to claim her soft, sweet mouth. Every molecule in his body pulsed. Tomorrow wasn't guaranteed, so he'd appreciate every moment of today.

And every moment would be spent showing her how deep his love for her was.

❧❧

12 Dec 1944
1400 hrs

Dear Maggie,

Please share this message with Ma and Pop, too. As I suspected, we got the orders that we're moving, and you may not hear from me for a while. I don't know where we're going but will let you know when we arrive. This letter is brief because I want to spend the remaining free hours with Annie. Will write when we reach our destination and settle in. My heart is breaking at the thought of leaving my dear sweet girl behind, but I knew this day would come. I can only pray that I can see her again soon.

With love,
J.P.

❧❧

John tipped his head forward to force the drizzling rain to run off the brim of his hat and away from his face. If he'd been able to choose, his last day in Paris with Annie would have been under a bright, cloudless sky so they could walk through the park where they'd first met, stroll along the river or maybe take a small rowboat onto the Seine River. He didn't want to share her with anyone else tonight. He needed to drink in what he could, enough to sustain him until he could get back to her. He only prayed his unit wouldn't be shipped too far from France.

When he reached the tiny school next to the convent, he took the steps three at a time. They had four precious hours before he had to report back for the train. His heart pounded with urgency. Every minute, every second, counted now.

He rapped on the giant, carved wooden door then hunched against a chill from his wet uniform. Everything he sensed was chaotic. The blaring horns of the cars with impatient drivers. Fresh rain mixed with smoke from fires in furnaces, a desperate attempt for warmth against the dampness. Even the umbrellas carried by pedestrians jumped and swooped as the people wove a pattern around one another.

After a moment the door squeaked, and he stepped toward it. There was a sliver of an opening that barely revealed part of a face that was framed by the white and black habit of a nun he didn't recognize.

"*Oui, Monsieur?*" the nun questioned, unwilling to compromise the tiny school's security by opening the door more than mere inches.

"Sister, I need to see Annie right away, please."

"*Mademoiselle* is with the children now. Please return after 6:00." She started to close the door, but John threw his palm up to stop it.

"No! Please!" He quickly glanced at his watch. Four o'clock. If he waited until six o'clock then he'd only have two hours, at best, to spend with her. It wasn't enough.

"*S'il vous plait!*" His heart tripped. The clock was ticking. He couldn't be denied Annie now. "I must see her, now. It's urgent." Even he could hear the tortured pleading tone of his voice, but he didn't care.

If he could just see her then maybe she could arrange to get away. Sister Eloise Marie would understand. She'd watched their relationship blossom over the last few weeks. In fact, she had encouraged Annie to go out with him. But this particular nun had never responded warmly to him. Finally, the woman nodded slightly, then closed the door.

Ticking. Ticking. With every passing heartbeat the time for him to leave drew closer. He tapped his foot. Turned to watch the activity in the street. Yanked back his soaked sleeve and checked his watch again. His nerves quivered until he thought the volcano inside him would erupt.

Just when he thought he could stand the pressure no longer, the door opened, and his heart lurched at the sight of Annie.

"*Zhaun*? Is everything all right?"

Her beautiful accent. Lord how he'd miss it.

"Can you get free, Annie?"

"Now?" She glanced toward the sky as if the rain was the reason she couldn't get away, then beckoned for him to step inside.

He moved toward her, wanting to seize her hand and pull her to him. Ticking. Ticking. The blood pumped through his veins hard enough to pound at his temples.

"We're shipping out, Annie."

A panicked look replaced her puzzlement. "When?"

"Tonight. Nine o'clock."

She gasped, covering her mouth with her hands. As if on cue, the drizzle turned to a downpour.

"Oh, no! So soon?" Her hands muffled her voice.

"Please." He closed the door to keep out some of the gloominess. "Can you ask one of the Sisters to take the children? There's so little time."

She nodded slowly and backed away, looking shocked. She disappeared into the chasm of the school.

Within minutes she had returned in a long, heavy coat and carrying an umbrella.

"Let's go." There was a sense of panic in her abrupt actions; the way she yanked open the door, forced the umbrella up and ran down the few steps to the sidewalk. She turned up the street as if she had a plan.

"Where are we going?" he asked, ducking under the umbrella with her. He put his arm around her and she snuggled into the curve of his side. They fit together perfectly.

She shivered. "I just want to be alone with you. To pretend for a few hours that it's only us and that you are not really leaving."

He realized then that she was taking him to her apartment. That was a good choice because he didn't want to share *her* with anyone tonight, either. It took only a few minutes and they were there, tucked inside, wrapped in each other's embrace. Four hours. It could be the last hours they'd have together for weeks. Maybe even months. Or, it could be the last hours they'd have together forever. His heart ached with the possibility of the latter.

She shook against his chest, sobs that surprised him. Through discussions about her parents' deaths and her missing family, she'd always remained stoic. Only a mistiness in her eyes ever belied the depth of her hurt. He held her close and allowed her these few minutes of loss of control. He felt the same way, but through his experiences, he'd learned to detach himself from those strong emotions. For now, at least.

Eventually she pulled back from his chest and wiped at the streaks on her face. "I don't want to cry anymore.

Allow me to make you a wonderful dinner before you leave, *Zhaun*. You should carry away happy thoughts."

His stomach gurgled, but eating was the farthest thing from his mind. He didn't care what they did as long as they were together. They worked side by side in the kitchen. Out of cupboards that were almost bare she managed to put together a brothy soup laden with carrots, onions, and potatoes. She cut up and stirred in the last piece of meat that she had in her small ice box, a chicken thigh Sister Theresa had insisted she take home the day before.

She stepped away from the stove and reached into the icebox, pulling out the opened bottle of Chardonnay from their dinner at a nearby restaurant two nights before.

"Maybe we can share a glass of wine while we wait, because the soup will need to simmer," she said.

When she set the bottle on the counter, John stepped closer and turned her toward him, settling his hands on either side of her jaw. Cupping her chin so he could lift her face and meet her gaze, he whispered huskily. "Do you know what *I* need?"

Her eyes bore into his, but rather than speak, she slowly shook her head.

"I *need* you to know that tonight isn't goodbye." He gave her a soft kiss on her forehead, before pulling back to look into her beautiful brown eyes again. Moisture gathered at the edge of her lids, and a knot inside him tightened. "I *need* you to know that I'll be back as soon as I can." Another kiss on the tip of her nose. "I *need* you to know that I could never love or need another woman as much as I love and need you." Tears slipped from the corners of her eyes and raced down her cheek, but he had one more thing he had to say. "Annie, sweetheart, *you* are my everything."

He heard her breath hitch in her throat before she swallowed hard and took hold of his forearms, squeezing her fingers into his flesh.

"After all the death and fear of the last several years, I never thought I could feel alive again, but you have changed that." More tears streaked down her cheeks. "I love you, *Zhaun.*"

Her words sucker punched him, leaving him breathless. She had never said those words to him before.

"Oh, Annie. How can I leave you?" He wiped away her tears with his thumbs before covering her mouth with his. He drank in the sweetness of her lips as he let his hands slip across her shoulders then down to her waist so he could pull her full length against him. When she slid her tongue along his lower lip, he groaned.

Without breaking their embrace, she lifted one of his hands to the zipper on the back of her dress and guided him to the clasp. Currents of desire shot from his fingertips and torched his body.

He shuddered as the tiny piece of metal slid down. When it reached the bottom, he knew they were at the point of no return.

CHAPTER FIVE

13 Dec 1944
0545

Dear Annie,

I'm sorry if my handwriting is shaky but I'm doing the best I can on the train. I don't know how to describe how I'm feeling. I've started and stopped several letters to you in the few hours since we left Paris station. I never thought I would find myself writing a letter like this. I'm struggling to find the right words because I feel so guilty for what I've done. I decided I would just come straight out and say it.

Our last few hours together before I left Paris were the best hours of my life. Every minute was like being in heaven. But my guilt has been eating at me. I'm so sorry for what happened, not because it wasn't beautiful, but because I took advantage of how upset you were when you found out we were shipping out. I've never done anything like that before with any woman. My head wasn't clear, and I took advantage of you.

Please know how much I love you. Even though it's been a short time that we've known each other, it feels like forever. I want you to know that I'm not the kind of man who takes advantage of girls. What am I saying? You're not a girl! You're a beautiful woman who made me feel more like a man than any tour in the army ever could.

I can still picture your tears after we made love. I wish you had told me why, but I can only hope they were tears of happiness, because if I hurt you it would kill me. If you were crying because you thought I only told you I loved you because of what we had just done, then you're so wrong. I believe in love at first sight, because I've loved you since the first time I saw you in the park with the children.

I'm sending you a present for Christmas, just a small token really, but I don't want you to think I'm doing it as payment for what happened. I'm sending it because I want you to have something to remember me by until I return. And I will return as I promised. I just don't know when. I promised to help you find your family, and I will do that.

I hadn't planned for our last night together to go the way it did, but while I feel guilty, I'm not sorry. Our time together is a memory that will help me keep my head up, and I'll look forward to being reunited.

I'm so thankful to have photos of you to help get me through the dark days. YOU and your love are what keep me going. I'll start and end every day by looking at your photo, and I'll always keep them in my breast pocket – next to my heart.

Please forgive me, my love. I pray you don't hate me.

Forever yours,
John (Or, to you, – Jean)

15 Dec 1944
1100 hrs

Dear Annie,

Do you have any idea how much I miss you already? It seems like weeks, not days, since we left Paris. I'm not sure how to begin this letter because I worry about how long we'll be apart. I'm concerned that you'll think that what we had is over and my commitment I made to you is false. It's not, dear one. I WILL be back. I promise. Even if it's not until this war is over, I will be back, and we will find your family.

I keep going over in my mind what our brief time together was like. Even today I can picture the first day I saw you in the park. You were as beautiful as the Madonna, surrounded by the small children who looked up to you as if you were their mother.

I smile to myself when I think of Benjamin and his difficulty listening. He didn't learn from his experience falling out of the tree, did he? The children are all so wonderful. Maybe someday we can adopt all of them. They are just innocents and deserve to have a family.

The other fellas have been razzing me since they saw us dancing at the club. They're just jealous. When I close my eyes, I can still feel you in my arms, swaying and twirling to the music. It's like we were meant to meet. I'm aching, sweetheart. Inside everything is a knot because I feel like I just found you and now I'm losing you. I left my heart there with you, love.

You know that Billie Holiday song I asked them to play for us in the café? 'The Very Thought of You'. I can't get that song out of my head because it's how I feel. I see your face everywhere.

As soon as we're settled in Belgium I'll send you my new address. That's where we'll set up the next hospital, but they never give us concrete timeframes for these things.

I'm getting tired, so I'll close. I love you, Annie, with all my heart. I am forever yours.

Until we can be together again,
Jean

January 3

Dearest brother-in-law,

I was happy to finally get a letter from you. What happened to that good friend of mine who wrote every day or two? I think maybe you have been busy with other things if your last letter meant what I thought. Annie sounds wonderful but Goodman does not sound very Irish — or French for that matter. Tell me more about her.

Christmas was solemn for us this year with you and Timothy gone. I went to the midnight Mass Christmas Eve because it's something Timothy and I have done together since we met. It was not joyous for me. It was very hard to sit there without him. Father Michael said that Mass. He did a wonderful job.

I hope you received the small gifts your mother and I sent to you. It was not much but we did not want Christmas to go by without some reminder of home.

Keep safe and know that you are in our prayers.

With love,
Maggie

5 Jan 1944
0600 hrs

Dearest Maggie,

As you know, I am no longer in France. We left the next
day after my last letter to you. This time they moved us to
Liege, Belgium. I suspect we will be here for some time. At first,
we were at a school but that was bombed, so we were forced to
move. Now they've put us up in the Citadel. It's a prison up on
a hill. So I have gone from Paris to prison. Don't tell Mama
and Pops or Pops will have a heart attack. Ha! I'll sugar coat it
in my letter to them.

Living arrangements are a bit cramped but it's still better
than a tent or the open ground. Our bunks are in the prison
cells and we have eight of us sleeping in the little room. The
doors to the cells have been removed so at least we don't have
to worry about someone locking us in while we're sleeping.
Knowing some of these pranksters, it's exactly what they
would do.

It's much different here from Paris. The Germans haven't
given up even though they have been chased out. We never
know if a buzz bomb is going to hit. The bombs look like
miniature airplanes with little engines on them. When we hear
them overhead we all run out and take bets on where the
engine is going to stall and it will drop. It's a helluva thing to
live with, but I guess we would all go crazy if we stopped to
think about how easy it would be for one of us to be killed.

The war is even more real to us here. We go over into

Germany where we see shells of buildings that used to be there. Just walls standing with rubble inside. Once in a while we see someone living in a basement but otherwise I keep wondering where all of these people have gone. These were towns with thousands of people and now they're just piles of stone and sticks. Pray that a war is never again fought on American soil gal because it is hell.

Yesterday a couple of Jews ended up in our hospital. They had escaped a prisoner camp and walked hundreds of miles to get away from the Nazi occupied areas. They were so thin and sick that we could see the outline of every rib and their shoulder blades. I've seen mutts on the streets back home that looked better than these guys did. I won't go into detail because it's horrific, but they told us about being dragged from their homes, watching family, friends, and neighbors killed in the street. Homes and businesses burned. All just because they're Jewish. Their stories turn my stomach.

I miss my Parisian angel. I just wish I didn't have to leave her behind. I can't wait for the day when I can bring her to meet all of you. I know you'll love her.

Time to hit the bunk. Thank you for listening. You're the best!

With love,
J.P.

Daniel folded the two pages of faded stationery and tucked them back in the envelope. The letters had him on a rollercoaster of emotions. If this was what it was like to read about their lives, he couldn't imagine living it.

His stomach growled at the same time he heard movement on the stairs. A few seconds later Liz peered around the corner, her forehead creased with concern.

"Do you know it's 6:00?" she asked.

He laid the letter back on the pile. "I'm taking the day off."

Her eyes widened, and she stepped into the den. "Are you sick? Is something wrong? It's not like you to take time off before the holidays."

"No, nothing's wrong. I just kept thinking about these letters during the night and decided to come down and look at them."

She quirked one eyebrow, then looked at the crate. "And?"

"I still don't understand why my mother was so insistent that I read these now. I don't understand what this has to do with what's between me and Liam."

"No insight, huh?"

"Not really. The closest I can come to thinking there's a connection is a letter that I just read in which it was revealed that my uncle fell in love with a woman in France who apparently wasn't Irish, and if I'm picking up any clues, she might have been German."

Liz ruffled her tousled hair with her fingertips while she stretched. "And given that Protestant was the dominant religion in Germany at the time, chances are she wasn't Catholic."

"I'm wondering if that's a comparison my mother is trying to make between that love affair and Liam getting engaged to a Jewish girl." He shook his head. "But, that doesn't make sense. Protestants have most of the beliefs that we do, so it's not the same. Christmas is Christmas.

Easter is Easter. But Passover and Easter are definitely not the same."

"Okay, then, I'm back to the fact that she wasn't Irish." Liz furrowed her brow, indicating she needed more information. It was something she'd always done, a gesture he loved.

"Well, that generation definitely stuck with the Irish clan." He shrugged, then scrubbed his palm across his eyes before looking up at his wife. "I want Liam to be happy, Liz. I know he is now, but what happens later? Where will Mora stand when we have Christmas dinner? Or Easter, especially? I don't want this to divide our family." Daniel shook his head. "Hell, it already has."

"That's on you, Daniel."

His shoulders tensed.

"Thanks for your support." His sarcasm thickened the air between them.

"It has nothing to do with support and everything to do with you accepting that times are changing. Gone are the days of only marrying within your religion. Come on! Lines are blurred everywhere now with religion *and* ethnicity. It's the whole melting pot effect. The 1960's effect." Liz kneeled next to the crate and shuffled through the photos. "I'm putting my trust in your mother on this one. She's a wise woman." She picked one of the photos he'd been looking at earlier with the woman in it. "Who's this?"

"I'm guessing it's Annie Goodman."

"And Annie Goodman is..." Liz's voice trailed off as she studied the woman's image.

"The woman my uncle fell in love with. She's a teacher at an orphanage connected to a convent. If I'm reading between the lines right, the children were sneaked out of Germany at the beginning of the war after their parents were killed by the Nazis. There were a lot of Jewish sympathizers in the country, and if they were caught helping Jews, they were often shot on the spot. No questions asked."

"How awful." She pulled the photo a little closer. "She's very pretty," Liz remarked before returning the picture to the spot where she'd found it. Peering into the crate, she picked up a few letters. "You have a lot of reading here."

"No kidding. That's why I took the day off. But at least my mother bundled the ones she thought were most important."

Liz stretched, then stood. "I'll let you get back to this. I hope it helps."

There was a little pull in Daniel's chest. "Me, too."

Liz started to turn away, but Daniel reached for her hand and held her by her fingers. Her skin was still warm from sleep. What he wouldn't give to pull her down on his lap and hold her tight, kissing her thoroughly. When she twisted to look at him, he decided to attempt something smaller.

"Honey? How about a kiss to start my day off right?"

She hesitated, and his heart lurched. If she rejected him it would tear him apart. But she didn't. She leaned over and brushed her lips across his. He closed his eyes, savoring the brief contact, breathing in her scent.

"I love you, Liz," he whispered, his voice tight.

"I love you, too, Danny, but I can't side with you on this thing with Liam." Suddenly her eyes glistened, on the verge of tears. "I hope your mother is right about those letters helping. It's Christmas. Our family is supposed to be happy."

His throat constricted. All he could do was nod. She withdrew her hand from his grasp and slipped from the room. He could understand how his uncle had fallen in love so easily. It had been the same way with him the first time he saw Liz more than thirty years ago when she was a soda jerk at Hinsch's in Bay Ridge.

Daniel believed in love at first sight, because that's how he'd felt that August day in 1963 when she'd looked at him from across the counter with those gorgeous green eyes and asked, "What'll you have?"

That was it. The sound of her voice, and he was hooked. He'd leaned forward on the counter, smiled his best smile, and said, "How 'bout a date with you?"

She'd tipped her head and tapped the eraser of her pencil against her lower lip before answering, "Gonna have to work harder than that, honey."

By the third time he'd gone into the diner and insisted on ordering only from her, then tipped her double the total of his bill, she capitulated. Later she told him that she'd have accepted the first time he asked except she wanted to wait to see what kind of tipper he was.

"It told me everything I needed to know about your character," she said with a coquettish wink.

And they were married as soon as she graduated college.

A lump settled in his throat, and it hurt when he swallowed against it. He needed to mend this rift.

He lifted the next letter, one from the mysterious Annie Goodman to his Uncle John, and removed it from the envelope. "Please give me answers," he mumbled.

Jan 12

My dearest Jean, my love,

When I saw the envelope with your letter to me today my heart sang. I am happy to have your address.

First, I must share that I was saddened to read of your remorse. You are worrying for nothing. I am not angry with you. I was worried that you now thought less of me. It is true that you were my first, but I have no regrets. I feel your love in so many ways. I keep it inside me to light my days. So, please, dear man, know how much I love you and I would not change anything. I'll cherish our last hours together every day until we meet again.

If I am to be angry about anything it is that we were brought together only to be pulled apart again. My heart hurts with concern and loneliness.

Thank you for your gift, though it was not necessary. The exquisite ruby teardrop necklace is beautiful. I wear it always because it keeps you close to me. Before I go to sleep each night I hold it and think of you, hoping for dreams with you in them.

I enclosed a petal to the rose you gave me so long ago. It fell off the day after you left, and it made me cry because I do not want to lose you or for things to change like this rose has. I want everything to stay the way it was when you last touched it.

I buy a newspaper every day to watch for news that might

come out of Belgium. I worry that there will be bombings or fighting near you. Even though you are medical corps that does not make you immune.

The children at the orphanage ask for you now. They think you are wonderful just as I do. I have been teaching them geography and show them where you are. It is not the same with you gone. Sometimes I have trouble remembering what life was like before I met you. I only know that it is immensely better now. You are a brave and honorable man.

You have shown me that there are good, kind, loving men still. I feared that you would think less of me because you are such a man of faith, and now I learn that you feared I would think less of you. Please can we look at this as an act of love so that our memory of that last day together is joyful?

I will change the subject and we will never speak of this guilt again.

You will be happy to know that some of the children under my care are now finding homes with local families. It is a bittersweet time. Because I have taken care of them for so long, I feel like they are my own. These children have lost so much and must be adopted by families who understand their past. Please keep them in your prayers as they find their way.

I have decided to take classes at University again. You have given me the courage to continue to pursue my dreams. I am excited to become a nurse so that I can do good in the world. Who knows? Maybe someday, I will even become a doctor.

I pray that we will be together again soon and that I will be with my brother and sisters, too. We can all be a family.

I'll write again soon. Be safe, my love. I need you to come back to me.

With deep affection,
Annie

26 Jan 1944
2100 hrs

Dear, dear Annie,

You have no idea how relieved I was to receive your letter. I didn't think it was possible to love you more than I already did, but you've proved me wrong. We have so much to look forward to.

We had a near catastrophe here at the hospital yesterday. One of those buzz bombs the damn Nazis love so much dropped in the middle of our complex. It skidded along a few hundred feet before it hit a corner of the building. It tore a hole in that end of the building, but luckily no one was killed. We had to evacuate patients from that section. Now they're crammed into even tighter quarters. What a mess!

My brother Timothy sent me a note saying they'll be shipping to Europe, too. For all I know, he could already be here. I'm hoping his wife will be able to tell me where. I know it will be hard for them to be apart, too. We're so lucky to have Maggie in our family. She's our rock right now who is keeping us connected to home through letters.

Hub is still acting up here, too. He's on extra KP duty because a couple of nights ago he decided to take a jeep into town. It wasn't bad enough that he went without permission, but add to that he took our C.O.'s jeep! (C.O. is commanding officer). If Hub doesn't end up court martialed before the end of the war, it's going to be a miracle. But you know what, he's a swell guy and he keeps everyone laughing. That's probably the only thing that saves him from bigger trouble.

Give hugs to the children for me. I'm glad they'll be getting homes soon. I look forward to your next letter. You're forever in my heart, and always on my mind.

With all my love,
Jean

28 Jan 1944
2030 hrs.

Dear Maggie,

I'll try to not sound too down in this letter, but the last few weeks have been the hardest of my life. It may seem fast, but my love for Annie is deep and it was hard to leave her behind. Life isn't fair, I know. Who am I to complain when you're missing your husband?

Let me think more positive thoughts. I can't wait for you to meet Annie. You asked me to tell you more about her. Maybe writing about her and sharing her with you will make me feel like she's closer to me. Her family is from Germany. She came to France in 1938 when she was sixteen to live with her grandmother who worked at the university.

Annie's a brilliant woman. She wants to be a nurse, but when the war broke out she had to stop her studies. She tried to return to Germany to her family, but there was no way to get back safely. Then her grandmother died and the nuns at a local convent took her under their wings.

Annie learned that her parents were killed in 1942. She

found this out through a cousin who sneaked out of Germany and found her in Paris, but shortly after she lost contact with him. Her younger brother and sisters are teenagers, but she doesn't know what happened to them. She's praying they were taken in by a relative. She's been looking for them, and I told her as soon as I can, I'll help her. She hasn't seen them in six years.

What did you think of Annie's pictures? She's beautiful, isn't she? I keep one of her pictures in my breast pocket so she's always near my heart. It wasn't easy to find a place to get them developed but it's amazing how money talks.

This probably all sounds like silly ramblings to you, but you did want to know about her. You'll love her. I hope that it will be soon.

There's a small church near here. I'm hoping to attend Mass tonight. It never worked out for Annie and me to attend Mass together while I was in Paris. I wanted nothing more than to go before God in His house and declare my love for her. In His sight, our love would have felt blessed.

I know I've said it many times before but thank you so much for writing to me. In the days when I wonder if this is all worth it, your letters remind me of what our country is fighting for.

I apologize that my letters aren't as frequent anymore, but there's little down time. It's also hard to get motivated to write when I miss everyone so much. All of you but especially Annie. I've only been in Belgium for a short time and already I feel like a big part of me is missing.

The last couple of months have been the toughest of my life. It was just so hard to leave Annie. Even though Belgium and France border each other, I feel like Paris is a whole world away. It will be almost six hours by truck or train. Let's hope

*this damned war will end soon so we can all be reunited with
those we love.*

*When I was in Paris I told the nuns in the convent about
my brother the priest. It still seems funny to call him FATHER
Michael. I should be used to it by now. I was surprised to hear
that one of the priests at the church knows him. They met on
the same visit to the Vatican just before the war started and
have remained somewhat in contact. The world is smaller
than we think.*

*Have you heard from Timothy? How about any other
news from back home. You probably know more about what's
happening on the warfront there than we do here in the
middle of it. It doesn't look likely that we'd be mobilized for any
front-line action soon. It's bad enough when we get the guys
who come through our hospital. I see the shape some of them
are in and wonder if they just wish they'd died. I shut off my
feelings so I can deal with it objectively, but there are very sad
cases.*

*My best to you, Maggie girl. I couldn't ask for a better
sister-in-law. I'll pray that your dreams come true.*

God bless,
John

֍

Daniel returned the letter to its envelope, careful to not
bend the tanned, brittle paper. He brushed away the tiny
pieces of what he now knew were from the rose petal
mentioned in the earlier letter. The loneliness they all
must have felt was sad, but, then he thought of what else
was happening in their lives, and it warmed him.

New love. He remembered the giddy feeling when he and Liz started officially seeing each other. Every date seemed like a new adventure, even if they were only going out for a malt or burger. He couldn't fathom what it must have felt like to fall in love in the middle of a war half a world away.

And, the situation between his uncle and Annie was complicated. He admired his uncle's virtue, his desire to do right by this young woman he had fallen in love with. And his mother. How difficult it must have been for her to stay positive when food was in short supply, her husband was away, faced with finding work to keep the rent paid, and helping take care of her in-laws. She was truly a remarkable woman.

The reference in the letters to the plight of the European Jews tickled his conscience. Mora had mentioned on a couple of occasions that she had family members who had been victims of Hitler's bedlam. Daniel had only seen it as a piece of tragic history in her family, but reading these letters gave him a different perspective from just hints his uncle gave.

If Liam and Mora did marry, and if they had children, then that family history would be *their* history, too. Could he condemn his own grandchildren the way Hitler persecuted the Jews? The whole scenario was preposterous. He'd never condemn *anyone* over their religion. It wasn't Christian behavior.

The hairs on the back of his neck prickled. Was he picking up on yet another point his mother was trying to drive home through these letters? Did she want him to make comparisons between what Hitler did to the Jews and his objections to Liam and Mora's engagement?

His jaw tensed. The two situations weren't the same. He wasn't condemning Mora for her religion. He was doing his duty as the wise father who had experienced more in life. Had seen more. It was his way of protecting his oldest son from the possibility of a life-altering decision.

Daniel glanced back down at the crate and the dozens of still-unread letters. What happened if he read all of them and didn't get whatever message his mother hoped? At the very least he would have learned more about his own family — about the uncle he'd never met but who had been a presence larger than life since Daniel was born.

He knew better than that. His mother wouldn't insist on him spending time on something trivial, especially during the busiest time of year. Whatever he was going to learn, he had no doubt it would have a huge impact on something in his life.

He took a few more letters onto his lap then lifted the footrest of the recliner. To anyone who might see him, his body position indicated he was relaxed, but he couldn't ignore the little knot of foreboding that tugged in his gut. He sensed that these letters were more than sweet, innocent love stories.

CHAPTER SIX

February 14

Dear John Patrick,

I hope you are safe and doing well. The holidays are a very hard time to be apart from our loved ones. I'm sorry I haven't written in some time but it has been very hard. Timothy's unit did finally ship out. I hope somehow the two of you can get together while you are both in Europe.

He was home last month. My heart is broken. That was his last visit. Even though he was gone before, knowing he will be an ocean away makes me so lonely. We had two beautiful days together. Bittersweet days. It is so hard when you know you are going to be apart for a long time.

We were relieved to have your letter arrive. The newspapers have been full of the news about the Battle of the Bulge and we thought it was where you were. In his Fireside Chat a few weeks ago, President Roosevelt tried to calm our fears. It is very difficult to not be worried when we are waiting for news from you.

Did you hear that Peter's wife had a baby last month? I did not know if I told you that in the last letter. They had a little girl. Peter got to see her while he was home on leave. He was shipped to the Pacific right after that.

I must get ready for work. I am sure your mother shared most news from here so I will not repeat it.

Every day I wait for the postman to arrive in case there is a letter from Timothy or you. William is no longer delivering our route because he enlisted in the army and left two weeks ago. Now we have a very young man who limps. His name is George. I watch him hobble down the street and admire his determination to perform his job. I do not know if he was injured in war or if he has a defect that kept him from going. He is very conscientious and he now smiles all the way up the sidewalk when he has a letter from Timothy.

I hope you are hearing from Annie. I can not wait to meet her. Anyone who can make my dear brother in law so happy has to be very special.

Please take care of yourself and stay safe.

With love to you,
Maggie

Tucking the letter back in the envelope, Daniel couldn't help but smile. The loneliness and sadness of the time was evident, but he couldn't mistake the timing for what was to come for his parents — something easy for him to see after the fact. His mother mentioned in letters about her desire to be a mother.

Mission accomplished on his father's last visit home before he shipped out, because he was born nine months later — October 14, 1945.

Over the years his mother had told him on many occasions how fortunate they felt to have him. He, in return, was fortunate to have them for parents. He had never wanted for anything — especially love.

He opened the next letter, still not making a connection to the situation with Liam but beginning to appreciate this unique opportunity to see into his family's life before him.

∞∞

8 Mar 1945
0230 hrs

Dear Maggie,

I apologize that it's been some time since I wrote. I think of my family often, especially with the holidays. I told Ma in my last letter to her that I got the fruitcake she sent me for Christmas, but don't tell her it wasn't good by the time it got here. My mail got backed up with the move, then somehow the cake got wet in the package so it was moldy. On the bright side, I fed it to the birds because I knew it would make her happy considering how much she loves the birds

It's the middle of the night, but I can't sleep. In fact, I haven't slept for a while. The world's gone crazy around here and I'm trying to make sense of what we've endured.

Here the Battle of the Bulge is called the Battle of Ardennes because the Krauts surrounded the Ardennes Forest. Because our news is sometimes spotty, at first we thought there were two separate battles. Just when we think maybe we're making headway and this war might end, something more happens.

We haven't heard specifics, but based on the number of casualties that came through our medical unit, we must have lost tens of thousands of soldiers. So many guys died in my arms before we could get them the help they needed.

I thought I'd seen the worst when we came in after the Normandy invasion. I can't even tell you how bad this was. One day a bad snowstorm hit and piled up fast. We were trying to bring the wounded in and we'd run over a mound of snow, only to discover it was a body.

All that day we never got inside for more than a few minutes at a time. Our hands and feet were so soaked and cold that they froze stiff. The only way we could catch any warmth was to duck into a doorway of a damaged building and huddle together for a few minutes. All I'll say is frost bite hurts like hell.

Before it snowed, the air smelled like death. I imagined we'd gone to Hell and Satan was burning bodies. I hardly ate for several days, because my stomach couldn't hold anything down.

How is your job working out? I did send a letter to Timothy using the address you sent me. Hopefully his unit doesn't move before he gets it, but even if they do, it will eventually catch up with him. I hope he has been able to keep you informed of where he is so you don't have to worry.

I miss Annie terribly. After the way Patty crushed me, I never thought I could feel this way again so soon. I guess it took a very special woman to get me to let my guard down. And Annie IS that woman. Her heart is bigger than the sun *and shines even brighter. I wish you could see how she is with the children. She is going to be a wonderful mother someday. I pray each night that her future is with me. I promised her I'd be back and that when I got out of the service my priority would be to take care of her. I want to bring her and her brother and sisters back to America and away from the terrible memories here. Only God knows if that's in His plan.*

I know it must be hard for you stateside to hear all that's happening over here and to know how it affects us. Compared to most units, ours is safe. Being a medic, I don't see action on the front, only the terrible after effects. It's horror, for sure, but after you see it constantly you force yourself to forget these are human beings. You just see them as broken bodies. Some you can fix and some you can't. I disengage my brain from what it really is. It's mental survival.

Sorry for the grim ending. Be well.

My love to all,
John Patrick

☙❧

Daniel let his hand with the letter rest on the arm of the chair, and he leaned his head back to close his eyes. The way the war period was recounted in these letters brought vivid images to his mind. His history teachers had taught lessons on World War II, but they'd either purposely glossed over the brutality, or, he wondered, didn't even know how bad it had been.

Not even Mr. Randolph, a veteran of the European campaign, had shared specifics. He had to have seen some of these horrors. Daniel was sure if his teacher had given the kinds of details he was reading in these letters, he would have remembered. But, then, his own father had always skirted around the topic.

How many times, as a child, had Daniel asked his father if he'd ever killed someone? Had he ever shot his gun? Had he seen others die? What did it look like where bombs were dropped? What did he see? Was he scared? Did he think Daniel would have to go and fight in a war, too?

Daniel opened his eyes to look at the photo at the center of a grouping of family pictures on the wall opposite him. There wasn't bright light on the one he looked at, but it was one he'd seen so many times since childhood that he'd memorized everything about it. It was of his father and uncle, taken the last time they were together.

Both in uniform, they stood next to each other, assuming a pose that conveyed the pride they felt wearing their country's uniform. Daniel could only imagine the emotions going through their minds, despite the stance of bravado. He wondered if they'd known then that one of them wouldn't come home, if they might have stood closer together with arms over each other's shoulders, instead.

The only questions his father ever answered were about friends he made in the service and the good memories he made with them. Daniel had heard a couple of stories about families his father had helped, and he often recounted his only visit back to Ireland to visit while he was stationed in England. But that was it. No stories of valor. No stories of horror. No stories of fighting. It was as if his father had erased it all from his memory.

He sighed, suddenly feeling the weight everyone must have felt at that time. The challenges and horrors seemed to outweigh the blessings, but he could see how his family continued on each day, expecting — praying — life would get better. Living on this side of that time period, he knew the outcome, but he admired their faith.

Picking up the next letter, he thought of the questions that still swirled in his mind. He'd never imagined that love letters would be so full of information, and he looked forward to reading more.

March 16, 1945

Dear Johnny,

I hope me calling you that made you smile.

I was happy to hear that your girl is writing to you. You deserve a wonderful woman. Timothy has told me how difficult it is for all of you to be so far from home. He is very lonely as I am sure you are. It is a relief to know that at this point neither of you is on the front lines.

You telling what it is like being a medic reminds me of the terrible stories that we are hearing from over there.

Steven Leyton wrote to his mother from radar school in Georgia. He said there were many Poles there. He met one who was in Russia after Poland fell and the man told him all he wants to do now is kill Germans. He saw the German officers cut his mother in half just because she asked where they were taking her husband. I am horrified by such evil and hatred. It upset your mother when she heard it because you are so close to Germany.

In Timothy's last letter he said when he gets a few days leave he plans to go to Ireland to see your grandparents. They will not recognize him since he was born after your parents came to America. If he has time he will go to see my mother too. I am jealous because it has been so long since she moved back there and I miss her terribly. I know she will love him as much as I do.

My job is fine but I am having trouble keeping up with the hours and helping your sister and brother take care of your parents too. I am exhausted all the time.

When I was in the grocery yesterday I overheard a man in a fight with Mr. Gilbert, the man who bought the store from the Legarios family. They were harping on him because the price of the cigarettes was so high and he had only a few packs left. There is such a shortage of cigarettes for civilians and it is making the smokers crazy.

I must end this. I need a nap before I make dinner for your parents and go to work. Please tell your Annie that I am looking forward to meeting her someday.

With love,
Your favorite sister-in-law

31 Mar 1945
1900 hrs

Dear Maggie,

Right now, the letters from home are finding me quickly. I hate it when they are stopped somewhere so then we don't get *them for a while. I haven't received letters from Annie lately and I'm wondering if that's what's happening with her letters. I miss her so much.*

I wish I could go with Timothy to Ireland. I sent a letter to him last week. He's not as good about writing as you are.

I knew about the cigarette shortage, because Hub got a letter from his mother and she told about it. Some of the guys say "P.F.C" (Poor Free Civilians) should roll their own cigs, and if they still complain, they should sign up to join the army so they can get their cigarettes cheap. They only cost 60 cents a carton for a G.I. Sometimes the government gives them to the guys on the front lines for free. Tell that to the "P.F.C." complainers.

I just looked back over what I wrote, and it didn't sound very nice, but it's hard to think about people being safe in their own homes back in the U.S. and complaining when there are guys dying over here. They just don't know how good they have it, and it's all because of the guys who died in wars to keep them free. Guess I better change the subject.

I sent another money order to Ma in a letter I wrote to her just before this. Can you check to make sure she got it, please? That's a lot of money to lose. It's the $44 pay from January and the $66 from February. They got backed up somehow, so I got both at once. I know it's a lot of money, but I kept enough out for me in case I can get liberty to go to France to visit Annie. I want Ma to put it in the bank for doctor bills for Pop. I don't want them worrying about money.

I wonder about the guys down at the precinct and hope everyone is okay. I miss walking the beat and seeing the people in the neighborhood. Sometimes I imagine what it must be like there at night right now with the blackout orders. Easy for criminals to get away with things that way.

Hub just came in and wants to go into town. Guess I could use the distraction. I'm sorry this is so sloppy. I'm writing this on my knees since I don't have a table.

Love,
Johnny

❦

The aroma of fresh-baked muffins permeated Daniel's senses and drew his attention from the letter he had just finished. Replacing the stationery in the faded envelope, he set the last few letters on the finished stack in the crate. He rolled his shoulders to pull himself out of the mental time warp of the correspondences.

The writing was so vivid that it transported him back to an era he'd heard about his entire life and now felt he was reliving vicariously.

He glanced at the antique cherry mantel clock on the bookcase. It was almost 7:00. Usually by this time of the morning he had a train loaded with passengers and was halfway through his first run across Manhattan. Liz always left for school around this time — a comfortable routine since she'd returned to teaching science at the high school. In fact, every aspect of their life had settled into a comfortable routine.

From his perspective, their children's upbringing had been idyllic. Just like when he was growing up, their mother was with them whenever they were home. Those times when Liz had meetings after school, the children went to his parents' house three blocks away where they received a heavy dose of their Irish heritage. His mother spoiled them with traditional treats. A favorite was the sweet, rich raisin cake. No one made it like his mother and grandmother. His mouth watered just thinking about it.

"I'll never be as Irish as you are, Danny," Liz had said with a carefree laugh after each failed attempt at making foods that were foreign to her. Her father was Irish, but her mother was Swedish and Danish. Her favorite comment was that at least she was 100% "ish" when the three ancestries were combined.

Even his father's mother had lived to the ripe old age of 96, so the children had learned about their heritage from three generations of Irish throughout childhood. His children came home from visiting Great-Grandma Coughlin speaking with an exaggerated Irish lilt. Daniel knew they weren't mocking her. Instead, they were emulating. They were being raised with a healthy appreciation for their heritage and traditions.

Traditions. What would Liam and Mora do when the family attended Mass together? Would Liam attend without her? Would she attend for his sake? Would they bring their children? Or would Liam drop his own traditions and religious beliefs so the children could be raised in the Jewish faith? The knot in his stomach returned with a vengeance. So many unknowns. So many possible changes.

A timer rang in the kitchen, then he heard metal against metal as he assumed Liz removed the muffins from the rack in the oven. He set the current stack of letters on the arm of the chair. He was hungry, but more than that, a few minutes with Liz, sharing what he'd read so far, would also keep it all fresher as he moved forward.

After a quick stop to wash his hands, he started down the hall toward the kitchen. He came up short when he heard Liam's tenor voice mixing with Liz's in conversation.

He peered into the kitchen. Liam, in his navy-blue police uniform, stood in the doorway to the back porch. His thick patrolman's jacket was unzipped, and his right hand was perched on his hip above the gun holster, holding the jacket flap back. His uniform hat dangled from the other hand.

Daniel only heard the end of his sentence.

"...sure everything is okay."

Liz moved in front of the hall door to put her lunch bag on the counter. "Sure, honey, everything's fine. Why?"

"I was patrolling the area and saw Dad's car in the driveway..." Liam's voice trailed off.

Trepidation rippled across Daniel's shoulders. Act naturally, he said to himself as he stepped into view in the kitchen.

"Good morning, Son." He crossed to the cupboard nearest Liam and took a cup from the shelf.

"Want some?" he asked as he poured from the pot.

Out of the corner of his eye, Daniel saw Liam drop his hand from his hip and shift his weight from one booted foot to the other. When Daniel looked up to meet Liam's gaze, Liam shifted his attention to his mother as if she had spoken.

"No, thanks. Can't stay. I'm pulling a double today to help a buddy. Shift changes in less than an hour, and I have some paperwork to do before I start the next shift."

Daniel stopped pouring and looked at him. Liam filled out his uniform well. He looked authoritative in his stance. Pride skittered through Daniel. He couldn't be prouder of the man Liam had become.

"Five minutes?" he pressed, topping off his cup. "Maybe have a muffin?"

"They don't get any fresher," Liz interjected, reaching for a hot pad hanging next to the stove. She picked up the full muffin tin and moved it to the wooden cutting board on the table.

Liam tapped the brim of his hat against his palm. "No, thanks, really." He stepped into the kitchen to give Liz a quick kiss on the cheek. "I'll talk to you soon."

Moving to the back door, he pulled it open, but hesitated before going out. With his back to them, he cleared his throat and said, "I'm glad you're okay, Dad. I was worried when I saw you didn't go to work."

Then in two steps, with a whoosh of frosty air heralding his exit, he was gone.

Daniel pushed the mug of coffee away from the edge of the counter and hurried to the door, pulling it open almost as soon as Liam closed it.

"Liam?"

Liam stopped at the bottom of the wooden stairs and turned. "Yeah."

"Maybe we can sit down and talk this through. You know, man to man."

Liam cocked a dark brow. "Talk *what* through?"

"This situation with you and Mora."

Daniel sensed Liz step behind him, but he kept his focus on their son.

Liam dropped his chin, pulled his top lip between his teeth, and shook his head. After exhaling loudly, he lifted his gaze.

"Mora and I don't *have* a situation, Dad. It's *my* life. *My* choice. *My* future. I love Mora. She's an amazing woman. I've asked her to marry me. The end." He sliced his hand through the air on the last two words as if to punctuate his staccato sentences. "I feel like I don't even know you right now. Where's the guy who made every one of my friends feel welcome, including Mora? She's good enough to be my friend but not my wife just because she's Jewish?"

Daniel bristled. "Whoa! You're out of line, Liam."

Anger flashed in Liam's eyes, but he kept his tone even. "*I'm* out of line? Did we learn nothing from World War II regarding religious intolerance? You're the one implying that my fiancée doesn't measure up to our *good* Catholic standards, Dad. I think *you're* out of line. I suggest you do some real soul-searching, and maybe then we'll have something to sit down and talk about. I'm not saying anything to Mora because I'm praying to God — yours, mine *and* Mora's, because it's the *same* one — that you have some kind of awakening."

Daniel stared, speechless, as Liam pivoted and stalked to his patrol car, pulling away from the curb without looking back.

A frigid breeze swept around Daniel, bringing goosebumps to his arms. He turned in time to see Liz wipe away tears that streaked her cheeks. She pivoted away and hurried across the kitchen.

"Liz?" he called, but she was already into the hallway. He closed the door and followed her. "Honey, Liam and I will work this out. It's just a misunderstanding."

She snatched her black pea coat from the closet and slipped it on, again wiping her face before grabbing the strap of the overstuffed satchel full of papers she'd spent hours grading the night before. She slid the strap over her shoulder, moved past Daniel to take her lunch bag off the counter in the kitchen, and headed for the same door Liam had just used.

She pulled open the door then stopped and turned toward him, nodding in the direction of the den.

"You better keep reading or read more carefully, Danny, because if your mother is right and the solution to this disagreement is in that crate, you need to find it before this *misunderstanding* is irreparable."

He moved down the hall toward her. "I'll stop by the station and see Liam when he gets off shift. Maybe take him to breakfast so I can talk with him."

"No," she said, squinting at him as if she were confused. "That's not the answer. What's changed in your mind between now and a few minutes ago? Nothing." She shifted the satchel to her other shoulder and opened the door wider. "Put yourself in Liam's shoes, Danny. How would you have felt if your parents hadn't accepted me when you told them we were getting married?"

The question sobered him. He couldn't imagine that. Stepping toward Liz, he gave her a kiss. "It will work out, Liz, I promise."

"Go back to the letters. I'm trusting your mother on this. As mysterious as it all seems, obviously there's something she wants you to know." She stepped into the cold garage and called over her shoulder. "Early dismissal today for conferences, but I don't have any, so I'll be home early."

She tossed her satchel on the back seat of her Camry then got into the driver's seat. Daniel watched until she pulled out of the garage and the door automatically descended. He backed away from the inside door and closed it. Despite the enticing aroma of the apple cinnamon muffins, his appetite had evaporated with Liam's harsh words.

He returned to the kitchen and put two muffins on a plate, anyway. After cutting them in half and slathering a pat of butter on each side, he lifted his cup of coffee to his lips, taking a sip as the steam curled around his face. There was something soothing about the way the hot brew slid down his throat. He savored the taste, then with his free hand he picked up the plate with the muffins and returned to the den.

He sat in the recliner and set the muffins and coffee on the lamp stand next to him. Liam's angry words about an awakening echoed in his mind. Picking up the handful of letters he'd left on the chair's arm, he untied the red braided cord holding them together and removed the top one.

Was it one letter that held the answers his mother insisted were here, or would the message be cumulative? As he removed the letter, his fingers tingled with a sense of urgency. There was only one way to find out.

CHAPTER SEVEN

End of March 1945

John Patrick laced his fingers behind his head and lay back on the hard, musty pillow on his thin mattress. As usual, his thoughts settled on Annie. His feelings vacillated between euphoria and worry.

He reached under his bunk to feel for the box he kept there, then pulled out last year's calendar, flipping it open to October. The tiny little date squares contained the small check marks since he'd left Paris. Since he'd last seen Annie. Kissed her. Held her. Enjoyed the intoxicating scent of her hair. Some also contained little stars marking when he'd received letters from her. He glanced at the wall to the small calendar from Loftus Hardware that Maggie had sent him in one of his *family love packages*, as she called them. She'd sent that and a precious pair of new socks. Now, from a distance, he quickly calculated how many days in this new year had also gone by without letters.

He kept them all and had read them so many times that he'd practically memorized every sentence.

A pang of loneliness shot through his heart. What had changed?

For the first weeks the letters had come every couple of days. Then, there was a week between letters, and now, it had been three weeks since the last one. He'd wanted to call the orphanage, but he'd been unable to get the number. His letters hadn't been returned, so he assumed she received them. So why did hers suddenly stop coming?

For now, all he could do was wait and imagine the worst. Were they being confiscated by the army mail service? Had she become ill? Were the censors stopping her letters? There'd been no military activity in Paris, so the concern over bombings wasn't there. Had she decided to go back to Germany to look for her siblings without him?

An invisible weight crushed his chest. Maybe she'd just grown tired of waiting for him. There'd been no hint of those feelings, had there? He rolled toward his bag of belongings and retrieved the last letter from her. He loved everything about her, even her handwriting that was so meticulously set to paper. Unfolding it reverently, he savored the thought of her delicate fingers pressing each crease. Once unfolded, he held it at an angle to catch the dim light from overhead and read it again twice even though he'd read it so many times before that he'd practically memorized every word.

When finished, John carefully refolded the letter,

slipped it into its envelope and pressed it to his heart. He drew in a deep breath, sure he could smell her beautiful scent on the paper. Did she contact the escort and leave without telling him? In his return letter he had begged her to wait so he could go with her when he had accumulated leave for a few days off. The trip could be dangerous, especially if they entered an area where the Germans hid. Her chances for safe travel would be better if she was with an American soldier.

Hub entered the cell and dropped onto his bunk. For the most part, John enjoyed his irreverence about everything. 'Rules were made to be broken' was his mantra. And the fact that his promotions and demotions over offenses made it look like his army life was on a see-saw, only proved his resolve to live by that mantra.

"Jee-zus Christ!" he muttered, throwing his forearm across his eyes. "What the hell are we doing here?"

John hadn't seen him since early morning when they'd gone their separate ways for assigned duties. Hub worked the wagon duty, transporting men from the battle zones, a job that was an ironic mixture of thrills and morbid scenes.

Although reluctant to put it away, John returned Annie's letter to his bag. "Rough day, mate?"

"We didn't bring back one living soul. Jee-zus Christ!" Hub rolled over in his bunk and hunkered down, a clear signal to John that he wasn't interested in talking. He understood. Some days it was hard to get up knowing that maimed bodies and death were routine.

More than fifteen minutes passed before Hub finally rolled onto his back. He snatched the pack of cigarettes and book of matches off the crate next to him.

"Looks like I'm going to make Private again," he said, tapping the ends of the cigarette against his knee before striking a match and lighting it.

John chuckled and swung his legs over to sit on the edge of his cot. "Again? What'd you do this time?"

Gray plumes of smoke rose from Hub's pursed lips. "Nothin'."

"Nothing, huh? How long were you a Private First Class *this* time?"

Hub rolled his head to squint at John. "You mockin' me, Irish?" he asked, using the nickname he'd pinned on John from the moment they'd met. "'Cause, if you are, you gotta know I broke my own record." He pulled in another drag, then spit tiny pieces of tobacco toward the floor. "Hell, I was PFC almost three weeks this time. You should be proud of me."

"I'm gonna pin a medal on your chest, Hubbard." John pointed toward the concrete near his friend's bunk. "And don't flick your damn ashes on the floor."

Hub whistled. "Kinda prickly, aren't ya, Irish?"

"Prickly?"

"How 'bout crabby?" Hub leaned up on his elbow. "You like that word better?"

John shrugged and tucked the letter from Annie back into the box then slid that under his cot. "A lot on my mind."

"Get a letter from your gal today?"

A tiny lump caught in his throat, and he had to swallow it away before he could answer. Now his voice was quiet. "Unfortunately, no."

"You know what I think, Irish?" Hub said. "I say we hop the train to Paris. We both need to get away and I think you need to see that gal. Find out once and for all if she met somebody else and she's holding out on you."

Anger flared in John's gut. He clenched his fists, in his present state of mind needing very little provocation. He knew Hubbard was purposely goading him, probably to release some of his own frustration from a grueling day, but he'd picked the wrong fight. "Annie's not that type."

"Hell, Irish, you only spent a few weeks with her before we shipped out. How well can you know somebody in that amount of time? Especially a dame, for Christ's sake."

Leaping to his feet, John stalked toward the cell entrance, afraid he'd have his fist in Hub's face if he didn't move. "She wasn't looking for *me*. I found *her*, remember? I'm the one who pursued *her*."

Another match was struck from behind and cigarette smoke curled into the air in front of John's face. He heard Hub again spit the tiny pieces of tobacco that came off the end of the unfiltered cigarette. John bristled and shook his head

"Cheap crap they're giving us these days," Hub muttered.

John twisted to look at him. Hub was obviously in one of those moods where nothing was going to make him happy. John could argue with him until he was blue, but in the end, Hub would always consider himself right anyway.

"You could quit smoking."

"Quit? And be deprived of the only damn pleasure I'm getting' in this war? Hell no!" He drew in several long drags from the cigarette, leaving a hazy cloud in the dimly-lit cell. "Look, I was serious about going to Paris.

Maybe a couple of nights of drinking, dancing and a roll with a good woman would help my disposition."

John leaned against the metal bars and let the cold sink through to his skin. "I don't even know that Annie's there. She wanted to go look for her family in Germany."

"Christ! Germany? Not exactly a friendly destination." He spit a few more pieces of tobacco out. "So, let's go and find out. What's the difference whether you worry from here or there?" As he finished talking, Hub blew small smoke rings into the air above him. "Unless of course you think I'm right and she's dumped you."

"Go to Hell, Hubbard!" John ground out.

Hub erupted with a short, boisterous laugh. "Christ, Irish, I thought I already was in Hell. This sure ain't Paradise."

John shook his head and left. He could never win with this guy. No matter what, Hub was always going to have the last word. And John hated to admit it, but Hub was right. It had been weeks since the last letter from Annie. The only way to get answers was to go to Paris. But it was easily a six-hour drive by truck. Who knew if he could catch a train.

He slammed the palm of his hand against the concrete wall as he walked by, relishing the shards of pain that shot through his wrist and up his arm. It at least dulled the pain that pulsed in his chest with each heartbeat.

With barely a nod of acknowledgement, he shouldered past a couple of guys coming into the building as he exited. The moon caught his attention, bright against the dusky sky. Was Annie looking at that same moon right now? Could he somehow will a message to her? His throat tightened.

He'd never imagined falling in love like this, not in the middle of a war, for sure. But, then, he never could have anticipated meeting Annie.

❧

April 5, 1945

Dear J.P.,

I am so happy to hear about Annie and you. Thank you for the picture. Now I do not have to imagine how she looks. She is lovely. Very lovely. She looks happy and I think that is probably because of you. If this love is meant to be God will make it happen. Trust Him to take you on the right path.

Last week your mother finished her mother's flag and hung it in the window. I think she did not want to hang it before because then she could pretend she did not have two sons in this war. She insisted on making it herself with red, blue and white fabric that her cousin sent her from Dublin. She believes using Irish cloth will bring better luck for your and Timothy's safety. She put the two blue stars just touching at one tip. I look forward to the day when she can take it out of the window.

Almost every day your mother asks me to walk with her to the library. The names of the soldiers who have died are posted there. It is so sad to see and it frightens me. The list is growing too long.

Today I finally was able to get more sugar. It takes so many ration stamps for so little but it is a treat. I made sweet biscuits to go with stew. Father Michael and Sister Siobhan will be at your parents' house for dinner and I will share the stew with them. Father Michael will give them communion since your father is too weak right now to go to church. We cannot get more gas for the car, so Father Michael starts the engine each week to make sure it still runs but we do not drive it in case we need it for an emergency. These are hard times with so much rationing.

I am sorry. I should not complain. We have much here and you and Timothy are in danger every day. Please forgive my selfishness.

My mother sent me a letter. Timothy was able to get a pass so he could visit her in Ireland. He had to hitch rides but he found people who knew our village. My mother loved him as I knew she would. Maybe now she will consider moving back here.

Please stay safe my dear brother. You are always in my prayers.

With love,
Maggie

8 April

Dear Jean,

I miss you so very much. It seems so long ago that we were together. I am sorry that I have not written, but I have been ill with the flu and the recovery is slow. It seemed I was sick for weeks and could not keep any food or drink down. The cold, winter days are short and I tire quickly. Some days all I want to do is sleep.

The nuns miss you at Mass. I think it is very sweet the way they think of you. Are you able to go to church there?

I did not start classes at University because I have been too ill and tired. Maybe with the next classes.

I have some good news about my brother and sisters. I have been in contact with someone who might know how to locate them. If this turns out to be true then I will hire a driver to get me as close to the German border as possible, then I can walk to our hometown since it is just on the other side. He does not think my family is in our village, but he said there is someone who has knowledge about where many of the children were taken.

I did not share with you why my parents were shot, but because of our growing relationship, I believe you should know. They were part of an underground group that was sneaking Jews out of Germany. I did not know that is why they were killed until this contact told me. They died for a just cause, and it is noble that they gave their lives and risked their own children becoming orphans to save hundreds. Pride is salve for my grief. They were honorable people.

I have no news to share. You are always in my thoughts and heart. I treasure your letters and eagerly await the arrival of each one. It warms me to know you feel the same. Our souls are united, my dear love. Tonight, when I look up at the moon, I will think of you in case you are looking at it, too.

My love is with you,
Annie

18 Apr 45
2100 hrs

My dearest Annie,

You can't imagine the relief I felt when I received your letter. I was going out of my mind with worry. I was glad to learn you are finally feeling better. My mind thought the worst when I didn't hear from you for so long.

I'm sorry that you couldn't find information on your brother and sisters. I'm sure it was very disappointing. I promise that I'll help you find them as soon as I can. I want to be with you so I know you're safe.

I'm trying to build up leave by trading off with some of the guys here. I want to get at least three or four days in a row so I can come to Paris. I'd ask you to meet me somewhere, but I never want you in harm's way.

Let me tell you a nice story for once. (I know it's hard to believe that there can be nice stories coming out of the war zone.) My outfit has adopted a mother cat with kittens. We found them living in the rubble of a building that had been bombed long ago. There were five kittens, but only three were alive. I think they might have been too weak from not enough milk because the mother was scrawny.

We took an old pair of fatigues to make a bed and then used a small crate tipped on its side as a little house. This at least gives the mother and kittens some shelter and warmth. We can't bring them inside because Arnie Miller is very allergic to them. We save scraps of our food and when we put it all together, it makes a decent meal for the mother. I hope we're here long enough for the mother to get fatter and the babies to wean off and eat on their own.

Do you ever think about the future — after the war? I know it's hard to believe that it might end, but with the progress we're making in Europe and the Pacific against the Krauts and Jap, maybe we'll see a surrender soon.

Thinking about the future is what keeps me going. OUR future together. I imagine us married, Annie, with children of our own. We'll have little girls with beautiful auburn hair like their mother. Maybe they'll inherit freckles from my side of the family. Dream this with me, sweetheart. I'll go wherever you want me to go it if means we'll be together.

This daydreaming is making me lonely. Somehow, I have to see you again soon. Please, please wait for me to come back to you. I'll be there. I promise.

You're in my prayers every night. Please take good care of yourself, my beautiful girl.

Forever yours,
Jean

19 Apr 45
0230 hrs

Dear Maggie,

I hope you are all holding up over there. We're still getting on fine here, but there are days when I wonder how much more we can take.

We got over into the northern part of Germany a few weeks ago. You'll never believe what we saw. It was a mass grave with hundreds of bodies piled on one another. We were told they could be Jews, but that many of them were probably resistance fighters. All these things make me more certain that if I come face to face with Hitler, I'll have no problem killing him myself. I don't think the devil can compete with his evilness.

There was a late spring snowfall here a few days ago. Hub, Kalzinski and I built a snowman with some local children. It was fun, and the children seemed to enjoy themselves, then suddenly, they started stabbing sticks into the snowman's body and yelling NAZI over and over again while they destroyed the snowman. We were shocked, but we can't blame them. We have trouble dealing with what we've seen, so I can't imagine how children feel. These people have been terrorized by Hitler's army. The one consolation for us is we know we're here to help them get their lives back. We're doing good, too.

I'm tired, but I can't sleep. I'm sorry to share such horrible news, but the world needs to know what's happening over here.

Another reason I've been having trouble sleeping is I'm so worried about Annie. Now that I've found the woman I know is the one for me to spend my life with, I worry that it's too good to be true and I'll lose her.

I received a letter from her that told me that she's been very sick with the flu and that's why I didn't hear from her in so long. I was going out of my mind with worry. Hub didn't help matters by suggesting maybe Annie was done with me.

Thinking about that isn't making me feel better, so maybe I'll think positively and tell you about her. Did I tell you how intelligent she is? She can speak German, French, English, and Spanish fluently. How does a person learn so much?

She told me her father was a banker in Germany. She had a picture of her family on her dresser. Annie has her mother's warm eyes and her father's smile. It's the only picture she has of them.

I was surprised when I got a short letter from Timothy a couple of days ago. I guess we've been here long enough that the mail could find us. I wish it would work out to meet up with him while we're both in this region. It would be swell if he could meet Annie. He'd love her for sure.

I'm going to try to get some sleep. I say TRY because the damn Germans are still sending their buzz bombs over here. Some guys seem to sleep right through them — until they explode. They sit straight up, then when they see they're still alive, they lie down and go back to snoring like nothing happened. I don't know how they do it.

Good night, my dear friend. Thank you for being there for me. I hope future letters have better news.

Give my love to all,
J.P.

20 Apr 45
2230 hrs

Dearest Annie,

It's late, and I should be sleeping but I can't get you off my mind. I know you probably just received a letter from me a day or two ago, but I needed to have a connection with you again, and this is the only way for now. I need your strength because it was an exhausting day mentally and physically. Annie, it scares me how much I've come to need you.

First, I have to tell you again that I love you with all my heart and soul. I hope you don't tire of me saying that. I hate the distance between us, but I thank God every day that He *brought us together. I trust Him to lead us back to each other again.*

It seems I learn some new horrible things every day. A couple of guys came through our hospital yesterday. They'd been helping Jews who had escaped from Poland where they had been in a work camp. They were nothing but skin and bones.

They told us that they were from Germany originally but not near your town. They were dragged from their homes and forced to watch the Nazis execute their neighbors who were part of the resistance against Hitler. Then they were dragged off and put on trains for hours. There were women and children on the trains, too. And no one knew where they were going. They didn't know what happened to many of them, but they were taken to a work camp.

They said in the camps they were beaten for so little as looking at a Nazi officer. They'd sometimes be given only bread and water even though they were forced to work in the fields harvesting food for the German soldiers from sunrise to sundown. If they were caught eating any of the crop they were shot in the field and left there. What the hell is going on in this world?

Their stories made me nervous for you. I thought of the stories of the journeys your parents made to smuggle the Jewish children out of Germany. My blood boils when I think of the horrors you must have seen in your attempt to do something good for the Jewish people.

Your parents are heroes. You know that? The more I listened to these men, the more I realized how dangerous that situation was for them and you. My heart swelled with pride when I realized what your family has gone through to help others.

I beg you to not put yourself in harm's way. Together we'll find your family. Wait for me. I know it must be hard but put your faith in God. And me.

I love you, Annie Goodman.

Your future husband,
Jean

April 21, 1945

Dear J.P.

I had to write to you and Timothy because I am just so shocked by the news. I cannot believe that the President is dead. I worry about what this means for both of you and all our men at war. There are rumors that he had a stroke at his retreat house in Georgia. He has not been well since he returned from a meeting in the Yalta with Joseph Stalin and Winston Churchill. Some say he was too soft on Stalin and allowed him too much power after all he has done. I do not understand politics, but I am worried that this could be bad.

Harry Truman was already sworn in as President. Did this news reach you?

So many changes in the world. So many frightening things happening. I pray the rosary every morning to get you and Timothy home. And now I include your Annie too.

I hope you are also getting spring there. I have seen daffodils already. It is a promise from God that better days are ahead.

I hope you have heard from Annie. I pray she is safe in France and just has not had the time to write to you. She sounds lovely. I wish I knew the right words to say to you to

*make you feel better. My heart aches for you. It is hard when
you are so far away.*

*Please write when you can so we know you are safe. We
love you and pray for you.*

*With affection,
Maggie*

28 April

My dear Jean,

*You are a dreamer, sweet man. I think with the war, we
are reaching for anything that will give us hope. We must be
satisfied with what we have and not make too many promises
for the future. You will make a wonderful husband for
someone. Maybe I am not the right person, though.*

*Until I find my family I will not be able to commit myself
to anyone or anything. They are a part of me that I cannot
forget. I dream of being married and having children someday,
too. And I hope I will be the nurse my parents dreamed I
would be. Maybe I will even be a doctor.*

*This is not meant to frighten you or make you think I feel
anything less for you. I do love you. You are a wonderful,
caring and intelligent man, but maybe we are only meant to
be best of friends for this life. We come from different worlds
and those worlds do not always fit together.*

*Please do not waste your precious leave time on me. You
deserve someone who can be there for you. Your dreams of me
moving with you to America are wonderful, but I cannot go
without my family. I will NOT go. I hope you can understand.*

I cannot stress enough that it is not because I do not love you. It is because I love you so much that I feel I must do this. Through fate, we grew up worlds apart in so many ways. I want you to understand this now. I will not hurt you that way.

I am sorry I allowed this to happen. I should have told you before you left, but it was so easy to fall in love. You are a dear man. You will make a wonderful husband and father someday.

I will forever hold a part of you with me. I can promise you that. Please find it in your heart to forgive me for hurting you. I never meant for this to happen.

I do remember the song "The Very Thought of You." Whenever I hear it I cry because it makes my heart ache with loneliness. Your love will always be with me because I will see you in the stars above as the words in the song say.

I am letting you go, but you will be in my heart forever.

My love goes with you.
Annie

10 May 45

Dear Annie,

No! I can't let you go! I WON'T let you go.

What happened? Did I say something wrong? Did I scare you with my dreams? I won't take you away from France if you want to live there for the rest of your life. Wherever you are is where I want to be. If I could get out of Belgium right now and come to you, I would.

I don't know what to say. I thought my heart was going to burst it was beating so hard when I finished your letter. I CAN'T give you up, Annie. I have a lifetime to wait for you, to *help you find your brother and sisters. We WILL find them. Together. Give me a chance to come back to you. PLEASE!*

I understand how much your family means to you, because my family is important to me. You know how much I talk about my brothers and sister and my parents and Maggie. They have always been the center of my world, but that center changed when I met you. I have never felt such a connection to anyone in my life. I close my eyes at night when I'm in my bunk and all I can see is you. Us together. It's what keeps me going.

We have so many memories that we share. Remember when you showed me the Arc de Triomphe? You were so excited to tell me the history. Remember the time I was able to get you extra sugar so we could make cookies for the children? We cut our names out of the dough. And the songs you sang to me. Even though they were in French and German, I loved hearing your sweet voice. Even if they weren't love songs, to me they sounded like it. Sometimes I can imagine the warmth of your hand on my cheek or in my palm. You're with me, Annie. Every minute of every day you're with me.

Please, Annie. I can't let you go. I love you. Please please write back to me and tell me you didn't mean what you said. Maybe it's loneliness that makes you feel this way, or maybe you're just scared. I'm scared, too. But now I'm scared that I'll lose you.

I feel like a babbling idiot. I'm sorry if I've done something to hurt you. I love you. PLEASE!

Forever yours (and I mean that),
John

CHAPTER EIGHT

Daniel shook off a surprising chill that cascaded through his body. If the implications weren't so sad, he would think it humorous that his Uncle John had received a *Dear John* letter from Annie. But there was nothing funny about it.

While reading, an empathetic sour feeling settled in his stomach. His uncle had poured his heart out to Annie. He'd laid himself out and promised her a future —certainly a better life than she had in France during the war. So, why was she suddenly spurning his professions of love and desire to marry her?

He was surprised at how much he cared about their relationship. How sad that the love was so short-lived. His uncle died in a car accident in southern France in December 1945. He wondered if Annie stayed in France after his death or if she married.

Glancing down at the crate, he considered the letters he had yet to read. There were so many questions surfacing. How many answers would the letters provide?

He had a new respect for his mother, too. He'd always admired her, because she was such a good woman, an excellent mother, and devoted wife. When his father was diagnosed with lung cancer, she had stood by him, caring for him at home for just shy of two years before he succumbed.

Those hours before his father's death flashed back to Daniel as if it were yesterday. His mother had summoned Daniel, as well as his father's siblings — Father Michael and Sister Siobhan — so they would be with him at the end.

As soon as he entered the house, Daniel knew his father was ready to die. His mother bustled around, preparing the home for visitors. The foyer and living room were warmed by the heat of the oven where she'd baked several loaves of bread over the course of the afternoon. It was a special request from Timothy. Later she'd told Daniel that his father had sensed death was near and he'd begged Maggie to bake so he could be comforted by the aromas of everyday life. He didn't want his passing to be extraordinary.

"I'm a common Irishman," he'd declared weeks earlier. "When I go, I don't want to go with fanfare. I want everyday life around me so when you think of me, it will be during the ordinary times of life."

So, the four of them had gathered in his parents' bedroom with only the dim light from the reading lamp next to the three-generation-old oak rocking chair in the corner. An old cassette player from the seventies played upbeat Celtic music. The established mood was as his father wanted it. He clung to Maggie's hand and smiled faintly as his body relaxed past the pain.

"I'm ready to go Home, Maggie," he said in the raspy voice of near death. "It's my time, and I've made peace with this. I want you to know I couldn't have asked for a finer wife. You stood by me and my family through everything." He drew in several ragged breaths before continuing. "I have no regrets. The hard decisions were the right ones."

His gaze lingered on her before he shifted his attention to Daniel.

"I'm trusting you to take care of my girl. She's done right by you. Now, you need to do right by her." His eyes snapped closed and his body tensed. Daniel saw his mother's grip tighten on her husband's hand, and he squeezed in response. His chest rose with a rattle that unsettled them. When Timothy opened his tired eyes, he retrained his focus on Daniel.

"Son, do you know the meaning of your name?"

Perplexed by his father's choice of final conversation, Daniel could only shake his head in stunned silence.

"The Irish translation means attractive. And, that you are. You were always a handsome boy, but there's another, more important translation." After a long pause, he winced and swallowed hard.

Daniel leaned across the bed and patted his father's shoulder. "Dad, you don't need to talk right now. It's not important."

His father's eyes widened. "But it *is* important, Daniel. I won't go to my grave with this left unsaid." As if hit with a burst of energy, his father leaned up off the pillow, and, with his free hand, grasped Daniel's forearm. His fingers were bony, his body half its original, hardy size because of the ravages of the cancer. He spoke in earnest.

"I want you to know the Hebrew translation of your name." Timothy lowered his head to the pillow, and he loosened his grip on Daniel's arm. A peaceful look settled on his face.

"It means judgment of God. God my judge. You, Daniel, you were a gift from God. Out of the ugliness of war —" he broke off to take rattling breaths — "and Hitler's hatred, God gave us you. Innocent people were unfairly judged for their beliefs. I saw it for myself." He sucked in a breath, and his lips quivered. "You were a gift to remind us that the future could be better — without judgment."

Daniel glanced toward the others, but they were focused on Timothy. Almost too focused. Daniel leaned a bit to make eye contact with his mother, but her worried gaze was trained on her husband.

Timothy wet his dry, cracked lips. "That means nothing to you now, son, but some day..." His voice trailed off as he rolled his head toward Maggie. "It will be your decision, Maggie. You'll know when the time is right to share the letters with Daniel. Promise me, Mag, for his sake."

Daniel frowned. Letters? He didn't want to intrude on his parents' precious moments, but when he had a chance, he would ask his mother what that request meant.

The sheen of tears in Maggie's eyes glistened as she bent to kiss her husband. "I love ye, Timothy Coughlin," she whispered, her Irish accented words dovetailing with the plaintive tune drifting from the cassette. "I give ye me word."

"You know, love, I'm not going away," he said, his

breathing increasingly labored. "I'm just going to Heaven, so I have a better vantage point to watch over you." He winked, and the depth of love relayed through his wrinkled smile filled the room with extra warmth.

His attention slipped over Daniel, Father Michael, and Sister Siobhan. "I love all of you," he said before settling his gaze back on Maggie. "But as I have for all of these years, I love you most of all."

Timothy drew Maggie's hand to his lips and kissed the back of it. "I've always been the luckiest man alive, Maggie." A sharp breath rattled his chest, then he winced, and his eyes drifted closed. "So damn lucky."

Maggie sat on the edge of the bed and leaned over to rest her head on his chest. His uneven breaths lifted the light gray hair along her forehead. The two of them had made peace with the dying process. Although Daniel had tried to prepare himself, the reality in the moment was harder than he'd anticipated.

Father Michael came around the bed and took hold of Daniel's elbow. "Let's give them some time alone."

Sister Siobhan was already gliding out the door, wiping at tears streaking her face.

Later, when Daniel went to check on them, he found his mother lying next to his father, stroking his face with her fingertips and humming an Irish lullaby. To Daniel, it looked as if she was etching his profile into her memory. She asked Daniel to change the cassette to one of love songs from the forties. Then he left them to be comforted by their memories.

Over the next two hours, his father slipped away. Only minutes before he passed, they all gathered again at his bedside. Father Michael gave them communion, placing a drop of the wine on his brother's tongue. Then Father Michael administered last rites while Daniel stared at his parents' clasped hands. He couldn't miss it when his father's hand tensed, then went limp. A few seconds later, the patriarch of their family gasped the last reflexive breath of air before his chest stilled and his body settled into the folds of the mattress and pillow.

With tears slipping down her face, Maggie laid her palm against her husband's cheek and pressed a kiss to his forehead. She twisted to the nightstand next to the bed and from the drawer withdrew a strand of rosary beads.

Without looking up, she said, "Will ye all pray the rosary with me?"

She didn't wait for an answer, but instead held the crucifix in her fingers, made the sign of the cross, and, in a tight voice, began the recitation of the Apostle's Creed. Daniel stepped behind her and rested his hand on her shoulder, staring at his father's lifeless body for the twenty minutes it took for his mother to complete the prayers.

When she finished, she wound the rosary among Timothy's fingers and rested his hands just below his chest. He looked at peace.

As he'd instructed, in the tradition of the old time Irish wake, within an hour of the call to relatives and friends that he had passed away, the house was teeming with people, mostly fellow parishioners of the church.

Dishes of food filled every space on the counters and table. The loaves of bread Maggie had baked were sliced, slathered with butter, and sprinkled with sugar. Maggie was determined to give the love of her life the kind of

Irish sendoff he remembered having for his own parents. Tradition. His family thrived on it.

The wake and funeral also had been the celebration his father wanted. After the burial, friends and family returned to the house. Daniel and Liz pushed the furniture in the living room to the outside walls so the worn hardwood floor in the middle was clear for grandchildren to perform Irish step dances. Food, music, dancing and laughter were enjoyed out of respect for Timothy's wishes.

Daniel pulled himself back from the memory. A sad time made happy because of family traditions. For a moment his mind drifted and he stared out the window toward the street where cars hurried by. How would those traditions be changed with a mixed-faith marriage? Daniel tried to picture Christmas with grandchildren. First communions. Catechism. All those faith-based traditions that were so important to who they were.

He sighed and glanced at the photo of his parents that hung on the wall above the rolltop desk. Only five years since his father passed away, but the memory was already a bit hazy. In his mind, he tried to recall the conversations with him. Bits and pieces came back, then with clarity that he hadn't had in years, he recalled word for word something his father had said.

Daniel sat up straight and looked back at the crate. The letters. *You'll know when the time is right to give him the letters.*

After the funeral, Daniel had questioned his mother about his father's comment, but she'd told him it was too soon to talk about it. He'd respected her wishes and waited weeks before broaching the subject again. That time, she'd dismissed them as just a bunch of old love letters, and her father's death was still too fresh for her to share them.

Since he was busy with work and the kids' plethora of activities, he accepted that. Although his father had seemed adamant at the time, Daniel wondered if, in his final moments, his father's mind had conjured the pleasant times in his life, and those love letters were part of that. Then Daniel's everyday life pushed the memory farther back until he'd forgotten about it entirely.

And, now, here he was, reading them and being told they were relevant. Impatience rippled through him. Maybe he should take a plate of those blueberry muffins to his mother's house. If she knew he was this far into the letters, perhaps over a muffin and cup of coffee, she'd give him the rest of the details.

But he knew his mother better than that. She'd raised him to believe that anything worthwhile was gained through the effort put into it. So, he'd continue reading. He thought of the last letter — the one he thought of as a *Dear John* letter. He hoped the next ones would shed light on Annie's sudden change of heart.

14 May 1945
0700 hrs

Dear Maggie,

I received your letter yesterday. Thank you for your continued support.

I don't know if the family was notified of my injuries, but I am recovering. I'm sure they didn't give any details. We had been back staying at a Catholic girls' school because a bomb destroyed part of our quarters.

A week ago, while we were sleeping we heard a buzz bomb. The next thing we knew the engine cut out overhead. Some of us had time to scramble to a wall for protection, but others were killed in their cots. Despite falling concrete and plaster, I managed to crawl out of the area. There were some guys trapped in a room below us. We heard them yelling. Those of us who weren't injured as much dug down through the rubble to get to them, but there were a lot of bodies in between.

When I got out I was covered with blood and my clothes had been shredded. My blood had dried by then and the pieces of clothing stuck to it. It hurt like hell when the other medics tried to separate it from my skin. I was a lucky one. At least I got out in one piece. We dug for two days searching for survivors, but with the cold and rain, they didn't have a chance.

I wanted you to know this in case a letter came from the government. I don't know how that works. I'm okay now.

What do you think about the news about Hitler committing suicide? It feels unchristian of me to tell you this, but we all cheered when we heard the news. The man was living, breathing evil. I'm only sorry he won't have to face the consequences for what he's done.

So many Germans were brainwashed by his promises of making the country better again. How could they turn a blind eye to what the man was really doing? I'll never understand. We all have to do our part to make sure this history doesn't repeat itself.

I waited until the end to share my hard news. I received a letter from Annie, and it wasn't good. She told me she didn't *think we could have a life together. She said her world is too different from mine and she doesn't want me to come back to her. I'm sick about it, but I won't give up.*

The good news is things have settled down again and I'm up for a weekend pass. As soon as it's granted I'm hopping a train to Paris. I've got to see Annie. Hub keeps telling me to just forget her. He doesn't understand what we had. I believe God brought us together for a reason. I'm not giving up on her that easy. I have to see her, and if she tells me in person that she never wants to see me again, then I'll leave her alone. But I at least have to see her one more time for my own peace of mind.

It's time for me to go on duty so I'll sign off and try to send this off in today's post. I haven't said anything to Ma about Annie, so please keep this between us.

As for the injuries, I'll probably have a few small scars from the attack, but at least I'm in one piece. I have every intention of leaving this war alive.

I'll write again soon, and hopefully by then Annie and I will have worked things out.

Love,
John

∽✑❀

Daniel looked back at the date of the letter. May 14, 1945. He knew from his history classes that Adolf Hitler committed suicide at the end of April. He laid the letter on top of the others and went to the history book about both World Wars that he kept on his desk. It had been a Christmas gift from Liam, Cathleen and Brendan five years ago. It was clearly laid out with timelines that were easy to reference, with directives of where to find the corresponding details about that event in history.

Turning the pages to the section about April 1945, Daniel skimmed through the events, paying closer attention to those he felt were more pivotal. He was horrified to read that Adolf Hitler enlisted five thousand Nazi youth, some as young as twelve years old, to defend bridges against the Soviet army as they moved toward Berlin. Almost 4,500 of them were killed or wounded.

He glanced at the shelf above the desk where he kept a photo of Liam and Brendan in their Boy Scout uniforms when they were in their early teens. He couldn't imagine them in battle against heavily armed army units. What kind of evil mind could justify that action? Daniel shook his head to clear the image of a battlefield strewn with the bloodied bodies of boys who hadn't even reached puberty.

And meanwhile, according to this book, on April 20th Adolf Hitler celebrated his fifty-sixth — and his last — birthday in an underground bunker. Ten days later, a day after marrying his girlfriend, Eva Braun, the two of them committed suicide in his underground headquarters known as the *Führerbunker*. Daniel hadn't known that Hitler had lived in the bunker since mid-January of that year. The bunker, fortified by 16 feet of concrete and six feet of earth, was intended to protect Hitler from the war, but according to accounts, he could still hear the shelling as the Soviet troops moved in. But did the coward even know what was happening to the youth he'd sent to face those troops?

This was the world the Europeans of the 1940's had lived in, and many hadn't known what was happening around them until after. He blew a slow breath through his teeth and shook his head as he picked up the next letter. Heaven help the world if its people didn't learn from the past and willfully allowed history to repeat itself.

❧❧

May 14

Dear John Patrick,

Although we have not received letters from you recently, I am going to trust that you are safe but busy. Maybe you have sent one and our letters will cross each other over the ocean.

I often wonder what news you hear there. We heard that our soldiers freed many Jewish prisoners in a camp at some place called Buchenwald last month. The stories of what was done to these people are horrific. It is so frightening to think that one man could convince others to do that kind of evil.

I am sure the news of Mussolini and Hitler's deaths must be changing the outlook in Europe. Two evil men gone from this world. I pray this is the beginning of the end of the war in that part of the world, but I am not so sure about Japan since they are allies of Italy and Germany. It is sad how much hate there is in the world.

I am sorry to end my letter soon, but I saved the best news for last. Our prayers have been answered. I am proud to say you are going to be an uncle. Timothy knows because I sent him a letter as soon as the doctor told me. If all goes well the doctor said this baby will be born in the middle of October.

I waited to tell you until I thought it was safe. Blessed be the Virgin Mary for watching over us.

Of course your mother has already started knitting. It gives her something to do and look forward to. This baby is bringing such hope and happiness to our family. We will never take this miracle for granted. I am so grateful to God for what He has given us.

I am tired and need a nap so I will get this in the mail.

Please let us know that you are safe and give our love to your Annie. I will continue to pray for you both.

With love,
Maggie

◈◈

Daniel smiled. There it was. The announcement about his impending birth. He figured it was inevitable that it would show up in the letters at some point since he'd been born before Uncle John Patrick was killed. It gave him a sense of satisfaction to know that, even though they'd never met, at least his uncle knew he'd been born.

He picked up the last letter from John Patrick and the one from his mother to compare dates. As his mother suggested, the letters must have crossed in the mail since they had each written them on the same date. So, she wouldn't have known about the situation with Annie. Daniel wondered how his uncle reacted when he received this letter.

Mussolini's name stood out in his mother's letter, prompting him to pick up the history book again. He'd forgotten that the Italian dictator Benito Mussolini had met his own gruesome end just before Hitler died, but over the years Daniel had forgotten the details.

His stomach churned as he read the next historical account. In the German towns, as the Soviet troops overpowered the Nazis, they took out their anger over the atrocities the Nazi soldiers had committed against Soviet citizens by raping nearly 100,000 German women. Then fearing the wrath of the Soviet army as they moved across the region, more than a hundred thousand German, Austrian and Polish citizens took their own lives.

The April chronology included the execution of the Italian dictator, Benito Mussolini. His death was particularly gruesome, and Daniel caught himself wincing as he reviewed the details. After learning that Hitler was negotiating Mussolini's surrender, infuriated and fearful for his life, Mussolini dressed as a Nazi soldier and tried to flee to the Swiss border with his girlfriend, Claretta Petacci.

Fearing Mussolini would escape, Italian partisans took him and his girlfriend to a remote farm house where they were both executed by firing squad. His grisly demise didn't end there, as his body, along with several others who had been executed, was dumped in Milan Square.

The people took the bodies and hung them upside down from iron beams at a gas station for all to see. The residents of Milan took out their anger over decades of oppression under Mussolini's rule by hurling rotten vegetables at the bodies, then beat and spit on them.

It was this treatment of Mussolini that spurred Hitler to kill himself so his enemies couldn't do the same to him. His inner circle then cremated him to avoid the same retribution from angry German citizens, particularly the Jews.

The book wasn't thick, but suddenly it felt heavy. Daniel shuddered and closed the cover, unable to fathom the depth of fear and horror those people endured. He thought of Annie's letters to his uncle. When she wrote them, did she have any idea what was happening all around her? Or did she purposely avoid writing about it as a way of mentally protecting herself?

He moved back to the chair, taking the book with him. He wanted to go between the letters and the timeline in the book to try and understand the world around them as they wrote the letters.

He removed the next stack of letters from the crate. It was amazing to think that the love between his uncle and Annie flourished despite all the obstacles the world events put in their paths. Knowing what else was happening in the world at the time made the letters even more compelling. Even though his mother insisted he would get answers to his own problems with Liam from reading them, for the moment, he was more interested in putting together this puzzle created by the information he was garnering from the letters.

He slid a yellowed letter written by his mother from the envelope. Once again, the odor of old paper swirled around him.

June 1

Dear John Patrick,

I just opened the mail and received your latest letter. I am so sorry to hear about the trouble with Annie. I am sure the war is confusing for her and makes it difficult to trust and love. I pray the two of you can work this out.

I went to the doctor yesterday and he said this baby's heartbeat is very strong. I can feel the kicks so I know it is all real. I am not showing very much yet but my clothes are starting to get tight. Timothy and I have wanted this for so long. I hope me sharing this is not upsetting to you.

Your mother and I baked some cookies for your friends at the precinct. We split the sugar from our rations to make a small batch. Just enough for each policeman to get one cookie. They appreciated the treat and it made us feel good.

Father Michael picked me and your parents up Monday afternoon and took us for a ride to the shore. He has been careful to not have the car out on the road to save the gas and tires from wearing down but he wanted to make sure to take a trip to keep it running properly.

Sean Kelly was brought back home after being badly wounded in the Battle of Bautzen. He lost an arm and part of his jaw. I have not seen him Father Michael visited the family. He said Sean will recover but of course his life will never be the same.

David Webster came home last week. He has served since Pearl Harbor was attacked. I remember when he enlisted in the Navy the next day like so many others. You are all brave souls.

I must close this letter. I pray the next letter from you will have better news about Annie.

Be careful. We want you and Timothy back home soon.

With love,

Maggie

≈⌘≈

John Patrick raced from the train station to hail a cab before other riders took them all. Several were pulling away from the curb, but luck was with him and one was coming down the street. The driver didn't have time to pull onto the side of the street before John ran to the back door and yanked it open.

"Thanks," he said as he threw his small duffel across the back seat and jumped in.

"*Où?*" the man asked.

Where? John recognized the question and gave the driver the directions to Annie's apartment.

The driver gunned the accelerator to join into traffic, and John sat back against the seat, trying to catch his breath. He prayed this surprise visit would make her happy.

The streets of Paris teemed with people enjoying an unusually warm spring day. John stared out the window, watching as the cab passed sights that had become familiar to him during his short time in the city. The place where he had fallen irrevocably in love with a woman with a heart of gold. Just thinking about her brought a smile to his face and warmed his skin. He couldn't believe he was finally back here again.

After a few minutes, they approached the church and the orphanage where Annie spent her days. It conjured memories of her with the children and the nuns who were so welcoming to them, saving their lives.

Suddenly he leaned forward and grabbed the driver's shoulder, making the man jump.

"Sir, can you stop here?" he asked, pointing across the front seat toward the church.

The driver slammed on the brakes and swerved to the curb, causing John to jerk toward the door. His arm slammed against the handle, but he bounced back and grabbed it.

"Please, wait here," John said, throwing open the door. "I may only be a minute."

He raced along the sidewalk to the back entrance where he knew it was more likely he'd could get the nuns' attention. At the top of the small set of stairs, he grabbed the cord to the interior bell and yanked it hard to make sure it would be heard. A few moments later, the door swung open, and Sister Irene peered out. Her eyes widened as soon as she saw him, and she threw the door open wider.

"*Monsieur* Coughlin, you are back," she said, sounding as surprised as her expression suggested.

"Sister, is Annie here?"

Her eyes shifted as if she was nervous. "No, she is not." Sister Irene took a step outside and looked toward the street. "Is she expecting you?"

"No," John said, moving backwards off the steps, fully aware that the cab driver was counting every minute he was idling. "Is she home?"

Sister Irene shrugged. "I do not know, but she is not here."

"Thank you." John held up a hand to wave goodbye as he ran down the sidewalk. "Taxi is waiting for me. Thank you, Sister."

He turned to sprint back, relieved to see the cab still sat where he'd gotten out. He dodged traffic as he ran across the street, then jumped back into the rear seat.

"Please continue to the address I gave you," John requested.

The cab driver maneuvered into traffic, driving as if he sensed John's urgency. When they passed the park where John had first seen Annie, a flood of memories washed over him. That park would forever be his favorite spot in Paris, even winning out over the Eiffel Tower and the Arc de Triomphe, because it was where he'd first seen Annie and fallen in love with her before even knowing her name.

A few minutes later, the familiar neighborhood came into view. The century-old brick buildings had withstood enemy bombings, and now the residents were reinvigorating them with renovations and greenery. John tapped the cab driver on the shoulder as the car approached the end of Annie's street.

"I'll get out here," he said, fishing his wallet from the pocket of his trousers. "How much?"

He didn't know if the driver even spoke English, so he spread five bills like a fan and indicated to the driver to take his fare from it. The man removed one bill, and nodded, then John pulled out one extra bill and handed it to him.

"*Merci!*" the driver acknowledged with an appreciative grin.

"Same to you," John said, grabbing his duffel, then shoving open the door.

Only a few hundred feet stood between him and the love of his life, and he wanted nothing more than to hold her in his arms. The cab driver made a U-turn and sped down the street, and John jogged toward Annie's building.

At the top of the stairs that led down to her apartment, he stopped to straighten his uniform and hat. Every nerve in his body tingled. In his mind he conjured the look on her face when she saw him at her door. It would be worth the long, overnight train ride to get here just to see her reaction. With a shrug of his shoulders and a deep breath, he descended to her door and rapped on it three times.

He drummed the fingers of his free hand against his thigh as he waited, the moments feeling like hours. Finally, the small curtain moved a little, and he just barely had a glimpse of Annie's face before the curtain dropped down again. When he didn't hear the lock being flipped or see the doorknob move, his lungs froze, full of a breath he couldn't expel.

Why wasn't she opening the door?

"Annie?" he called, tapping on it again. A moment of panic overwhelmed him. Was it possible she didn't want to see him?

Finally, the doorlatch clicked, and Annie pulled it open, and he saw her full length.

The shock that zapped through him had to have registered on his face, because her eyes immediately filled with tears and she dropped her hands to her swollen belly.

"Annie?" he choked out, barely aware of the handle of the duffel bag slipping through his fingers. It hit the ground with a small thud, but then there was no other sound as they stared at each other.

Finally, his muscles unfroze, and he stepped forward, laying one of his hands atop hers on her stomach.

His heart hammered against his chest. "My God, you're pregnant!"

She drew in a ragged breath and dropped her eyes. "I am sorry," she whispered.

"No! No," John said, scooping her against him. "Don't be sorry." He kissed the side of her hair. "If anyone should be sorry, it's me." He leaned back and lifted her chin. "It is my baby, right?"

As soon as the words were out of his mouth, he regretted them. They sounded cheap and accusatory.

Pain flashed in her eyes.

"Oh, God!" he said, tightening his grip around her waist. "That was a stupid question. I don't know why I asked it. I'm so sorry." His whole body reacted with a mixture of remorse and embarrassment. How could he have been so insensitive?

Annie sniffled. "There could never be anyone but you, *Zhaun*." She wiped the tears streaking her face and pulled from his embrace. "Come. Come inside."

John snatched his duffel from the cobblestone stoop and followed her in. When she closed the door, he turned to her, unbuttoning his uniform jacket, needing more room for his chest to expand with breaths.

"You should have told me, Annie. I would have been here for you."

"I didn't know you were coming," she said quietly.

"That doesn't matter," he shot back, realizing his voice sounded harsh. He took a breath and continued. "How many letters have you sent me since you've known? What if I hadn't been able to come? When were you going to tell me that I'm going to be a father?"

Her lower lip trembled. "I didn't want you to worry about me when you needed to concentrate on staying safe."

"Okay, so I'm back to the question, when *were* you planning to tell me?" What if her plan had been to disappear and never tell him? He fought the annoyance brewing in his gut.

She brushed past him and sat on the couch. "Please sit with me, *Zhaun*. You must be tired. Do you need anything to eat or drink?"

He hooked his hat on the doorknob, removed his uniform jacket and laid it across the back of a chair, and then joined her. His eyes were drawn to her protruding belly, still shocked that she was carrying *his* baby.

"*Were* you going to tell me?" he persisted, putting an arm across the couch behind her.

She reached for his other hand and held it between both of hers.

"Yes, but it was difficult." She dropped her chin. "I started and ripped up many letters, because I was afraid you would feel obligated to me, and I didn't want that."

"Obligated?" he said, dipping to look her in the eyes. "Annie, I love you more than I can ever show or say. This isn't what we planned or expected, but I'm not the kind of man to shirk my responsibility. I'm proud to be this baby's father. He or she was created out of love. Our love. And, we have enough to share with this child, and many more in the future."

He noticed her sudden jerk and sat back.

"What's wrong?"

She smiled and pulled his hand to her abdomen, splaying his fingers across the hard swell protecting the baby. "Your child heard you. He kicked when you said that. Hold your hand here. He will kick again."

"He?" John said. "What makes you so sure it's a boy?"

She shrugged and moved one hand to her chest. "My heart has told me. The world needs another fine, loving man like this child's father, and I believe we have created one."

His throat thickened. "You are a beautiful person, Annie. Inside and out."

He slanted his head to press his lips to hers. Her eyes fluttered closed as her lips parted, and a sigh escaped just as they met. He closed his eyes, too, wanting to fully experience all the sensations she brought out in him. He breathed in her fresh scent. Felt her soft breath against his cheek. Lord, he couldn't love her more.

And, suddenly, he felt the flutter of movement under his fingers. He snapped back, looking down at her stomach as she burst out in laughter.

"You just met your child, my love," she said.

John looked toward the ceiling and exclaimed, "Oh, Lord, I've died and gone to Heaven!"

The sweet sound of Annie's laugh filled the room. He looked back at her, coming within inches of her face.

"I love you and this baby with every cell in my body," he whispered. "And, mark my words, Annie Goodman —" he tapped the tip of her nose — "I will convince you to marry me."

❦

20 May 45
1900 hrs

My dearest love,

This train ride is an eerie echo of another a few months ago when I had to leave you in Paris. My emotions are so mixed that I can't think straight. For me, I need to write this letter so I can make sense of everything that happened while I was with you this weekend.

On one hand, my heart is bursting with pride and love for you. On the other, I am confused and angry, but not at you, my love. More at myself for what I've done to your life.

I wonder, if you had known I was coming, would you have gone into hiding? And I worry that somehow you will slip away from me now.

My promise is serious. I want to marry you, not just because it's the honorable thing to do under the circumstances, but because I love you so deeply. My mind can't comprehend you being out of my life, especially now.

I can't describe the shock I felt when you answered the door and I saw your rounded belly. I'm ashamed to admit that at first I feared that you had betrayed our love and been with another man. Instinct told me that was not the case, but with all my uncertainty the last few months and not hearing from you, my mind wasn't clear. Then I saw you, and the love I saw in your eyes said it all.

When you put my hands on your belly so I could feel the baby — our baby — I thought my heart would explode.

Daniel's eyes widened, and he pulled the letter closer, as if that would change what he'd read. The back of his neck prickled, and his breaths intensified as he re-read the last line. Wow! He dragged a long breath through his teeth and let it out slowly. His uncle had a baby with this woman? He couldn't believe no one had ever slipped and shared that secret. Was it because they were ashamed of him having a child out of wedlock? Was that the real reason that he never returned home after the war?

The paper shook as a tremor hit his fingers. What other bombshells did these letters hold? He found the last line he'd read and continued from there.

I understand your shame at being unmarried and expecting a child. But I love you, Annie, and I will not let you live in shame. This child, our child, will be raised by his mother AND his father. He or she will know nothing but love because we love each other so much. I could tell as we held each other that that hadn't changed. It's stronger than ever.

These last few months have been hell for me because you stopped writing. I know you said you thought it was best to break all contact and let me go, but I can't live that way. I thank God I was able to get to Paris to see you. I have a responsibility to you and our baby.

When I get back to Belgium, I'm going to talk to my C.O. and see if there's a way for me to return to you sooner. We can be married then. In the sight of God, in the Cathedral, we can become man and wife. I want that with all my heart, Annie. God has seen fit to make us a family, and I was raised to not question His plan.

I'll take care of both of you. Even though you said you don't expect anything from me, I'll send you money so you can take care of yourself and our baby. I don't have much, but what I have I'll give to you so you'll be healthy and comfortable.

Although this isn't what we planned, I can't lie and say I'm not proud. I'm going to be a father. I'll admit I wish we were married, but we will be. Soon!

I'm sorry our time together was so short. But, soon we'll be together forever. Hold onto that promise. I'll write again soon. I love you with all my heart — forever.

Your future husband,
John

20 May

My love, Jean,

You are on the train on your way back to Liege right now. My heart is sad that you had to leave again, but I feel fortunate to have spent the days with you this weekend. I apologize again that I worried you for those many weeks.

I felt like a thousand pounds of weight lifted from my shoulders when I opened my door to find you standing there. You looked so handsome in your uniform, but I could see how tired you were. I wanted to keep my arms around you and never let you go, because you make me feel so safe.

After our conversation, I realized how wrong I was to not tell you about the baby. I did not want you to feel obligated to me. I know you want to do the right thing, as you say, and be married, but life is not so simple. We still have much to learn about one another, and although my heart is full of my love for you, I cannot agree to marry. Someday I can explain, but the time did not seem right when we were first reunited.

Selfishly, I wanted to enjoy our time together without anything ruining it.

I so enjoyed the walks along the river and our special dinner in the café where we first danced together. When I am with you, I can so easily forget the problems in the world and my life. You comfort me like no one else I have ever known. It is what makes me love you so much.

I will close this with a thank you for your persistence. I am relieved you know about our baby. I have lived with guilt for months, but I felt it was the right thing to not burden you. I will treasure the time we spent together as a warm memory to lull me to sleep at night.

I do love you, and no matter what fate brings to us, I will always love you. And I love this baby because it is a part of you that I can always keep with me, especially now as it grows so close to my heart. But please realize our future cannot include marriage. I know you love me, and you love our child, but I have not had the heart to tell you there are things about me that I have still not been able to share with you. I am sure what you learn will change your feelings for me and this baby because of your devotion to your faith.

Please be safe, and do not let this distract your thoughts and put you in harm's way.

With deep affection and appreciation,
Annie

❦

Daniel scrubbed his hand across his face as if that would change what he was reading. He knew all about families having "skeletons in their closets," but these revelations were more like his family had a sealed crypt. How had no one ever slipped and revealed any of this over five decades?

His mind spun with a myriad of hypotheses about why the two couldn't marry: maybe government agents were after her because she helped hide the children; maybe she worked for the German government and her stories had been a cover, but now that she'd fallen in love she felt guilty about the deception; maybe she had a husband fighting in the war and expected him to return.

That last idea shoved out the others, because it made more sense as to why this was such a secret. It also explained why Annie and the baby had simply disappeared when his uncle was killed.

Daniel stared into space, imagining the last scenario. Somewhere, possibly in Europe, he had an aunt and a cousin — that was, if they were still alive. He wondered if his cousin knew about his or her American family.

Was this his mother's purpose for having him read the letters? Did she want Daniel to search for this long-lost relative?

How that connected to the situation with Liam was a mystery, but he had to assume she saw it that way. He hoped more letters would make it obvious, so he picked up the next one to continue.

27 May

My dearest Jean,

I had a wonderful surprise today. Your brother Timothy is in Paris and he used your instructions to find me. It was such a wonderful surprise. What was not a surprise is that he is a kind and intelligent man like you, Jean.

When you describe him, I picture a man who is much bigger, but he is not tall like you. Sometimes when I looked into his face, especially his eyes, I felt I should pinch myself to remember it was not you. Your look is similar enough for people to think you might be twins. Do others tell you that, too?

He showed me a picture of his beautiful wife, Maggie. She looks as lovely as you have always made her sound.

Do you remember little shy Helga from the orphanage? She has a new family. She will live in a home with brothers and a sister, just like the family she had in Germany. Her face was bright with excitement as they left. I envy the innocence and resiliency of a child. I will always have a part of my heart that will ache without my family.

Please be safe. I do not want anything to happen to you.

Until we meet again,
Annie

May 30

Dear John Patrick,

Thank you for your recent letter.

We are still saddened by the news that our beloved President Roosevelt is dead. For days after his death, every Mass was full, and all you heard was people sobbing. It is like we have all lost a member of our own family. We have to thank the radio for this. I think we felt he was part of our family because he came right into our homes in his Fireside Chats.

He has done such good for my adopted country. He will be missed. President Truman has already been in contact with Stalin and things did not go well. Truman was much tougher in his demands. I hope this does not make the war last longer.

It is good news about the surrender of Germany. I hope that makes it easier for your Annie to get back there to search for her family. I cannot imagine the emptiness and fear she must feel every day because she does not know if they are dead or alive.

Everyone is talking about the story and photos in the issue of Life magazine that came out last week. It showed the horrible camps that the Nazis held Jewish people in. I have been avoiding upsetting news, but we were at the neighbor's house and they showed me the pictures before I knew what I was going to see. It made me sick to my stomach to see how thin those poor people were. How did they even survive? What would make someone do such horrible things to others? How did we not know this was happening? It makes my heart hurt.

Have you been back to see Annie? Timothy wrote and told me of his plan to visit her as they will be near Paris for a time. It would be wonderful if you could be there together.

I went to the doctor and he said everything is still fine with the baby. We are both healthy. In some ways October seems not very far away, but sometimes it seems like it is forever from now. Timothy and I have decided on the name Maureen Mary if it is a girl. If it is a boy I like Martin. Timothy is not so sure about that name. Until we have a birth certificate we can still decide. Right?

Stay safe, my dear brother-in-law.

Love,
Maggie

1 June 1945
2030 hrs

Dearest Maggie,

I'm sending this letter to you, but I'm asking you to share it with Ma and Pops. You'll understand why when you read more. I trust you to find the right way to tell them what I'm about to share with you.

I've stared at this paper for almost an hour, because what I have to write is difficult. I'm petrified, but it has nothing to do with the war. I'm afraid my actions will be an embarrassment to the family. I worry that you will all be ashamed, but I have no shame. My fear is that I won't do the right thing.

This letter is about Annie and me and our future. Her letters, her strength, and her love have kept me strong. She's a wonderful woman who expects nothing from anyone or the world.

I'm sure you're wondering why I feel it's important to preface my letter with this, but I need you to understand the depth of my feelings for her. She is the most remarkable woman I have ever met. Her love for others comes before her own pleasure or safety, and in this case, that includes me. Children, regardless of how they are conceived, are precious gifts from God. The child YOU are carrying is a gift that our family will always treasure.

I have been likewise blessed, and I hope our family will understand the happiness I'm feeling and be happy for me. There is no simple or easy way to say this. My beloved Annie is carrying my child. She is due in September, but I've asked her to marry me as soon as I can get back to Paris on leave. I want our baby to carry the Coughlin name.

Annie is resisting until she has found her family. They will become my family, too, so I hope that she'll see this is the right thing to do. I would die if I couldn't be in my child's life. I trust Annie to not rob me of a future with our baby.

I hope you don't view this news as tragic or unfortunate. Though it most definitely wasn't planned or expected, I already love this child with my whole being. It gives me even more reason to survive this war. I won't abandon Annie or our baby. They both deserve better than that.

I sent a letter to Timothy. I'm hoping there's some way for him to be in Paris to see us married. I pray you will give us your blessing. I know you will love her as I do.

God bless all of you and keep you free.

With affection,
John Patrick

05 June 1945
1030 hrs

To my one and only love, Annie,

I received your letter today, and I'm not sure what to think. Our weekend together was perfect. I feel so comfortable with you that I can't understand why there would be something so important that you wouldn't share with me. If your concerns are because of your family, please don't let that become an obstacle to us becoming our own family. I promised you I would help find them, and I will. Please don't shut me out again.

I lie on my cot each night and close my eyes so I can picture you with me. My imagination is so clear and strong that I can almost smell the clean scent of the soap on your soft skin. I have the picture of you in front of the Eiffel Tower pinned to the wall above my pillow. It brings me a little closer to you.

You have no idea the relief I feel knowing you're all right. It seemed wherever I went I would see someone from a distance and get a start, thinking maybe you were there. Of course, I had to deal with the disappointment when reality told me that wasn't possible. But we are together again, Annie. As it should be.

It appears I'll be able to get another short leave in three weeks. When I come, I'd like to arrange to be married. I know you have concerns, but we can face them together. I'll live wherever you and our baby are.

Please reconsider and accept my proposal. I'm sorry this isn't romantic, but I promise I will give you a good and secure life. You won't lack for love.

I look forward to your next letter.

Forever yours,
Jean

18 June

Dear Jean,

I can only write a brief note to you today. I do love you, but you must trust me that we cannot be married. Our lives *are too different, and wishing and dreaming will not change that.*

I would like you to be a part of our baby's life. I do not intend to take that away from you. It will be your decision regarding the blending of your future and ours from there. I can promise you I will love your baby and give him or her the best life possible.

In my heart we will be married, my dear man, but a true union will never be possible. These words are not intended to hurt you. As I said before, there is much you still must learn about me. I promise when you next come to visit, that you will understand my position.

You are in my heart every minute.

With love,
Annie

❧ ❦

Daniel picked up the photo that he assumed was the one of Annie Goodman and her baby in the corner of the crate. Was this one of the children from the orphanage, or was this his uncle's child?

He set the picture on the edge of his desk and picked up the phone. Before reading another letter, he needed to talk to his mother. The story the letters revealed wasn't just about history anymore — at least not world history. This was his family. Why did they keep this baby a secret for more than half a century?

He tapped his mother's number into the keypad, then pushed end before it rang. This conversation wasn't one he wanted to have over the phone. He needed to see the reaction on her face when he asked his questions.

It only took him a few minutes to change into jeans and a shirt. A few flakes of snow drifted haphazardly past the window, but the sun was trying to peek through the clouds. At the bottom of the stairs, he grabbed his jacket from the closet and shrugged it on. When he opened the front door, the brisk December air whirled around him, breezing along the exposed skin at his neck. He yanked the jacket zipper higher and took the sidewalk around to the driveway.

He brushed the snow from his car, and climbed in. As soon as he turned the key, cold air blasted him from the vents. He turned the fan down and glanced at the clock. 9:45. His mother would be back from Mass, and, knowing her, was probably elbow deep in flour in her oven-warmed kitchen.

He backed into the street, his mind on the encounter ahead more than the task of driving. He wasn't leaving his mother's house without answers.

CHAPTER NINE

His mother's sidewalk and driveway had already been cleared of the overnight snow. Daniel had no doubt his mother had shoveled it herself, probably before sunrise. Her energy put them all to shame.

He bounded up the front steps, glancing at the statue of the Blessed Virgin Mary in the tiny garden area to the right. He couldn't remember a time when a statue hadn't set there, even though over the years, it had been replaced a few times. The current one had been a Mother's Day gift from his children to their grandmother a few years before. He could still picture their excitement when they found one they thought she would love. And she did.

When he opened the front door, the little silver bell on the inside knob jangled, heralding his arrival. It had hung there since he'd learned to walk. It was her security system to let her know when anyone was coming or going.

As a teenager, he'd learned how to open the door

holding the handle tight to minimize the sound, so when he came in past curfew, no one would know. Occasionally his tactic was successful, but usually even the slightest jangle and his mother appeared in a doorway. Her stern look of disapproval warned him he wouldn't escape the consequence of his recalcitrance.

At the time, he hadn't appreciated his parents' strict discipline, but once he became a parent, understanding dawned. Those same disciplinary tactics he'd found most annoying in his parents were the same ones he used for his own children. The damned thing was, he was proud of it.

The aroma of fresh-brewed coffee surrounded him as soon as he stepped into the front hall. He took off his coat and hung it on the closet door handle.

"Ma?" he called, surprised the bell hadn't already summoned her.

"Danny?" He could hear the surprise in her voice. It came from the direction of the kitchen at the back of the house.

"Yeah, it's me." He wiped his feet on the small welcome rug just inside the door. The aroma of fresh-baked bread momentarily transported his mind back forty years. It was an every-other-day ritual when he was a child, and to this day she still made her own bread.

"I'm in the kitchen." She appeared at the end of the short hallway, drying her hands on the ever-present apron.

Daniel met her at the doorway and bent to kiss her cheek. At six foot three, he dwarfed her. He was the only one on either side of the family to breach the six-foot height until Liam and Brendan nearly matched him in their late teens.

His mother put her warm hands on his cheeks and looked deep into his eyes. "Are ye all right? Why aren't ye at work?"

"I took the day off." He glanced past her, surprised to see his aunt, Sister Siobhan, sitting at the table. He waved in acknowledgement, then lowered his voice. "I started reading the letters."

Slowly, almost imperceptibly, she lifted her chin, then nodded. "So, that's why ye've come, is it?"

"Yeah. I have some questions."

She tipped her head and ran the tip of her tongue across her lower lip. "Ye haven't read 'em all, though, have ye?"

"No." He cleared his throat, feeling like a grammar school child confessing to the teacher that he hadn't finished his homework. "But, maybe this isn't a good time since you have company."

"Ye haven't got anythin' ta keep from yer aunt. Come and have a cup of the coffee." She pivoted and bustled across the kitchen to a cupboard where she removed a mug. "I have ta leave ta take Sister ta a doctor's appointment, but we have a few minutes."

She filled the mug with coffee then set it on the table. "Sit! Sit!" she ordered.

Daniel pulled out one of the heavy wooden chairs that had sat around the matching kitchen table since he was a boy. The pinewood set had come from his mother's family in Ireland, crafted by their father.

He sat adjacent to his aunt and took a sip of the

coffee. "I hope the doctor appointment is routine," he said.

Sister Siobhan nodded. "It is. I thought perhaps *you* were ill."

"Oh, no, no. I'm fine. Just took a day off because —" He glanced at his mother.

She had refilled her own cup and was returning to the chair between them. "Daniel is readin' the letters," she supplied.

His aunt arched her brows and looked from his mother to him. "I see."

"Wait!" he said, looking between the two women. "Am I the only one who didn't know about the existence of these letters?" He looked back at his aunt. "Have you read them?"

"No." Sister folded her hands on the table. "They were always meant for you."

Daniel put his hands around the mug and stared into the dark contents. "I remember just before Dad died, he said something to Ma about knowing when the time was right to give me something." He glanced up at Sister. "You were there. You must have heard him."

She nodded. "I did."

"Weren't you curious?"

She shrugged.

"Do you know why Ma gave them to me now?"

Sister nodded slowly.

He sat back in the chair. "You think I'm wrong, too?" She didn't respond, so he continued. "You, of all people, should understand what our faith means to us. What our traditions mean. I'm looking years down the road. Will Liz and I be able to give our grandchildren Christmas gifts? Take them to the Christmas Eve Mass? And Easter." He blew out a breath of frustration. "The holiest of holidays, and we might not be able to share it with them."

His mother and Sister Siobhan listened but neither commented.

"There won't be pre-Cana classes. They can't raise children in both religious traditions without causing confusion." He splayed his hands on the table and looked at them. "Their marriage may not even be sanctioned or accepted as legal in the Church's eyes. I know there are some who wouldn't care, but I do. I want Liam to be in a marriage that will succeed."

"Compromise," Sister Siobhan said quietly. "That is the only way it can work. And that compromise may need to start with you. You are being closed-minded."

He stared at the steam rising from his cup. It mirrored how he felt. Everything inside him heated up when he thought about the situation.

"I'm being realistic."

His comment hung in the air between them. They sipped their coffee, but for a few minutes, no one spoke.

Sister Siobhan drained her cup, then looked at him. "Tell me about the letters. What have you learned?"

The shift in topic was a relief. Daniel looked at his mother. "Well, I can tell you one thing. I came to appreciate just how much my parents loved each other. It's coming out loud and clear in the letters."

A small smile creased his mother's slightly wrinkled skin. Did her cheeks just grow rosier? He couldn't resist a wink, and with that she dropped her gaze to the cup in her hand.

"But, I'm also learning what a nice relationship Ma

and Uncle John Patrick had, too." His mother lifted her eyes to look at him again, and Daniel could see how they'd softened with the topic. "Were you and Uncle John Patrick always that close?" he asked.

She tipped her head in a slight shrug. "The war time was difficult for all of us. We needed ta hang on ta each other the best we could. I loved him like he was me own brother. There wasn't anythin' we would not have done for each other."

His mother shifted her gaze toward the side kitchen window, with a far-away expression that seemed to take her back half a century.

Daniel continued, enjoying the opportunity to connect with his mother in this way. "I also learned how excited Ma was when she found out she was pregnant." He looked at his aunt and smiled. "Not many people get to read firsthand about their *very* early days of life." He chuckled.

Siobhan returned his smile. "You were the light of her life from the moment she first laid eyes on you and held you in her arms. Her love for you is beyond question. What else have you learned?"

Daniel recounted the details of John Patrick's and Annie's meeting and growing love. Then, he pushed the barely touched mug of coffee forward and leaned his arms on the table. "But now I have more questions than when I started reading." He stopped and corrected himself. "Well, maybe I should say, different questions."

"And they would be?" Sister asked.

"I'm assuming you know that he had a child with Annie Goodman."

She nodded.

"That is," he said, lowering his voice, "if he's actually the father of the child."

His mother's head snapped up. "'Twas his child."

"Then where's Annie Goodman?" Daniel pressed. "Where's their baby? We know Uncle John was killed in an auto accident, but where did they go? The point I'm at in the letters, it's only another few months and he's going to die, so the baby was born before he was killed. Where are they?"

Mist filled his mother's eyes, and Daniel regretted being so blunt. Even though it had been so many years, it was clear the pain of the loss was still with her. She grabbed her and Sister's coffee cups and pushed her chair back to stand.

"Ye still have much more ta read, Danny. The answers will come." Turning toward the sink, she deposited the cups and ran water into them. She sniffled, wiping the back of her hand across her eyes.

Daniel went to her and put his hands on her shoulders. "I didn't mean to upset you, Ma."

She shrugged and turned toward him, reaching behind her back to untie the apron strings. "'Tis as hard on me as ye, but ye need to learn it through the letters." She folded the apron and laid it on the counter before taking hold of Daniel's wrists and squeezing. "Cutting corners serves no one. I want ye ta understand how the past is tied ta the present because it affects yer future, and the letters are the best way ta learn that."

Daniel frowned. "That's pretty cryptic, Ma."

Her hands slid from his wrists to his hands and she squeezed once more. "Ye've always been me pride and joy, Daniel. I don't want ye to ever forget that."

"Thanks, Ma, but —"

"'Tis time to take Sister ta her appointment," she said, dropping his hands and sidling past him. "We're goin' in ta see the tree at Rockefeller Center, then to the Christmas show at Radio City after. Ye can join us if ye like."

Daniel shook his head and turned to get his coffee mug from the table. "Guess if I have to read more letters, I better pass. I won't be able to take another day off before Christmas."

He dumped the remaining coffee down the drain and started for the front door as his mother and aunt put on their coats. The lack of new information was disappointing, but there was one thing he wanted to know more than anything else.

"Ma, can you answer one question for me?"

With her hand on the front door handle, she turned toward him. The little bell jangled just a bit. "What be it?"

"Do you know where Annie and her baby are today?"

Her gaze pierced him. "Yes, Danny, I do."

CHAPTER TEN

June 24, 1945

Dear John Patrick,

A baby! Oh my! What a surprise! I pray for you and Annie each night, and now my prayers will include your baby.

I am sure you want to know how your parents took the news. I must be honest. At first your mother cried. Your father said nothing and still has said nothing. It is hard for me to find words for how I feel. I agree with you that you must get married. It is what is right and you love her. Your mother is having difficulty with this but I think she and your father will come to give you their blessing. They will love their grandchild. Both of their grandchildren equally I am sure.

She spoke with Father Michael. They prayed together and he encouraged her to be accepting of this innocent child as it carries her blood, as well. She found comfort in his words. His spiritual guidance is wonderful. There is a natural calmness in him that makes even the most difficult situation less troublesome.

You have my blessing dear man. You deserve happiness after all you have been through. I trust in God that He had a plan when He sent this child to you and Annie. To everything there is a purpose. Out of this difficult time I trust good will come.

I hope Annie will change her mind and you can be married. I will add that to my prayers. God be with you, my dear brother in law. Be safe.

Love,
Maggie

15 July 1945
1715 hrs

My love, Annie,

This letter will be very short and I hope you receive it soon. I have secured a three-day pass for next week. It's unusual to be able to get one again so soon, but I pulled some strings to make it work. That means in a little more than a week I'll be holding you in my arms again. I'm hoping you receive this letter before I arrive so you're expecting me. I'm anxious to see how our baby has grown.

I pray that you are well.

Forever yours,
Jean

1 Aug 1945

0700 hrs

Dear Maggie,

Thank you for your letters. I appreciate you taking the time to write to me. We're having trouble with letters getting through again, so I get so much news late. I hope you and your baby are doing well.

Ma isn't as faithful about writing as you are. I haven't heard from her since May, but maybe there are letters lost and I don't know it. I worry that it's because of my news about Annie. I don't want to embarrass my family, but like I said before, I'm not ashamed. It's not what we planned, but it was love that created this baby and he or she will always be loved.

It drives me crazy that I can't be with Annie, so I just have to trust that she is doing okay. Now that I've gotten used to the reality that I'm going to be a father, I'm eager for our child's arrival. I'm sure it's the same with you with your baby.

I do have some good news. When I got to Paris, Timothy's unit was still in the area, so we were able to meet. He already met her on a previous visit. He loves her.

She is looking very pregnant. I think it makes her look even more beautiful. The nuns have been taking very good care of her to make sure she has plenty of food and time to rest. She has seen a doctor who said she and the baby seem to be in good health.

Even Timothy tried to convince her to marry me. But she is very stubborn. I think I'll go and talk to Sister Eloise Marie at the convent and see if she can help me convince Annie.

I go on duty in half an hour, so I must close. I'm hoping to have a shower before. Kind of a funny thing, but at home I took for granted the opportunity to bathe regularly. That's not the case here. Sometimes we get pretty ripe. It's probably dangerous because I imagine the enemy could smell us from a mile away. When we do get a shower, it's usually very quick. Oh, the things I never knew I'd miss.

You are not one of those things, though. I always knew I'd miss all of you and Brooklyn. I can't wait to be back on the beat.

Give my love to all. I'll write Ma and Pops later this week.

Your devoted brother-in-law,
J.P.

2 Aug 1945
2000 hrs.

Dearest Annie,

This letter will be a different kind of letter. I don't know why, but I feel different today.

I don't think you truly understand the depth of my love for you. It's been almost a year since I first laid eyes on you, and you become more beautiful each time I see you. (Which is NOT enough.) If I was a better writer, I would write you a wonderful poem. But I'm not a poet, so instead, I'll just make a list of all the ways that I love you.

#1. I love the way you look at me with your beautiful cocoa-brown eyes as if I'm the only man on Earth.

#2. I love the gentleness of your voice, and the way each word you utter sounds like a love song on the breeze.

#3. I love the way you take my hand and lay it on your stomach so I can feel our child moving in your womb.

#4. I love the way you take the time to notice the beauty

around you. To you, each fragrant blossom is a special gift from God.

#5. I love the way you stroke the hair on my bare chest as we lie next to each other in the quiet hours of the night.

#6. I love the fullness of your body and your willingness to allow me to admire your newly sculpted beauty.

#7. I love stroking your full breasts, knowing they will nourish our baby.

#8. I love telling people that you are the mother of my child. You are truly beautiful inside and out.

#9. I love that you accept people for who they are, and you do not judge them.

#10. I love the way your dimples crease your creamy skin when you smile at me with love.

#11. I love you more than life itself, and no words can ever convey the depth of my feeling.

My love, I wish I could pen beautiful, flowery, and flowing words that would make you melt. You deserve better than me, but I will give you anything to make you happy. Our time together is so full of sweetness that returning to Liege is like going to the depths of Hell. Each time I leave you is harder and harder. I struggle to eat because there is such a void from loneliness in my stomach.

I wish I could be with you when our baby is born. I'm filled with guilt to know I probably won't be able to get back there that soon. I have a calendar, and I cross off each day that brings the time closer to our baby being in this world. My promise to you is that I will always be there for you and our child. Neither of you will ever be abandoned by me.

Take care of yourself, love. I will return as soon as I can. Please remember how much I love you.

Yours forever,
Jean

～⚬～

Daniel skimmed through the letter again. He knew his mother hadn't given him all of the letters from the time period, and from the ones she had given him, he was beginning to think that his uncle found more opportunities to get to Paris to see Annie than the letters revealed. The funny thing was, he realized he cared that they were able to see each other. It made him happy to know that they could be together.

The list of the ways John Patrick loved Annie was surprisingly romantic. Because he was sure there were letters missing, he attributed the exponential increase in comfort expressing this depth of feeling to the fact that there was more to this story than his mother had shared.

Daniel stared at the gray crate and the worn, brown canvas that obscured the majority of correspondences. Just hours ago, reading the stacks of letters tied together had seemed like a daunting task. Now, he caught himself wishing he could read all the letters, not just the ones selected to reveal the untold story of his uncle's and father's time in Europe. It wouldn't be today, but after the Christmas rush, he would read a few of the other ones each night.

For now, he'd follow his mother's wishes. He'd never thought of himself as a terribly romantic man, but the way he was feeling as this story unfolded indicated otherwise.

All he could do was keep reading. He was sure at

some point he would get to a letter announcing his birth, considering what a momentous occasion it was for his mother and father.

⋞⋟

16 August

My dear Jean,

Thank you for such a lovely letter. Even though you do not think you are a poet, to me, what you wrote was just as beautiful. I could feel your love through your words. No man has ever loved me as you do.

I am now counting down the days to our child's arrival. I feel myself growing restless and it becomes more difficult to get comfortable. I am hoping for an early delivery.

When I think about us, I realize there are still so many things we do not know about each other. This war has forced millions of people to think differently and to hide from themselves.

There is something that has been prickling my conscience since you first told me you loved me. I don't know why, but I feel I must tell you now. It is something I should have done many times since we met, but I was selfish and didn't want to ruin our time together. I was fearful that it would change the way you feel about me. I hope it does not hurt you, but I think it will help you understand why I have resisted your proposals for marriage.

When I was still living in Germany, there was a man in my life. He was a wonderful man who was a banker from Berlin. My father had met him on a business trip and was impressed with him, so he hired David to work at his bank. Because his family was in Berlin, David spent a great deal of time at our home. Even though he was several years older than I, we became very close. And, yes, we fell in love. We planned a wedding for the second weekend in November in 1938.

A few days before our wedding, he was attacked because it was discovered that he was part of the resistance group against Hitler. Someone informed the Nazis that the group was secretly meeting in the back of a restaurant in the town next to ours. The Nazi youth group, under orders from Hitler, found them and beat everyone at the meeting. Some died that night from their injuries. David died three days later — on the day we were to be married. I was devastated by his death and all of the growing horrors around us.

The following week is when my father sent me away to France to live with my grandmother. He feared they would come for me because of my ties to David. My dreams before I met David had been to become a nurse, or maybe even attend medical school, so out of the ashes, I struck a fire to do something to help others in the world.

Those first years were difficult. It seemed my family was cursed with one horror after another. When my parents were killed, and then my siblings disappeared, and then my grandmother died, I was not sure I could go on.

Then, like an angel from heaven, you came into my life. You, dear man, gave me hope that the world was not all bad.

I'm sorry I did not tell you this before. The time never seemed appropriate. Even if fate means we will not be together forever, I feel blessed to have had this time to love you and be loved by you. I will always cherish the child we created, because he or she was conceived in love during a hateful time.

If this angers or upsets you, I will understand. This is but one obstacle for us. There is one more that I feel safer to share with you now. When we are together next, I will make sure there are no more secrets between us.

Please forgive me, Jean. I do love you.

With deep love and gratitude,
Annie

August 17

Dear John Patrick,

I hope you are doing well. Here we are all doing fine. Your father is much stronger than he has been in some time. I can see the relief in your mother's face. The baby and I are doing fine too. It is hard to believe that in two months I will finally hold this precious child.

I am enclosing newspaper clippings about the bombings of Hiroshima and Nagasaki because I do not know if you see newspapers there. It still does not seem real that we have done this to those innocent people. Thousands died because of the decisions of their government. I do not know if this was the right decision for President Truman to make or not but I hope that finally this war will end. There has been enough suffering and death.

I received a letter from Timothy yesterday and he said it looks good for him to be home by the beginning of the new year. I so hope that is true but I know to not count on anything. I keep praying it will come true.

We have new neighbors now. Their name is Brennan. They are a young family with seven children all under ten years old with another on the way. I can not imagine how busy Aileen, the mother, must be. Her clothesline is filled with laundry every day that it is not raining.

The children are very active and spend much time in the yard so I get to watch them play. The two oldest are boys and the other five are girls. Sometimes the boys wrestle but I think they are just playing. I have not met her husband as he travels for work. (Maybe he should travel more unless they want many more children. I am only joking. They seem very happy.)

Maybe our baby and the one she is due to have will play together. That will be nice.

I am taking dinner to your parents today so I am going to close now. Your mother is guessing this baby is a boy because I am carrying him low. We will see if she is right. All I care is that I have a healthy, happy child — like the Brennan children.

Be safe.

With love,
Maggie

❦

Daniel shook his head and smiled as he refolded the letter and put it away. The Brennan family lived next door until well after he was out of high school. He remembered those days well.

He was always closest with Caitlin, the red-headed daughter who was born just three months after he was. They spent many hours playing in the treehouse her father had built in their tiny backyard. Caitlin was the first girl he'd ever kissed — and it was in that treehouse.

It was a shy, quick peck on the lips, but he'd never forgotten it.

Years later, he'd asked her to be his date for junior prom. She was one of his best friends, and despite that first kiss, there had never been anything romantic between them. They were each other's confidante and encourager.

Now, she also had her own family, and his kids and hers all graduated from the same high school. Their paths crossed at school events, but otherwise, he and Caitlin had drifted apart when he'd fallen in love with Liz.

He smiled at the memories. Lord, but he'd had a great childhood. His hope was that his children looked back on their own and felt the same way. Liz was a phenomenal mother, and he'd always had a close relationship with his kids, too.

Until this problem between him and Liam. He sighed and picked up the next letter. Where was the answer his mother promised he'd find?

4 Sept 1945
1830 hrs.

Dear Annie,

I received your letter, and first I want to tell you that I was very surprised, and my head is spinning with all of it, but it doesn't change the fact that I love you.

I trust that you had your reasons for not sharing your engagement. It isn't my place to judge the decisions you made.

I'll admit I'm a bit nervous to learn this other secret, but whatever it is, we'll face it together. As a family. Next to my faith in God, being with you gives me an inner strength like nothing else. We will overcome this obstacle, too.

I'm sorry for your loss of David, but like Patty leaving me, I feel God has a bigger plan for us. I still believe He intended for us to be together.

I'm concerned that my unit will be moving again soon. I'm afraid I won't get to see you again before we ship out. The good news is, the government has started making the arrangements to draw down the troops since the Japs surrendered. Our commanding officer told us about the discharge point system that's been put into place.

Soldiers receive points for having children, for months of service, medals, and citations earned. There are many ways to earn points. I think Timothy will be mustered out before me based on that system. Since he and Maggie will have a child soon, also, that will give him extra points. Even at that, we were told it will take close to a year for most of the guys to receive their discharge orders, but at least there's hope.

Hub told me he'd give up his leave for me so I can swing extra time when you have the baby. I'm not getting my hopes up, though, because I don't think the army looks too kindly on bartering.

I have guard duty soon, so I'll have to close. I wish I didn't have to stop, because I feel so much closer to you when I'm writing a letter. It's the best I can do for having you here with me. Soon, my love. I promise.

Love,
Jean

7 Sept

Monsieur Coughlin,

I am writing on behalf of our dear Annie. She has given birth to a son. She had a very difficult labor and delivery and is very weak. The child survived. We are doing all we can to help her. We wanted you to be informed, and we will attempt to keep you updated on her condition. Please keep her in your prayers. She insisted the child be named Joshua.

God be with her, the child, and you.
Sister Eloise Marie

❧☙

A lump jammed its way into Daniel's throat as he stared at this short missive. He wondered if this was why he'd never been told about Annie or the child she and his uncle had. Based on this news, and considering the time period, there was a good chance that neither Annie nor her baby survived.

His eyes stung, and he rubbed the back of his hands against them. He hoped this wasn't the end of their story.

CHAPTER ELEVEN

John Patrick paced like a caged animal outside the Citadel. He'd gone to his commanding officer to plead for emergency leave to go to Paris to be with Annie and his son, but the request was denied. He had no legal ties to Annie or their child. Frustration over his powerlessness clawed through his body.

He lifted the letter from Sister Eloise Marie, but his hands shook so badly that he could barely focus on the words.

She has given birth to a son. She had a very difficult labor and delivery and is very weak. The child survived. We are doing all we can to help her.

He glanced again at the date at the top. The letter had taken almost two weeks to reach him. Anything could have happened in two weeks. Had Annie recovered? What if, God forbid, she had died? His throat tightened, and he gulped in a shallow breath. He'd never be able to live with himself for doing this to her if she didn't survive. And what about their son?

John studied the letter, as if looking at the baby's name would make it all more real.

She insisted the child be named Joshua.

Joshua. The only discussion they'd ever had about names was for him to assure her that whatever name she chose would be perfect.

Joshua Coughlin. John let the name roll around in his mind. Had Annie also given the baby a middle name? Did Joshua even carry the Coughlin name?

"You okay, Irish?" The question from Hub was accompanied by a jab to John's back.

John wheeled toward him, the first break in his half hour of pacing. He held up the letter.

"I just received this. Annie had the baby."

Hub grinned and stepped forward to grasp John's shoulder. "Well, well. Look at that! You're a daddy, Irish. Congratulations! Let's light a cigar."

John shrugged from his grip and stepped back, pressing the letter to his chest. "The news wasn't good."

Hub's eyes rounded. "They're dead?"

"No! I mean, I don't know." John shoved the fingers of his free hand through his hair. "The letter's from one of the nuns. She just said Annie had a rough time and wasn't strong enough to write to me herself." He pivoted and resumed the pacing. "I feel so damned helpless."

"What the hell good does it do to pace?" Hub asked. "Get in there and write a letter to the nun. Or to your girl. You won't get answers by pacing."

John halted and whirled toward him. "It could take weeks before I get an answer."

Hub shrugged. "It'll take weeks if you write it and send it tomorrow, and it will take weeks if you write it and send it next week. But, if you send it tomorrow, it'll get there sooner, and maybe you'll get an answer sooner, too."

The matter-of-fact suggestion snapped John from the haze of confusion that had taken over his brain the moment he'd read the letter. His response didn't have to be long. He had just one question: Are Annie and my son all right?

⋞⋟

Daniel held the letter that his uncle had received from the nun and stared at the brief message. He couldn't imagine the anxiety associated with being caught in a war zone, separated from the woman you loved, and learning that she and your child were in crisis and there was no getting to them.

Because he had already looked through several of the photos of the woman he assumed to be Annie, he also assumed she had survived, but back then, his uncle didn't have the advantage of seeing into the future the way Daniel did with the letters and photos.

Daniel riffled through the small stack of photos on top of the letters until he found the one he was looking for. This had to be Annie cradling an infant, her lips pressed to the top of the baby's head. The child's gender wasn't discernible because of the tightly wrapped blanket, but that kind of affection looked very maternal. He assumed it was Joshua.

He sat back in the recliner and stared at the ceiling as he calculated when this child was born and when his uncle was killed. He hoped in that four-month span that his uncle had been able to get leave to go back to Paris to meet his son.

Curious, he took the next set of letters from the crate. Once again, his mother had bound this small stack with a red cord and a note indicating he was nearing the end of what he was referring to in his head as the *required* reading. He recognized the handwriting on the next envelope as Annie's. If he was relieved, he couldn't imagine how his uncle must have felt when it arrived.

September 13

My dear Jean,

I know by now you probably received a correspondence from Sr. Eloise Marie. I'm sure that was very frightening for you, and I am sorry to have worried you. Obviously, I am much stronger now. Sisters Catherine and Eloise Marie begged me to go to hospital to give birth, but I wanted our child to come into this world in the same place where he was conceived in love.

I do not know how much Sr. Eloise Marie shared with you, but I had a very difficult labor and birth. But, I was very aware when Joshua was born. He arrived with wide eyes of surprise at the cold world he had entered. The sisters cleaned and bundled him quickly, and he has been happy since then.

Thank you for this beautiful gift you have given me. Since you gave me permission to name him, I chose a name that started with the same letter as yours. But, his name has more meaning than that. Joshua is Hebrew for he saves. Being a man of great faith, I am sure you know that Joshua was chosen to lead the Israelites to the Promised Land after Moses died. I believe our Joshua will also be a leader. And, he has saved me at a time when I felt all was lost.

He is a handsome boy, Jean. He has dark hair that is so perfect that he looks like he has already been to a barber. Right now, his eyes are blue, as are all babies, but I hope his stay blue like yours. I would like him to look like an Irishman because you are so proud of your heritage. Heritage is important, and we will find a way to blend yours and mine for him.

I am eager to be out of bed, but the doctor came to examine me and said I must rest a few more days. Soon, I will take our little boy to all of the places you and I have been together — all those places where we have come to love each other.

It is my prayer that you will be able to meet Joshua soon. I miss you so, and I want you to know him. He will want to know you, too.

I love you John Patrick Coughlin and feel so blessed.

Forever,
Annie

25 Sept 1945

Dear Maggie,

I hope you'll forgive me for not writing sooner, but I just received a couple of weeks of back mail today. I'm writing to you and Ma and Pops first.

A lot has been happening. I got a promotion to Sergeant. I'm not sure that it will make much difference, except it is a *higher pay grade. I'll continue doing this medical work. I never imagined this is something I'd be good at, but I find I am. Isn't it interesting that Annie wants to be a nurse and help mend people and that's what I do every day? We were truly meant for each other.*

It's difficult for me to write this next part, which is why I held off, because the news is bittersweet. I almost lost her. Annie gave birth to our son on September 7th. She named him Joshua. I'm hoping to get leave to go to Paris as soon as possible. Since we're not married, I have no claim for going.

I'm hoping Annie will allow Joshua to have the Coughlin name. As the first grandchild, and a boy, he can carry on the family name. (Of course, if your and Timothy's baby is a boy, there will be two to do that.)

I hope you are doing well. I'm looking forward to receiving a letter from you introducing me to my niece or nephew. I pray each day that your delivery will be trouble free — especially after Annie's experience. I'm still shaken up by that, but at least everything is fine now.

Sending love to all.
J.P.

≪❧

Daniel smiled as he refolded the letter. As the old saying went, *he was a chip off the ol' block.* Apparently, Uncle John Patrick had also been proud of his Irish heritage if Annie mentioned it in her letter. What she didn't mention was if she gave Joshua the Coughlin name. If she did, it might be easier to track him down — if he was still alive — than to try to track Annie down, because she could have married someone else after his uncle died.

It was becoming more apparent to him that this, perhaps, was part of the reason his mother wanted him to read the letters. There was a missing leaf in their family tree, and as an only child with no cousins, Joshua could be the only other Coughlin, besides Daniel, from that generation of the family tree. How that related to his situation with Liam, he wasn't sure.

He glanced at the next letter, sent by his mother in October to his uncle, and smiled again. There was no doubt what her news was — this letter would announce his birth. It would be fun to read about his mother's excitement over finally holding the child she'd so badly wanted. She'd been, and continued to be, the best mother there was.

October 18, 1945

Dear John Patrick,

I write this letter with a heavy heart. Timothy's and my beautiful little boy was born a week ago. It breaks my heart to tell you that he did not survive the birth.

Daniel jerked up straighter in his chair and pulled the letter closer, as if that would change what he'd read. *Hadn't survived?* What the hell was *that* supposed to mean? Of course, he'd survived. His heart pumped furiously. He was sitting here holding the letter. Was his mother playing a cruel joke on his uncle? Daniel tightened his grip on the paper and continued reading.

The labor lasted more than 28 hours and the cord was wrapped around his tiny neck. Because my labor was so long, he died before he even entered the world. It has taken me this long to write to you, because I still cannot believe this is real. I have cried myself to sleep every night, only to wake up in the morning and grieve more for the little boy we will never see grow up.

I do not have the energy or spirit to write more to you now. I feel as if there is always a lump in my throat the size of a lemon. I cannot eat. I cannot breathe. My heart aches every second. This baby was so badly wanted by us.

Please pray for your brother. This loss is very difficult on him, too.

Please tell me about your son. We need some happiness in our family. I feel like my whole world has collapsed. I have never felt such loneliness. Timothy and I have talked of this in the past because we had so much trouble conceiving, but I truly believe it may be time for us to consider other options to have a family. I cannot take more heartache like this.

Be safe and count your blessings when you are finally able to hold your child in your arms. There is nothing more precious than that moment of new life.

With love,
Maggie

❧❧

Daniel's fingers shook, then the shaking overtook both hands until he couldn't hold the piece of stationery still enough to read the message. A cold sweat popped out on his forehead, and he lay his head back against the headrest and closed his eyes, willing the whooshing in his ears to stop.

What the hell was going on? There was no way he could misread the letter four times. He was sure his mother had left out key words that would have made her message make more sense.

The letter crinkled as he tightened his grip and let his hands drop to his lap.

Dead. His mother wrote that her baby had died. It was impossible.

His heart pounded so hard he'd swear a herd of buffaloes was stampeding through it.

"Breathe," he mumbled.

There had to be an explanation. What was it that his mother wanted him to know?

The sound of a car engine cut through the noise of questions buzzing in his head. His eyes snapped open, and he leapt from the chair. Two o'clock. It was early for Liz to be home from school, but he saw just the tail end of her dark car as she pulled in the driveway.

He hurried to the door. Before she was up the two front steps, Daniel yanked it open. Frigid air swirled in, rustling the letters in his hand. Liz halted abruptly, her leather school bag hanging from her shoulder, and tipped her head sideways to narrow her eyes at him.

"Hi." She drew out the single syllable as if it were three. "What's up?"

"What are you doing home already?"

She squinted at him. "Early dismissal for conferences. You don't remember me telling you this morning as I was leaving?"

He stepped aside. "No, sorry. I was pretty distracted. It's cold out. Come on in."

"Okay." That word, too, became multi-syllabic. She moved past him, and once inside, allowed the bag to slip from her shoulder as she turned toward him. "What's wrong?"

"I'm not sure where to begin." Daniel pushed the door closed and turned back toward her. "It's been kind of a crazy day."

She stretched on her tiptoes to give him the usual welcome home kiss. The familiar gesture calmed him. At this point, he'd cling to anything that felt normal and uncomplicated.

After wiping her feet, Liz shrugged her left shoulder out of her wool coat, and Daniel stepped forward to help her out of the rest of it. "Thanks," she said, taking it to hang in the hall closet.

"Does this have anything to do with the letters? Did you get through many?"

He blew a quick, loud breath through his nose. "Enough for my head to be spinning."

She slammed the closet door and whirled toward him. "What do you mean *spinning*?" Like his mother, she placed a hand along his cheek and forehead checking for a fever. "Are you dizzy? Is your stomach okay? Any muscle soreness? There's a lot of flu going around at school."

He took hold of her hand and pulled it between them. "Honey, relax. I'm not sick."

She searched his face. "Then what's going on?"

"Come into the den with me." He took hold of her hand and led her there, pointing at the crate when they entered the room. "I'm really confused by these letters."

"Have you read them all?"

"No, but I'm close to being done with the ones my mother specifically wanted me to read." Once again, he held up the letters in his hand. "But these last two, I – I —" he rubbed his hand roughly across his chin. "They don't make sense — the ones that talk about my mother being pregnant. I want you to read a few of them, though. I want to know how you interpret them."

"Here, you sit in the chair," he said, guiding her to the recliner. "I'll give you a few of these letters, and you tell *me* if they make sense to *you*."

He knelt next to the crate and sorted through the letters based on date, guessing that he was pulling the correct ones. He also included a couple of letters between his uncle and Annie after she revealed she was pregnant.

"Make sure you read them in chronological order," he said, laying the stack on her lap. "When you get to the end, you'll understand why my head is spinning."

"Okay." She took the envelopes and leafed through them, looking at the postmarks. The strong, musty box odor permeated the room again. Finally, she removed the first letter from the envelope and unfolded the long, age-tanned paper. "I'm afraid I'm going to rip this."

"They're holding together fine. Can I get you anything? Something to eat? Drink?"

She laid the letter on her lap and smoothed her hand across it to work out the stiffness of the folds. "Water would be nice. Thanks."

"Do you want lime?"

"Yes, please." She lifted the letter and began to read.

He rose, kissing her on the cheek before leaving the den. All he hoped was that Liz picked up on some clue that he had missed.

By the time he returned with the water, she was already on the third letter. He set the glass on the stand next to her, then pulled the antique oak caned chair across from her so the crate was between them. He wanted to watch her face as she read.

Her hazel eyes scanned across the pages quickly. Occasionally, she scowled or frowned, and sometimes her lips curved into a small smile. Once, she sighed and put her hand against her heart. It hadn't taken her long to understand the love stories that had unfolded in the letters.

At one point she gasped. Her eyes widened, then as she read, grew even wider. She laid a hand against her throat as if she was having trouble breathing, though she clearly was not. Daniel craned his neck to see the postmark date on the envelope she'd just opened and realized she'd just read the letter where John Patrick revealed that Annie was pregnant.

Liz was so engrossed in the letters that her water sat forgotten on the stand. While she read, Daniel opened the letters and read each of them again. The line stating that his mother's baby was dead echoed in his head like a bass drum.

Finally, with several letters in the read stack, Liz laid the current one there, but stared at it for a moment. When she lifted her eyes, tears wavered on the lids. She sniffled and wiped at them.

"That's so tragic that Annie's first fiancé was killed in Germany. It makes me want to cheer that she and your uncle found each other. Their love is beautiful." Her eyebrows lifted. "How come I never heard about your uncle having a child?"

Daniel leaned forward, putting his elbows on his knees and folding his hands under his chin. "Maybe for the same reason I never heard about it."

"And that reason would be?"

He shrugged. "I have no clue. That's what's so confusing."

"Maybe it's time to ask your mother."

He sat up and dropped his still clasped hands between his knees. "Tried that. I went over this morning. She and Sister Siobhan were just getting ready to go to a doctor's appointment, and then they were going to see the Rockette's Christmas show after. They won't be home until late afternoon."

She took the glass of water and squeezed the lime slice into it. The pulpy fruit bobbed on the water's surface. After drinking a quarter of it, she set it back down. "So, no big deal. You ask your mother about your uncle's baby. Confusion over."

Without speaking, Daniel handed her the first of the two letters that were now committed to his memory. She read the first one.

"A boy. Annie and John Patrick have a little boy. That's so sweet." She smiled. "I wish I could rewrite the ending of their story and have them all live happily ever after." She sipped her water again, "but then, I don't know the real ending."

Daniel shook his head. "I'm curious about that, too,

but that question is nothing compared to the questions you'll have after you read the next one." He was disappointed that she hadn't picked up on some clue he'd missed. He handed her the last letter he'd read. "Here's the one that has me totally baffled."

The crease between her thin eyebrows deepened the moment she started to read the letter from his mother to John Patrick. He knew she couldn't have read more than a few lines before she flipped the paper over to check the signature.

"Wait! This letter is from *your* mother?"

Daniel nodded. "And look at the date she wrote it."

Liz looked at the date. "October 18th. This doesn't make any sense. You're sitting right here. How can this be possible?"

"I don't know." He slumped back against the ladder back of the chair. "I don't think I've ever been this confused in my life."

Daniel watched as Liz ran the tip of her tongue along her lips, her eyes staring off toward the window as she contemplated what she'd read. The grandfather clock ticked loudly in the living room, the only sound, besides their breathing. At one point she looked at the letter again, then bolted up in the chair.

"Oh, my gosh, Dan. I think I know what happened."

CHAPTER TWELVE

"I think you were adopted!"

Daniel blinked and stared at Liz. "What?"

She leaned forward, her expression serious. "That's what makes the most sense. And, back then, they weren't as open about adoption as they are now."

Daniel scratched his head, processing what she suggested. "I don't know —"

"It's the only explanation."

Skepticism crept in. "I was never treated like I wasn't a Coughlin."

"Being adopted doesn't mean you're not a Coughlin, Danny."

"But, I've always prided myself on my Irish heritage — the Coughlin blood running through my veins. If I'm adopted, I might not even be Irish, let alone have any Coughlin blood." His fingers tensed as the reality of the possibility sank in. "This is ludicrous. I don't even know what to think or believe.

"You know what? We're just grabbing at straws, crazy

straws." Liz looked at the crate. "How many more letters are there?"

Daniel picked up the last of the letters from the bundle. "Just these."

"Let's read them, Dan. We won't know if there's more information if we just sit here guessing."

"Here," she said, extending her hand. "Give them to me, and I'll read them out loud."

He handed them to her. She glanced at the postmarks.

"That's interesting," Liz mumbled. She picked up the previous letter from Maggie. "Is this the order your mother gave you for the letters?"

Daniel nodded. "Yeah. Why?"

"These letters go back before the letter she wrote to your uncle." She shrugged as she removed the next letter from its envelope. "I guess we just have to do as your mother asked." Her eyes flicked up to look at Daniel. "Cross your fingers that we get answers."

04 Oct 1945

My dear Jean,

I apologize if my penmanship is not good in this letter. I am cradling Joshua in my other arm, so it makes writing awkward. He is such a content boy. I do not have to hold him as much as I do, but I cannot believe this unexpected blessing. Looking into his tiny, peaceful face makes me believe that all will be right with my world.

There are some things about him that remind me so much of you, Jean. He has your chin and jaw. It is a little squared at the end. When he is awake, his eyes are always wide open as if he is amazed by all he sees. I love snuggling him after his bath each day, because I nuzzle his silky hair and skin just to enjoy the clean baby smell. I am surprised how content he makes me feel. I suppose he is filling a void in my life, just as you have.

Since meeting you, Jean, I have felt happy again for the first time in years. I miss my family, and I still feel the urgency to find them, but I no longer feel lost in this world. I have a purpose. A reason for being here for our son.

The doctor has finally allowed me to get out of bed. I went outside with Joshua this afternoon so the sun could shine fully on his face. It smelled so fresh because of a gentle rain we had this morning.

I was relieved you weren't angry to learn of my engagement. I was so worried that you would feel I had lied to you. It was a painful part of my past and talking about it opened the wounds that are still healing. Besides my family, you, my sweet man, are the only person who knows this about my past. Thank you for understanding the difficulty I had sharing it.

Joshua is stirring in my arms. I am sure he is hungry. I so look forward to the day when father and son can finally meet. I purposely did not give him a middle name, because I want you to have a part in this.

Be safe, Père. Your son and his mother need you. I hope we can see you soon.

With love,
Your Annie

❧❧

When Liz stopped reading, Daniel looked up.

Her soft expression made her eyes crinkle at the corners. "Aww, Danny, this is so sweet."

"Sweet doesn't help us solve this mystery."

"No, but coming from a woman's perspective, I would guess that your mother knows that you, as a man, would probably overlook the importance of these relationships. I haven't even read all the letters you have and can see how important each of these relationships are. Your mother is the anchor. She was holding down the fort at home while the men were off at war. She helped take care of your grandparents. She supported your father and John Patrick while they were away. She took care of everyone else."

Daniel shifted in the chair. "Yeah, so what about my uncle and Annie?"

"It's a love story. Clearly, Annie rescued your uncle after his girlfriend dumped him. And, now — "Liz held up the letter in her hand — "now she gives him a reason to live. And with a baby? Wow!" She shook her head and smiled. "It's an *inspiring* love story. Despite the ugliness of war, they found each other."

Daniel stared at her, and she looked back at him.

"Come on! Let your romantic side enjoy this moment. Besides, you're a history buff." She tapped the edge of the crate and arched her eyebrows. "This is a whole lot of history."

Smirking, he said, "Fine. Continue with the letters."

❧❧

16 Oct 1945
0645 hrs.

Dear Annie,

I have some good news. Since we've been working day and night, I'm up for liberty soon. I hate that you and Joshua are so close but so far.

I've been praying that when I come to visit that you will finally agree to marry me. It's what's best for Joshua and us. If you haven't already done it, I would like to have him christened when I'm there. When I give you a date, I hope you'll have time to make arrangements with a priest for both.

I can't tell you exactly where we are, but maybe if I tell you that if I knew where to look for your siblings, I would, maybe that will give you an idea. We WILL find them. I promise.

My unit recently went through several cities that were destroyed. Aachen and Dusseldorf were a couple of the worst. There was still so much dust that we had to wear scarves over our faces as we drove through.

The saddest part was seeing the people living in basements of destroyed buildings. Children were so frightened that they dove under collapsed walls to hide from military personnel. It was hard to leave the children behind. We didn't see any adults, so we wondered if they were Jewish children whose families had been taken to concentration and work camps. Hub, Artie, and I gave them three days' worth of our rations. It's not much, but it will help some.

When we arrived in the next town, there was an old man playing a clarinet in a neighborhood that had been bombed early in the war. He was actually quite good even though his fingers were badly scarred from burns. One whole side of his face was ragged with scars, too. Our interpreter spoke with him and learned that he had studied jazz in the United States in the 30's. After his home was bombed, all he salvaged was his clarinet.

I'm sure it was because of his music that I had a dream about you. God, it was beautiful! We were together, dancing to Benny Goodman. It reminded me of our wonderful weeks together in Paris. Being with you made them the best weeks of my life.

I miss you so much. Give Joshua a kiss from his daddy, and please tell him how much I already love him. He's lucky to have you as his mother, too.

With deep love,
Jean

30 Oct 1945
1600 hrs

Dear Maggie,

I don't even know how to begin this letter to you. I am so shocked and so sorry to hear the news about your baby. Timothy told me the news when I saw him in Paris. (I'll explain about that in a minute.) I know there's nothing I can do or say that will make this better, so I won't even try. Please take care of yourself. I hope Timothy can be home with you soon.

I'll get right to the point in this letter. Maybe Timothy already told you, but you have a new sister-in-law. Annie and I were married while I was in Paris. I know you will love each other because you're both beautiful people.

As I had hoped, Tim was able to get a day of R & R while I was in Paris, so he stood up with me when Annie and I took our vows. He also met Joshua.

The circumstances of our wedding are very complicated. For now, I'll just tell Ma and Pop that we are married. When Annie and I return to the States, then I'll be able to explain why we made the choices we made. We were not married in the Catholic Church as I had hoped, but, still, we were joined in the sight of God. The chaplain from Tim's unit was kind enough to perform the ceremony.

She was a beautiful bride. My favorite part of the ceremony was when we each took a candle of our own and lit a single candle in the middle to signify the joining of our hearts and lives. We are one, now.

When I entered this war, I didn't expect to come to Europe and find a wife, but God has a bigger plan than any of us can ever understand. I hate that I had to leave Annie and Joshua, but I'm sure we will be reunited soon.

It was good to finally meet him and hold him. I hope this doesn't hurt you since you lost your son.

Annie allowed me to give Joshua his middle name. I chose Timothy. It means one who honors God, but I also wanted to honor my brother. I believe this child is God's way of saying that love can overcome all obstacles. Annie and I will have obstacles to our future, but Joshua Timothy Coughlin will be proof that only God sits in judgement of others. It's our job to accept His will and accept all people for who they are not what they are. It's time for us to undo the damage done by Hitler's hatred.

I need to write to Mrs. John Coughlin now. I love the way that sounds. Everything happens for a reason, and now I know why Patty left me. God wanted to be sure my heart was open to love Annie. I'll try to write again, soon.

My heart aches that you and Timothy are going through this awful time, but I knew you would want to hear something happy.

All my love to you,
J.P.

"Well, I'll be damned," Daniel muttered. "They got married."

Liz replaced that letter in its envelope. "And your mother never told you about it?"

Daniel shook his head. "I'm guessing after Uncle John was killed that they lost track of Annie and Joshua, so what was the point?"

"I guess, but, he'd be your only cousin. You must be curious now. Don't you wonder where they are?"

"That's why I went over to my mother's earlier. I asked her if she knew where Annie is now."

Liz perked up even more. "Really? And does she?"

Daniel nodded. "She said she does, but she wouldn't tell me. She said I needed to keep reading the letters."

Liz lifted the last three envelopes and a telegram under those. "Well, then the answer must be here. Let's find it."

17 November

My dear husband,

This letter will be brief. I received a message from an old friend in Frankfurt that he may know where my brother and sisters are. He was told that Samuel, Ruth and Esther may be in Strasbourg at a house used for German refugees. Sister Eloise is trying to arrange to borrow a car from a parishioner.

I will leave Joshua with the Sisters while I travel. Even though I will not have to cross into Germany, it is still too dangerous on the border. I will keep you informed. Pray that this is true. I want so badly to have my family reunited.

Your loving wife,
Annie

3 Dec 1945
1930 hrs

Dear Annie,

That's great news from your friend, but please don't go without me. The thought of you traveling alone makes me sick. I agree that it's better to leave Joshua with the Sisters at the convent, because the trip would be too hard.

I'll talk with my CO to see if I can get emergency leave. I also know a local with a car and maybe I can swing a deal with him so I can come to pick you up and we'll go together. Please let me try before you go alone.

I promise I'll see you soon and we'll go and find your brother and sisters together. We're family. All of us, and my place is with you and protecting you.

I love you, Annie Coughlin.
John Patrick

5 Dec 1945
1745 hrs

Dear Maggie,

Tomorrow I'm leaving for Paris to join Annie on a trip to the German border. She received word that her brother and sisters may have been located in Strasbourg. I was able to get emergency leave and a car so I can take her.

I'm eager to see her and Joshua. The trip will take several hours one way, so we are leaving Joshua at the convent.

I'll write again after we return. I plan to write with good news that we have them. Then, as soon as this war is over, I'm bringing them all to New York. I can't wait for that day when my whole family will be together again.

Love to all,
J.P.

∾∾

Liz scowled and peered into the crate like a child inspecting the inside of an empty cookie jar.

"Are you sure that's the last letter you're supposed to read, Danny?"

"The telegram is the last thing in the bundled letters."

Liz opened the tanned telegram, its size about two thirds of a regular piece of paper. Daniel stood and moved next to Liz, settling on one knee next to her so they could both see the telegram sent to his grandfather, so she didn't have to read it out loud.

WESTERN UNION

EYA353   29GOVT-WASHINGTONDC   DEC 18

MR SEAMUS COUGHLIN=

BAY RIDGE NY=

THE SECRETARY OF WAR DESIRES ME TO EXPRESS HIS DEEP REGRET THAT YOUR SON SGT JOHN P COUGHLIN DIED OF INJURIES IN AN AUTOMOBILE ACCIDENT IN STRASBOURG, FRANCE 8 DEC 45

CONFIRMING LETTER FOLLOWS

STEPHENS ADJ GENERAL

Daniel leaned his elbow on the armrest of the recliner and looked at Liz. "I always thought he was killed during a mission with the army." He took the telegram and read it out loud. "Died of injuries in an automobile accident." He shook his head. "Every time I turn around, something I thought I knew turns out to be false."

"Did your family say he was killed while on duty?"

Daniel shook his head. "No, I don't think they ever did. I just *assumed* that's what happened. We didn't talk about it."

He nodded toward the telegram. "So, if this accident occurred when he and Annie went to look for her family, then what happened to Annie?"

Liz clutched Daniel's hand. "And, Joshua."

CHAPTER THIRTEEN

Daniel stood and turned away from Liz.

"This is so crazy! What was the point in keeping all of this a secret?"

Liz rose from the chair and stepped beside him, laying her hand on his arm. Her warmth comforted him. "With your uncle gone, and apparently Annie and her baby unreachable, maybe it was easier to save the family embarrassment by just not acknowledging it. Because your uncle is a legend around here, the family may have decided it was better to let him be an untarnished hero."

"A baby didn't change the good he did here as a policeman, or even during the war." He looked back at the crate. "And where's the confirming letter that was to follow the telegram? Could there have been more concrete information in that?"

"Maybe, but if this is what your mother gave you, she probably figured it was enough. She obviously wants you to know now, for some reason."

"I still don't see a connection to Liam and Mora being

engaged." He thrust a hand through his hair. "I wish she was home so I could ask her questions, because this is going to drive me nuts."

"Well, unfortunately, she's probably the only one with answers, so you have no choice but to wait."

He stepped away. "Yeah, I —" He whirled toward Liz. "No, she's not the only one who knows the details of Uncle John's death. Father Michael had to have known how his brother was killed, right?"

"He has Alzheimer's, Danny. It's unlikely he'll be helpful."

A glimmer of hope charged through him. "But, it's early stages. There are still times when he's totally lucid. Besides, don't they usually remember details from the past better than what they just ate?" He pivoted toward the door. "I have nothing to lose. And, maybe if he thinks I know more than I do, he'll tell more than Ma would."

"Are you going now?" Liz asked.

Daniel glanced at his watch. "Yup. There's no time like the present." He started toward the door, then stopped. "Wanna come?"

Her eyes lit up. "You bet I do. Let me grab my coat."

Within minutes, they were out the door and maneuvering through traffic across Brooklyn to Southside Manor. The highway was busier than usual for mid-afternoon. Daniel pulled around a slow-moving car, his mind barely on driving.

"It's hard to believe it's been just a few hours since I opened that crate. I seriously feel like a whole lifetime has passed today."

"I guess in some ways it has," Liz responded. She took

hold of his hand and leaned forward so he could see her face.

"I hope you're not getting your hopes too high, honey," she said, the concern obvious in her tone. "There's no telling what he'll be like today. The positive is that it's early enough in the day that Sundowners Syndrome shouldn't have kicked in, yet."

He squeezed her fingers. "Yeah, I know. I'm praying it's a good day, though. Besides, I've been so busy that I haven't been able to get over to see him in a couple of weeks, so if nothing else, that's important."

"Good. Keep it all in perspective." She returned her attention to the highway.

Daniel tried to focus on the cars darting in and out of lanes. The occasional blowing horn kept him alert.

At Southside Manor, many of the visitor parking spaces were empty since it was mid-afternoon. He swung his Buick into a space and cut the engine. Liz's seatbelt rolled into its holder before he'd even put the car in park. Apparently, he wasn't the only one eager to find out what Father Michael knew.

Daniel climbed from the car and flipped his jacket collar up against the frigid breeze. He met Liz at the back of the car, then they twined their fingers together as they crossed the parking lot. Puddles of water from snow that had melted earlier were glazing over with a thin layer of ice. They weaved around them until they reached the automatic sliding doors that led into the building.

A warm whoosh of air enveloped them as soon as they stepped inside. Daniel's stomach somersaulted as the distinctive medicinal odor of the home overpowered the fresh scent of the winter air.

They stopped at the chest-level faux marble counter where a visitor's book lay open. A small Christmas tree with tiny, bright, multi-colored lights adorned the other end of the counter. Next to that, the light from the electric candles in a golden menorah reflected off the shiny wall.

A balding man in his mid-thirties sat behind the counter, bent over a small stack of forms.

"How are you this afternoon, Sid?" Liz asked as she picked up the pen to sign them in.

"Fine, Mrs. Coughlin. And you?"

"Busy, like everyone at this time of year. I bet the girls are excited about Christmas."

Sid grinned. "They sure are. It's amazing how kids will bring back the excitement of the holidays." He looked past her to Daniel. "Hello, Mr. Coughlin. Nice to see you again."

"Nice to see you, too, Sid," he said as he put his hand on the small of Liz's back to guide her down the hall toward the north wing.

"I'll be off for a couple of weeks, so if you come back before Christmas, I might not see you," Sid explained. "We'll see you at Mass Christmas Eve. Hope Santa gives you whatever you want."

"Forget Santa," Daniel whispered near Liz's ear as he slid his arm around her waist. "I hope my uncle gives me the information I want."

They worked their way through the maze of halls. Paintings of various serene scenes dotted the peach-colored walls. They'd visited Father Michael at least weekly in the seven months he'd resided here, so navigating the corridors was easy.

Televisions blared from individual rooms, a

cacophony of programs blending into indiscernible noise in the hall.

It had taken Daniel months to learn to ignore most of what he heard and saw here. As with so many medical facilities, the home was understaffed and the staff overworked. They had to be saints to maintain their positive attitudes in this environment day in and day out. As difficult as the situations seemed at times, he also knew that, for the family's sake, there was probably no other option for their loved ones.

It was the case with Father Michael. When he was first diagnosed with Alzheimer's Disease just a few months after Daniel's father died, the parish nuns bravely vowed to care for him at the rectory. Their efforts were valiant, but as he declined, they couldn't give him the supervision he needed.

And that's when Maggie volunteered to take in her brother-in-law to stave off the need for a nursing home. Less than a year later, Father Michael's condition declined to the point that on his bad days he was belligerent — behavior that was out of character.

Fearing for Maggie's safety, Daniel and the family physician had tried to convince her that she had done all she could for him and that it was time for Father Michael to have twenty-four-hour care. In her stubborn way, she refused — until the day he threw a bowl of hot soup at her, insisting it wasn't warm enough. Fortunately, the burns were superficial, but she reluctantly agreed it was time.

Within days of his move, Father Michael became attached to a nurse named Regina whom he had baptized more than forty years before. In his good days, he even remembered her as a little girl. In the eyes of the Coughlin family, she was a heaven-sent angel. Daniel was sure God was reserving a special place in heaven for all these workers.

They rounded the last corner. Leaning toward Liz, he said in a stage whisper, "If I ever get like these people, promise me you'll just shoot me and roll me into a hole in the backyard."

She frowned in response. "That's so morbid!"

"No," Daniel replied, "I'm thinking of you. I don't want you or the kids to have to deal with all of this."

"For better or worse," she said, bumping her shoulder against his arm.

As they approached Father Michael's room, Regina stepped into the hall. Her hair was a different shade of red than the last time they visited, but then, the color seemed to change monthly, anyway. Her uniform today was a set of scrubs with little cats dancing in various forms.

"Hi, folks," she chortled, as good-natured as ever. Her green eyes sparkled behind the dark-rimmed glasses perched halfway down her nose. She stepped to the computer on a high cart just outside the door, inputting information as she spoke.

"Father Michael's having a great day, so he's down at the ice cream social in the dining hall. I was just on my way to get him. Hold on a sec," she finished, distracted by her work.

She pondered over her entry on the computer monitor for a moment, then clicked out of the screen and glanced back at them with a bright smile.

"Okay, come along, folks." Everyone was "folks" to

Regina, a trait she said she'd picked up from her grandmother who raised her in western Pennsylvania.

Daniel and Liz followed her down the hall, barely able to keep up with her brisk pace. She greeted every person by name and a pat on the shoulder, whether they were staff or patient. It was easy to see why Father Michael was happy here. Regina made everyone feel welcome.

"Are you folks ready for the holidays?" she asked over her shoulder.

"Close," Liz replied. "Need to get the tree up and wrap a few Christmas presents, a Hanukkah gift for our future daughter-in-law, and I'm done."

Daniel knew her casual mention of the gift for Mora was her way of proving her acceptance of Liam and Mora's engagement. Even though reading the letters helped him understand his uncle's acceptance, he'd be lying if he said that it changed his apprehension over trying to blend Christianity and Judaism in his own family.

Regina laughed. "Lucky you. I don't even have time to start shopping until the day before Christmas. Two days before if I'm really lucky. That's the joy of working in a profession where we're always short staffed."

At the end of the hall, they took another left, and then the dining room was in front of them. The bright, airy room was filled with four-person tables arranged haphazardly. Many of the tables had been vacated, but the empty dishes left behind were proof the room had recently been bustling with activity. A middle-aged woman rolled a cart from table to table clearing dishes.

At a table near the windows, Father Michael sat with

two other residents: a man, dressed in a blue-striped formal shirt with a red bow tie, and a woman in a wheelchair whose lavender dress accented her silver hair.

"Father Michael always asks to sit with Lester and Mildred," Regina said as they crossed the dining hall.

Father Michael scraped his spoon along the inside of his bowl to get the last remnants of vanilla ice cream, while the man talked animatedly to him. He glanced up when they approached but didn't acknowledge them. That didn't surprise Daniel. He remembered his mother saying that as the Alzheimer's progressed, Father Michael got to the point where, at times, he wouldn't even notice her if she was sitting across the table from him.

Daniel and Liz stopped to the side of Father Michael while Regina inserted herself between Lester and Mildred, affectionately draping an arm across each of their shoulders. "How was that ice cream, folks?"

Lester and Mildred nodded and mumbled approval, but Father Michael only looked up at her and smiled.

"These two love birds have been married for seventy-four years. Their anniversary is next month, and we're going to throw them a big bash." She squeezed them closer to her.

Daniel glanced at them, but then gazed at Father Michael's profile — the man who had baptized him so many years ago. He and Sister Siobhan were revered in the family for their commitment to their faith. For generations of Coughlins, those who chose to dedicate their lives to God were held in the highest regard in the family.

Regina stepped behind Father Michael's chair and

laid her hand on his shoulders while she leaned next to his ear.

"Father, did you notice you have company?" She seemed to apply pressure to direct his attention toward Daniel and Liz. They stepped closer to move directly into his view.

A smile lit his face instantly.

"Brother. How nice of you to visit."

Daniel's heart sank. Even though for years others had commented on Daniel's resemblance to his father and uncle, today it was disheartening. Did this indicate they hadn't caught his uncle during one of his lucid times?

Father Michael struggled to rise from the chair, so Daniel hurried to assist him.

"This is my brother," Father Michael continued, introducing Daniel to Lester and Mildred. He stood unsteadily for a moment, then seemed to regain his balance. "He's home from the war. He was in Europe."

Liz rubbed the small of Daniel's back, and he knew it was her way of supporting him in his disappointment. It was unlikely he'd get answers from Father Michael today.

"Father," Regina interrupted, "this is your nephew, Daniel."

As if startled, Father Michael drew back for a moment and stared at Daniel. The intensity of his scrutiny would have made most people uncomfortable, but Daniel prayed it would snap the priest back to the present.

"Yes, yes, you're right," he said, his voice suddenly sounding tired. "You boys all have such a strong resemblance to one another."

Daniel shot Liz a look of despair as the air in his balloon of hope seeped out.

"I'm Timothy's son," he said, knowing the disappointment in his voice was obvious. "Timothy and Maggie."

Father Michael narrowed his eyes as he studied Daniel. "Yes, yes. Of course, you're right. Timothy and John Patrick were so close that people mistook them for twins, but you do favor John Patrick."

Daniel forced a smile. "So, I've heard," then under his breath he added to Regina, "from everybody."

"Can you stay and visit?" Father Michael asked. "We can go to the parlor where it's more comfortable."

Daniel sighed, wondering if this was going to be a waste of time.

"Of course, we can."

Liz stepped beside Regina. "We can walk him from here, unless you're required to stay with him."

"Oh, no," Regina answered. "That would be great."

Liz hooked her arm around Father Michael's elbow. As if noticing her for the first time, he perked up.

"Elizabeth! I'm sorry I didn't see you before, you beautiful creature." To Daniel he said, "She's as beautiful as ever. You chose well, boy."

"Beautiful inside and out, Father." Renewed hope surged through Daniel. It was like a switch had been flipped, and now Father Michael was back with them in the present.

Father Michael looked at Liz. "And how are the children?"

"They're doing great," Liz said.

"Maggie told me about Liam's promotion," Father Michael said with a smile. "You must be proud."

Daniel shot a look at Liz, and she met his eyes and

nodded. That promotion was recent. Could they be so fortunate as to have caught his uncle during a lucid time, after all? Daniel said a silent prayer that God would keep his uncle's mind open at least for the next half hour. Just long enough for Daniel to get answers.

"We're very proud," Liz said. "And over the holidays, there's going to be an engagement party for him and Mora."

"Is that right?" Father Michael shook his head. "God bless them."

Even though no one else could see, Daniel raised his eyebrows. God bless them, indeed. They would need the blessing to get over the relationship hurdles of the future.

They made their way to the parlor, an intimate sitting room around the corner from Father Michael's room. Daniel knew this was one of Liz's favorite rooms because of its intimacy. The wallpaper was off white with rich burgundy stripes, making it feel homey. Two loveseats and two Queen Anne's chairs in the room complemented the wall paper with burgundy, forest green, and gold upholstery.

On the wall between the chairs hung a painting of a Victorian-style house, complete with porch, gazebo and tall trees hovering over it protectively. A dirt path snaked from the front steps around the side until it disappeared behind the house. It was the kind of picture that made a person wish they were in that place, and Daniel guessed that it was purposely chosen to remind the residents of their own homes.

Liz guided Father Michael to one of the loveseats and sat to his right. Daniel sat in the chair diagonal to them.

"Well, you're looking great," he offered, not sure

whether to launch into his questions or to work the conversation up to them. It seemed selfish to focus only on his purpose for coming.

"Thank you." Father Michael leaned back on the loveseat. "Is your mother well? She hasn't been here recently."

Daniel knew his mother had been in to visit Father Michael the day before, but he wasn't going to argue with a man who might not even remember that he'd just finished an ice cream sundae five minutes before.

"She's fine. She took Sister Siobhan to a doctor appointment this morning, and then they were going in to see the Christmas show at Radio City and the decorations in Rockefeller Center. I'm sure she'll be here tomorrow."

"Your mother is a good woman, Daniel. She's always been the glue to hold the Coughlin family together."

"And, she's no different today," Daniel agreed.

He thought of the crate of letters and his main purpose for coming, deciding there was no point in small talk. As with most Alzheimer's patients, the present was often foggy, but the past came with great clarity.

He cleared his throat, trying to decide the best way to approach the subject. He decided to start subtle and see if Father Michael reacted to any of the pieces of information.

"My mother gave me the crate of letters to read."

Father Michael stared blankly at him. Daniel glanced at Liz. She sat rigid, apparently as anxious as Daniel about what the priest would recall. Daniel moved a little more forward on his chair and pressed on.

"Do you know about the crate of letters that Uncle

John, my mom, and a woman in France wrote to each other while Uncle John was in the service in World War II?"

Father Michael shook his head and shrugged. "I know nothing of a crate."

Daniel's neck tensed. Was this going to be a dead end, after all?

"How about Annie Goodman? Do you recognize that name?"

"Annie —" Father Michael scowled. "What did you say her last name was?"

"Goodman," Daniel repeated.

His uncle shifted a bit as if uneasy. "No, I don't recall anyone by that name."

Now the muscles up through Daniel's jaw tensed. "Are you sure? Annie Goodman." He said the name louder and slower, as if that would make a difference.

"Show him the pictures, Danny," Liz urged.

The pictures. He forgot he'd put them in his pocket before leaving the house. He withdrew them and held them out.

His uncle took them and focused on them one at a time. Slowly, his lips lifted into a smile.

"Do you recognize her?" Daniel swallowed the sudden profusion of saliva.

"Ah, yes," Father Michael said. He made the sign of the cross. "God rest their souls."

Daniel leaned over and saw that Father Michael was focused on the photo of Uncle John, Annie, and the baby. The beat of his heart quickened.

"Do you know what happened to her?" He noticed even his breaths were coming faster.

Father Michael grimaced. "They're gone. Such a tragedy."

"Right. Uncle John died in a car accident in Strasbourg, France, but what happened to Annie and the baby?"

"Annie died in the accident, too."

"And their baby? Was he in the accident?"

His uncle gave him a bewildered look. "Their baby? Oh, no. He was left with the nuns at the convent."

"Really?" Currents of excitement shot through Daniel. "Do you know what happened to him after that? Did the nuns raise him in France? Does anyone have contact with him anymore?"

Father Michael furrowed his brow and his attention darted between the picture he held and Daniel. He lightly tapped his finger against Joshua's image.

"I helped bring him here."

Daniel straightened with a jolt of surprise. His gaze locked with Liz's for a few seconds before he leaned closer to Father Michael.

"You brought him to New York?"

"Yes. My parish sponsored him to bring him to the States."

That revelation sucked the breath from Daniel's lungs. Had Father Michael slipped out of reality without them realizing it? Daniel decided to take the questioning a bit further for confirmation.

"Do you know where Joshua is now?"

"Yes," Father Michael acknowledged.

"Where is he?"

A mirthful smile tipped the priest's lips, again. "He's here."

Daniel snapped his attention toward the doorway, expecting to see a stranger walk in. There was no one. He turned warily back to his uncle, positive now that the man had slipped back into his world of confusion.

"There's no one there, Father."

Father Coughlin's smile turned indignant. "I wasn't speaking of someone else. I was speaking of you."

Daniel looked at him incredulously. "What?"

Reaching out, Father Michael rested his feeble hand on Daniel's arm.

"You, my child, are Joshua."

CHAPTER FOURTEEN

Daniel dug his fingers into the arms of the chair in an effort keep himself steady in a room that was suddenly spinning.

"Danny, are you all right?" Liz moved from the couch and kneeled in front of him. "Dan, honey, are you okay?"

His throat tightened as he stared at his uncle. The man's dull blue eyes were locked on Daniel. Surely Father Michael had slipped back into confusion. What he said was ludicrous!

"I think we should go," he finally managed, pushing up from the chair. An invisible thick belt tightened around his chest as soon as he stood.

Liz stood and took hold of his hand. "Do you want me to take Father Michael back to his room and meet you at the car?" When he didn't respond, she squeezed his fingers. "Are you all right?"

He swallowed against the lump in his throat and thrust his shaking hand through his hair.

Lowering his voice, he said to Liz, "He must be confused, again. He's gotta be."

Liz tipped her head, gave him a sympathetic look, and whispered. "I'm sure you're right. He *was* confused about who you were when we first got here."

He pushed his palms across his thighs to relieve the tension in his hands. He couldn't think straight, and obviously, neither could his uncle.

"I bet you want to rest after your busy afternoon, Father. We'll take you back to your room."

Father Michael shook his head. "I'm not tired, and I'm not confused."

Daniel startled, surprised his uncle heard him and Liz whispering. There was no strength in his uncle's voice, adding to the question of the validity of what he'd said.

Attempting to remain patient and calm, Daniel sucked in his upper lip and pushed his teeth hard against the sensitive skin.

Finally, he said, "You have me confused with someone else. I'm Daniel."

When Father Michael started to shake his head again, Daniel straightened, took a step back, and held up a hand. "It's okay. Maybe I'm tired, myself. I'll come back and visit in a few days."

Father Michael drew in a loud breath and struggled to rise from the couch. Liz and Daniel hurried to either side of him to assist. Once on his feet, he looked up at Daniel. "It was not my intent to upset you."

"I'm fine, Father," Daniel lied as they started the slow walk out of the parlor. He was anything but fine. Shaken to the core was more like it, but there was no reason to upset his uncle.

Regina waved when she saw them approaching his room. "I'll be down in a minute. If you have to leave, he'll be all right until I come to settle him in."

"I can walk with him from here, Danny, if you want to go outside," Liz offered.

"No, I'm fine." He wasn't, but going outside and pacing while he waited for her wouldn't change anything.

When they entered the room, they found that Regina had already turned on the television to a local talk show. Father Michael's attention shifted to the screen and his face lit up.

"Ah, I remember that christening," he said, pointing to the show's middle-aged female host who was talking about a holiday toy drive for children in Harlem. His uncle chuckled. "She spit up all over my robe."

Father Michael shuffled to an olive-green vinyl chair next to the bed, and Daniel helped him settle into it.

He laid his hand on the man's shoulder. "Thank you, Father. We'll see you soon."

Without taking his attention from the television, Father Michael nodded. "She used to sit with her parents in the back of the church for every Mass. Why do you think they never came up front except for communion?"

"I don't know, Father," Daniel said, withdrawing toward the door. He waited while Liz gave his uncle a kiss on the cheek.

"Goodbye, Father," she said quietly. "We'll visit again soon."

Father Michael absently reached for her hand and patted it, never taking his attention from the television.

"Beautiful!" he murmured.

He wasn't aware of their departure. It was obvious he had already shifted to a different world.

The air outside had turned brisk. His mind was reeling with questions, so he was barely cognizant of Liz stopping to sign them out. When he reached the car, he laid his arm on the hood and dropped his forehead to his sleeve while he waited for her to cross the small stretch of parking lot.

Other than the whirring of the heating system on top of the building and cars in the distance, the only sounds were his deep breaths and Liz's feet as they crunched the snow and ice in the parking lot. When she reached him, she pressed her warm, bare hand against the back of his neck and kneaded the tense muscles.

"I warned you that he might not make sense, Dan. There's just no way to know when he's lucid." She pressed her face next to the small exposed part of his cheek. "He's confused." She took the keys dangling from Daniel's fingers and depressed the unlock button. "I'll drive."

He was too numb to argue. He opened the door for her to get in, then walked around the car and slid into the passenger seat. She fumbled with his keys until she had the right one, then put it in the ignition. The car purred to life, forcing cold air from the vents.

While the car idled, Liz looked at Daniel, but he couldn't look squarely at her. Every inch of his body was in a knot. Staring out the passenger window, he replayed in his head everything Father Michael said.

"Liz?" His voice sounded like a croak.

She laid her hand on his. "What?"

"How do we know if he was lucid?"

Tightening her grip on his fingers, she leaned closer so their coat sleeves barely touched. "It's just hard to tell, Dan. I wish we knew for sure."

Bile inched its way up his throat. Voicing his thoughts would be the end of the world as he'd known it for his entire life.

"I think — I think I believe him. Now that he's said that, I realize it was spelled out clearly in those last few letters." He turned to face her. "My parents —" He halted mid-sentence and sat up straight. "Jesus, Liz!" Clenching his fists, he pushed them against his thighs. This couldn't be real.

"If what Father Michael said is true, I can't call them *my* parents. Their son died at birth, while John Patrick and Annie's son lived. It said so in the letters." His heart pounded so hard he could hear the blood whooshing in his ears, and his eyes widened.

"So our adoption theory regarding me wasn't so far off, but is Father Michael *really* remembering it all accurately?"

He pulled the pictures from his pocket. In the still frigid air, his breath hung like a suspended cotton puff in front of him. Flipping through the photographs, he stopped when he came to the snapshot of John Patrick, Annie, and Joshua in front of the Eiffel Tower.

"Who the hell am I?" he rasped out as he stared into the eyes of the strangers. If this was true, then his whole life was a lie.

Liz's teeth chattered, pulling him from his trance.

"You're cold," he said, and she nodded.

"Just a tad."

He turned the heater dial to its highest setting.

"Let's get going," he suggested. "I'll leave you at home, then I'm going over to my mother's." He laughed, but not in amusement. "Ha! My mother's." The word mother came out in a mocking tone.

"I want to go with you, Danny."

He laid his hand against her cheek, relishing the feel of her soft, smooth skin. It grounded him, helped him realize that this was reality, not some kind of twisted nightmare that he couldn't wake up from.

"I think this is something I should do alone."

She pursed her lips, and tears shimmered on the brims of her eyes. "We've been a team for almost three decades. Whatever comes of this, we're in it together." She turned her face into his hand and kissed his palm. "I love you. What you might learn affects both of us." She grasped his fingers with her cold hand and slid them along her warming cheek. "And, it affects *our* children."

The lump returned to his throat, and an ache spread like a wave through his gut. She was right. This not only changed his past, it changed their future, too. He cleared his throat against the fear and anger that constricted it.

"Well, then, what are we waiting for? Let's see if she's back home."

⊰⊱

Fresh snow had fallen in his mother's neighborhood, and now it twinkled like minuscule diamonds in the car headlights. Liz pulled the car along the sidewalk in front of Daniel's childhood home. There were fresh tracks in his mother's driveway and footprints across the sidewalk and to the front door, but her car wasn't in the driveway.

"Damn it!" he cursed under his breath. He looked at Liz. "Do you mind waiting to see if she comes back soon?"

"Of course not," she answered, "but I'm leaving the car running to keep the heat on."

He reached for the door handle. "I'll start clearing her driveway and sidewalk while we wait. I can't just sit still."

"Want me to help?" she asked.

He waved her off. "No, you're not dressed for clearing snow."

She quirked one eyebrow. "Neither are you, but it's not like it's a blizzard."

"No," he said, pushing open the door. "I appreciate the offer, but she only has one shovel, anyway. You stay warm."

"Okay," she said, and settled against the back of the seat.

He found the shovel at the side of the house and made paths across her sidewalk before he moved onto her driveway. He only had a couple of swipes left when he saw her car coming down the street. She threw on her signal light and pulled to a stop at the end, then pulled in when Daniel stepped onto the sidewalk out of the way.

Behind him, he heard Liz cut the engine and get out of the car. He waited until his mother — no, maybe not his mother — cut the engine before he stepped up to open her door.

"Danny Boy. 'Tis a nice surprise ta see ye again." She climbed from the car, reaching back to take her purse and a cloth bag she used for shopping from the seat before getting out all the way. "I appreciate ye takin' care of me driveway, again."

"You're welcome, M—" he stopped, not even sure what to call her right now.

"I came back home but then had ta run ta the grocery because I remembered I needed more sugar."

Liz was halfway up the sidewalk when Maggie acknowledged her. "Liz, how are ye, me dear?"

"Fine. Thanks. So far avoiding the crud the students are passing around."

"Good. Good," Maggie said as she hurried to the front door and put her key in the lock. Before pushing it open, she took a few steps to the right and bent to wipe the fresh layer of snow off the statue of the Blessed Virgin Mary.

"How was the Christmas show?" Liz asked.

"'Twas wonderful," she shot over her shoulder. "You should both go with me next year. Puts ye in the Christmas spirit, for sure."

The small talk rankled Daniel, but he didn't want to have a conversation about his birth on the front steps. He waited while Maggie pushed open the door, jangling the bells on the other side.

"Come in out of the chill," she said, stepping into the warm house. "We'll go into the kitchen."

Of course, Maggie chose the kitchen to begin this conversation, because his whole life, the living room had been reserved for only happy memories, while the kitchen was where real problems were hashed out.

The air still held the hint of freshly-baked bread, and the aroma had a bit of a calming effect on Daniel's nerves.

He and Liz slipped out of their coats and he hung

them on the rack by the door while Maggie put hers and her purse in the hall closet.

She picked up the grocery bag and started for the kitchen. "Mebbe next year we can make a visit ta see the Christmas decorations and start to make it a family tradition."

Daniel rolled his eyes toward Liz and muttered, "Yeah, a *family* tradition."

Liz hit his arm with the back of her hand. "Stop it," she whispered. "Let's hear what she has to say."

He rolled his shoulders, hoping to release some of the tension building there. They followed Maggie into the kitchen. She bustled around to empty the sugar into the canister on the counter, and then she stuffed the cloth bag into a corner of a lower cupboard. Liz sat at the table, but Daniel couldn't fathom sitting when his nerves were this jittery.

When Maggie turned toward him, tears glistened in her eyes.

"I'm relieved ye still came ta me. Me guess is ye got far enough in the letters that ye know, now, don't ye?"

Daniel drew in a deep breath and let it out slowly. "Do I?"

Maggie clasped her hands in front of her in prayer fashion, closed her eyes, and tipped her face toward the heavens.

"Dear God, Almighty, be with us," she said quietly. She held her pose for another moment, then opened her eyes, blessed herself with the sign of the cross, and dropped her hands to her sides.

"Sit down, son."

"I'm not your son," Daniel snapped. Her passive acknowledgement of the apparent truth irked him.

Maggie narrowed her eyes. "I raist ye as me own, Danny. 'Twas me and Timothy who sat up and rocked ye all hours of the night when ye was sick with fever." Her voice started out low, and though the intensity seemed to change, her pitch and volume did not.

"'Twas I who fixed yer scrapes and wiped away yer tears when ye was hurt. 'Twas I who made sure yer belly was full and ye had clean, pressed clothes ta wear ta school. Do na tell me yer not me son. Mebbe 'twasn't me who birthed ye, but I was a good mother to ye."

Daniel was taken aback by the ferocity of her claim to parentage. He hadn't yet had time to mentally adjust to these stunning revelations. He had no idea how to react to his feelings. Or to her. Hell, he didn't even understand his feelings right now, because they were all twisted up in his gut.

Maggie squared her shoulders. "Ye've got a right ta be angry, boy, but there are always two sides ta a story. I suspect ye barely know one side, let alone mine."

His anger fizzled into submission. This was real. Somewhere deep inside, he'd convinced himself that she'd tell him that he'd misinterpreted the letters or that Father Michael had been confused. But she was implying he hadn't.

Awkward silence crowded the room as Maggie retrieved a green apron with bold sunflowers on it from a hook next to the refrigerator and tied it around her small waist. Patches of flour still clung to the fabric from the morning's baking session.

She picked up the scratched and dented kettle and

filled it at the faucet before returning it to the stove and lighting the burner. The flame licked at the drops of water, causing them to sizzle into oblivion before the streak reached the copper bottom.

Maggie turned toward them. "I'm goin' ta tell ye what ye want ta know." She glanced at Liz. "Did ye read them, too?"

"Only the last few," Liz answered. "The ones about the babies being born."

"Aye," Maggie said quietly. "I knew those would be the ones ta give ye the clues ye needed ta figure out the truth." She pointed toward one of the open chairs. "Sit, Daniel."

He complied, glad to be next to Liz. She was the one who took the lead in the conversation, and Daniel silently thanked her for it.

"We were trying to find the letter from the government that was mentioned in the telegram. It was a letter to confirm that a telegram was sent and giving details about John Patrick's death."

Maggie shook her head. "'Tis gone. Timothy destroyed it."

Daniel perked up, looking from Liz to Maggie. "Why?"

"'Twas a painful time." She sucked in her upper lip, the same way she always did when she was trying to remain emotionally strong. "We had so much ta look forward ta. The war was ending, John Patrick had found new love, and they were having a baby just like we were. Ye know from the letters how badly I ached ta have a baby for Timothy. It seemed finally everything in life was going right after those horrible war years."

She covered her abdomen with her hands as if there was a child nestled in her womb. Sniffling, she plucked a tissue from the box on the counter and dabbed it under her eyes and nose.

"Then, just as fast, everything in our world turned upside down. When I lost our little Martin while Timothy was in Europe, 'twas difficult for all of us. I had ta look at an empty crib day after day. All I wanted was ta hold me wee one, the only part of me husband I had ta hold onto."

She paused, and her lips quivered while she drew in deep, calming breaths.

"Timothy took it hard being so far away, and then before he could get over that, he lost his brother, too." Her pain-filled voice was weaker. "The government allowed him to bring John Patrick home to be buried, and for the first time, he stood at his little boy's grave." She dabbed her eyes again. "I'll —" her voice hitched — "I'll never forget that day as long as I live."

She paused, her eyes staring off toward the ceiling as if she was seeing it all again.

"He stood at Martin's grave and cried harder than I have ever seen any man cry. 'Twas the one time in our marriage when we were farthest apart. I wanted ta hold him and console him, but he wanted ta be alone with his grief." She gulped before continuing. "I felt so guilty for causing him such pain. At the grave, we stood two feet apart, but I knew his soul was a whole ocean away from me. His spirit and heart were broken. Later, when we got home, he took the letter from the sideboard about John Patrick's accident and tore it ta shreds." Her gaze lifted to look into Daniel's eyes. "He was grievin' hard. We were both broken."

Tears streaked down her face. Daniel wanted to get up and hold her, but he was too confused to respond. She used a corner of her apron to wipe her cheeks.

"I'm sorry," she said. "I've lived all these years knowin' this day would have ta come. I thought I would be ready, but bringin' out the truth is like opening a wound with a painful scab on it. It makes me bleed all over again."

The tea kettle rattled behind her as the water heated, and at the same time, the clock in the hall chimed the half hour. All these sounds were familiar and comfortable, reminding Daniel of his enviable childhood. A childhood lived in blissful ignorance.

Maggie continued, her voice subdued. "When Timothy returned to France to finish his time in the service, he and Father Michael worked out the particulars with the nuns ta bring ye home ta us. Before ye came, Danny, a part of us had died inside."

She pursed her lips and sniffled, this time not bothering to wipe away the tears that rolled off her cheeks and splattered on her lap.

"We went to see Father Michael," Daniel said. "He told us that Annie and Uncle John Patrick died in the same accident."

"'Tis true. They were run off the road near the border and the car was found smashed in a gully."

Liz gasped and covered her mouth. Maggie continued.

"The thought 'twas Nazi soldiers, but we'll never know for sure. They were missing for a week before the car and their bodies were found."

Liz laid her hand across Daniel's on the table. He turned his palm over and clasped her fingers in his, then glanced at her. Her eyes brimmed with tears. He wasn't sure which part of these revelations to react to. He was angry about the years of deception, but he also ached with empathy for Maggie's renewed pain.

"After we got the news about their deaths, we knew we had ta to find a way to bring ye home. Ye were like an angel sent from Heaven, Daniel. Havin' ye with us brought life back ta our family. When Timothy and Father Michael returned from France with ye, it was like yer father was a man born again. His brother was gone, but we had a precious piece of him that Timothy needed in order ta continue livin'."

She finally sat at the table, and with a smile, continued. "Ye gave me back the man I loved, Daniel." Her voice rose from the strain of keeping her emotions in check. "He brought ye home to us, but 'twas ye who brought me Timothy home to me. I will always be grateful for that."

As if the memories overwhelmed her, she buried her face in her hands and wept. Daniel scooted his chair next to hers and wrapped his arms around her shaking body. It was then that he realized the toll it had taken on her to make the decision to give him the letters. For him, it was unearthing his past; for her, it was unearthing a time of intense pain that she'd managed to push into a corner of the attic with an old crate of letters.

"'Twas months after John Patrick and Annie passed on before we could work through the details to bring ye home to us."

She took Daniel's hand, the intensity in her grasp

belying the depth of her pain. "They were the longest months of me life. Ye were cared for in the same orphanage where ye mother took care of the Jewish refugee orphans, but I wanted ye here where we would love ye."

Daniel conjured an image of a war-time orphanage but couldn't picture himself there. The nuns had saved Annie's life — his mother — and then they'd saved his. Fate had intervened in every aspect of his life. Daniel stared into Liz's soft green eyes and gulped against the thickness in his throat, then looked toward Maggie, again.

"But the dates don't add up," he said. "Joshua —" He blinked, thinking that would clear his mind. "I was born in September and Martin was born in October."

"Because ye were an orphan of the war, Father Michael was able ta work through the church to bring ye home even without birth records. Annie never registered yer birth, so ta the rest of the world, ye were never born. Once ye were here, we were able ta register ye using Martin's birthdate." She lowered her eyes as if embarrassed. "It might have been wrong, Daniel, but at the time it seemed right. Ye helped us over the heartache."

"You gave me his birthdate but why not his name?"

"Ye were not a replacement for Martin. He may not have taken a breath, but he was still our baby. No one else knew the name we had given him, and no one other than us knew that ye had been born. We only used his birthdate ta avoid questions from those who knew when Martin was ta be born. 'Twas only six weeks separating yer births. 'Twas easy for people to believe."

"Why didn't you and Dad tell me the truth before? Why the lies for almost fifty years?"

Maggie uncovered her tear-streaked face. "No, Daniel!" she said emphatically. "No one ever lied ta ye. Ye lived believin' certain things about our family's past."

"And you never corrected me." The edge of anger bit into his lungs, making his breaths sharp. "I had a right to know who my real parents were."

"*We* were yer parents. Timothy and me. Ye still have the Coughlin blood runnin' through yer veins. Nothin' changes that. We didn't take yer mother and father from ye, but we made sure the war and circumstances didn't keep ye from your rightful heritage as a Coughlin."

He blinked, taken aback by the reality of that fact. Had John Patrick and Annie survived, Daniel would have been raised by different parents, but the rest of his family was the same. Except his parents were really his uncle and aunt.

His chair creaked as he leaned back and drew in a slow breath. "I'm sorry. You're right. This is just all so much to take in. This morning, I thought I knew exactly who I was." He sighed. "Now —" he glanced at Liz — "now, I feel confused and lost."

The tea kettle murmured the beginning of its whistle, and before Maggie could get to the stove, steam spewed into the air and the piercing blast crescendoed to its peak. She turned off the flame below it, and the whistle slowly died out.

As if trying to regain her composure, she turned to them with a tiny smile. "Would ye like a spot of tea? Me mother used ta say tea was balm ta soothe a troubled soul."

Daniel held up his hand and shook his head to refuse.

"I'd love some," Liz answered. She'd been so quiet throughout his exchange with his mother that hearing her voice now was soothing.

Liz rose and joined Maggie, putting an arm across her shoulders and pulling her against her hip for a side hug. Maggie touched her head to Liz's shoulder, then smiled up at her.

"Ye've always been a blessing ta our family," Maggie said, her voice sounding tight.

Liz reached for one of the mugs that Maggie had pulled from the cupboard. "I've always felt blessed to be part of it, Mom," Liz responded, glancing over her shoulder at Daniel when she called Maggie Mom.

He got her point, but the mixture of emotions he felt right now couldn't be fixed with a cup of tea — or even a shot of whiskey.

The only sound in the kitchen for the next couple of minutes was the tinkling of spoons against ceramic. Liz returned to the table with her mug, but Maggie set hers at her place and remained standing.

"There's somethin' else I have ta give ye, Daniel. It came with ye when Timothy and Father Michael brought ye home." She started from the kitchen. "I'll be back in a minute."

The steps to the second floor groaned, telling them she was going up. Liz picked up the bottle of honey from the mini lazy Susan in the middle of the table, filled her spoon with the gooey, golden liquid, then swirled her spoon in the hot tea. While she stirred, she looked up at Daniel.

"This has been quite a day, hasn't it?"

He flicked his eyebrows up, then nodded. "That's an understatement. My head is spinning. I don't know if I'm coming or going." He shrugged. "All these years, and I had no clue." He narrowed his eyes. "They should have told me."

"Maybe the time was never right." She blew across the top of the steaming tea, then took a noisy, quick sip. "This isn't something you just happen to bring up on a Sunday ride or anything. 'Oh, by the way, Danny, we're not really your parents. Hope you don't mind.'"

She tipped her head in a chastising kind of way. "Besides, what would it have changed if you'd known? Your birth parents aren't alive, and you were raised with love, never feeling that you didn't belong."

The steps creaked again as Maggie descended. When she entered the kitchen, she struggled to carry a large, dark, wooden box. Daniel jumped up from the table.

"Why didn't you ask me to help you with this?" He reached to take the box from her.

"'Tisn't heavy."

"But it's awkward, and it wasn't safe coming down the stairs."

"Ta!" she scoffed, angling away to continue to the table.

She set it in front of his place, treating it as it if were a fragile, precious gem. Stubborn and independent.

"There's more than what ye think ye learned in the letters, Daniel." She laid her slim, wrinkled fingers on top of the box. "I told ye what ye learned might help heal the trouble between ye and Liam."

Daniel returned to his chair. "Well, you got that one wrong. I don't see how any of this has anything to do with

Liam, other than learning his grandmother isn't who he thinks she is."

As soon as the cutting words were out of his mouth, he regretted their sting. Maggie pursed her lips and dropped her chin.

"I'm sorry," he whispered hoarsely. "That was uncalled for."

She took a deep breath, then continued as she ran her hand along the lacquered finish on the box's lid.

"This box was yer mother's. The nuns took it when they cleaned out her apartment. Annie asked them to be sure that it stayed with you." She took hold of Daniel's hand and put it on the box.

"When ye open it, Daniel," she said, "ye'll learn who ye really are."

CHAPTER FIFTEEN

Daniel glanced from the brown, wooden box to Maggie.

"What's in here?"

She sank onto her chair and picked up her cup of tea.

"I never looked below the things on top when I checked ta be sure the letter was there. 'Twasn't mine."

"This belonged to —" he hesitated, unsure how to continue — "Annie?"

Even knowing the truth, he couldn't refer to the woman he only knew through decades-old letters as his mother.

"The nuns found it," Maggie confirmed. "'Tis a part of yer heritage."

"Is that how you ended up with all of her letters to Uncle John, too?"

She nodded. "The nuns found them and knew of no other family members, and since they were letters ta Annie, they thought we would want them for ye. The crate and letters were part of John Patrick's personal effects that the army returned ta us after his death. Yer grandparents took the other items that were in the crate, and I never knew what they did with them. I put me letters from John Patrick and the ones he wrote ta Annie into the crate after. Timothy insisted we nail it closed and put it in the attic. I did not look at them for all these years — until I separated them for ye,."

"Was this box in the crate in the attic, too?" he asked.

She shook her head. "Father Michael kept it at the church. When he left his position, he passed it on ta Father Prior ta hold for safe keeping. I picked it up at Mass after ye took the crate home so I would be ready for ye."

Clenching his jaw, Daniel attempted to rein in his sudden agitation. "Wait! What if this issue had never surfaced with Liam? These things would have been kept from me indefinitely?"

Maggie sagged a bit as if deflating. "I don't know. For all these years I've lived in fear that ye would find out and I would lose ye. Giving ye the crate, and this —" she indicated the small box on the table — "'twas the scariest thing I have ever had to do in me life. I understand if ye can na forgive me — us," she corrected. "We only meant ta protect ye."

Daniel glanced at Liz. This was all so surreal that he needed to look at her for confirmation that his entire world had not flipped upside down. She smiled and reached out to gently massage his shoulder. The heat of her touch radiated to warm the cold pit in his stomach. He needed her calmness to quell the rioting emotions clashing in his mind.

"Would you rather look at the things in the box

alone?" she asked. "We can move to another room, if you'd like."

"No," he croaked against the lump in his throat. He cleared it and finished. "I'd like both of you here."

"When ye open it," his mother said, "ye'll see I slipped an envelope in on top. I did not look at the contents of the box when I put it in."

He touched the box for the first time. His fingertips tingled, but Daniel wasn't sure if it was from fear or anticipation. He grasped the tarnished gold clasp that held the lid in place and pushed it loose. His heartbeat accelerated as he lifted the top. The small hinges resisted, then with a delicate squeak, they gave way, allowing Daniel to reveal the contents.

He was vaguely aware of Liz leaning in closer, and in his peripheral vision, his mother sat ramrod straight, worrying the end of her apron between her bent, time-worn fingers.

As his mother said, the envelope, whiter than he expected given its age, lay on top. He removed it, staring at the writing on the front. *To My Joshua.*

That's me, he thought, staring at the delicate script. The penmanship was beautiful, almost a work of art. He opened the seal and removed the letter.

His gaze slid from the greeting, down to the closing signature, and back to the greeting.

"My dearest son, Joshua," he mumbled, trying out the name. He glanced at Liz. "It's to me from —"

There was a strained moment when he pondered exactly what to say. He focused on Maggie, wondering if acknowledging Annie as his mother would be hurtful. Then, a shard of annoyance poked him. *She* wasn't the one who'd been kept in the dark all these years. She'd known all this time that Annie was his birth mother.

Even thinking the words *birth mother* gave him a mental start. Yes, this was all only minutes old, so he knew there would be a period of adjustment, but how did someone shift the way they saw themselves after almost half a century of believing something else?

When he looked back at the paper, the words blurred. He rubbed the pad of his thumb against his eyes to try to clear his vision, but that still didn't help. The words were a wavy mess of dark characters. He extended the letter toward Liz.

"Would you mind reading this out loud?" he asked.

She furrowed her brows and took the paper from him. "Sure."

Daniel clasped his fingers prayer style, then, setting his elbows on the table, rested his chin against his thumbs. He focused on the etched glass salt and pepper shakers in the middle of the table. They had come from Ireland with his grandparents nearly seventy years ago. They were reminders of his past, his ancestry, that he now knew was full of holes.

Liz began to read, the huskiness in her voice belying her suppressed emotions.

"My dearest son, Joshua,

If you are reading this letter, it means I did not safely return to you. I felt it important for you to know my thoughts and what you mean to me. The nuns can tell you, but it is not the same as seeing it in your own mother's words. Whenever you receive this, and wherever you are, I want you to know how very much you are loved.

It is 5:30 in the morning. You woke me an hour ago, crying and shaking. I took you to my breast to soothe you, but you could not be consoled. I wondered if you were shivering from cold or because you were frightened, somehow sensing I was leaving you. Even though your father and I will only be gone for a day or two, it breaks my heart to leave you behind.

This is not a decision we made thoughtlessly. We do not want to be separated from you, but we cannot expose you to danger as we travel to Germany's border. My hope is to return here with my brother and sisters — the only remaining family you and I have. I pray they are still alive.

Now, you are settled back in your little cradle, content once again, unaware of the peril ahead for me and your father. I look around at our little home, as simple as it is, and realize that, with you, I have already begun to rebuild my family. Your father arrived just hours ago, and it brings me comfort to know I at least have the two of you.

First, I must tell you how fortunate I am that your father and you have come into my life. For too many years, my world was ugly and frightening. My grandmother, and then the nuns, did their best to shield me from the worst of the brutality, but I saw it, anyway. Your father rescued me from that. He made me feel safe, protected, and loved. I have never known a kinder, gentler, more compassionate man. I pray you will grow to be like him.

When I came to France, I started a journal. Sometimes I forgot to write in it for months because life was so exciting. Then, the war came, and I didn't write for weeks because I could not put my sadness into adequate words. After I met John Patrick Coughlin, your father, I was filled with so many wonderful feelings that I began to write them down every day. When he was not with me, then I would turn to my journal to read the words I had written when we were together, and that gave me some solace.

Then, when I learned I was pregnant with you, my joy was bittersweet. Words cannot express how much I love your father, but at the time I felt we could never be together because of our differences. It was he who made me see that true love could conquer those differences.

Because of this war, I, and I hope the rest of the world, have learned a valuable lesson. Religion does not define who we are. One race or religious group is not better than another. We all pray to the same God. We are all His children.

Like your father, you are my world. Since the moment you were born, you and I have never been separated. You are so precious, and I am always frightened that something will happen to take you away from me. You are my bright light of hope that keeps me going.

I want you to know why I chose your name. In Hebrew, Joshua means "God is my Savior." He allowed me to be spared during this horrific war, and this meant you, too, would have life. I believe God must have a great purpose for you to have brought you into this world under these circumstances.

This is my message to you, dear child. Be open, as your father is, to the possibility that being different is not always bad. Religion isn't about right or wrong; it is about tolerance and acceptance.

My mother and father, your grandparents, sacrificed themselves to try and save others from Hitler's insanity. When family members started to disappear, my father's friend gave him inside information about what was happening to our people.

. . .

Daniel jerked up, dropping his clasped hands to the table top and interrupting Liz.

"What was happening to *our* people?" Tiny currents of shock shot through his body. Wide-eyed, he turned to Maggie. "By 'our people', she meant the German people in general, right?"

Maggie shook her head, and whispered, "No."

His chest tightened. It took him several seconds to recognize the only other choice. "Are you telling me that Annie was Jewish?"

Maggie tilted her head. "Yes."

His mind spun. His life was so ordinary and uncomplicated, and then, out of the blue, everything about it was different.

"Danny, are you okay?" Liz asked.

"Yeah," he croaked out, even though he wasn't sure he was.

How did he not see clues in Annie's letters that she was Jewish? He wasn't just Irish Catholic, as he'd believed all his life — he was half Catholic and half Jewish.

"The letter is almost finished, Dan. Do you want me to read the rest?" Liz asked.

He wasn't sure how much more his mind could take, but he nodded. He again steepled his fingers under his chin, concentrating on taking slow breaths to calm the whole-body quake that had followed the shock. Liz continued reading, her inflection more measured than before.

. . .

In case I don't return, I have asked the nuns to give you this letter and box. This box belonged to my mother — your grandmother, Ruth. It was a gift from her grandmother. My mother gave it to me when I went to Paris to school. If fate had allowed, I would have passed it to my daughter. But, should I not return, it is to go to you, and perhaps one day you will pass it on to your first born. If it is not to be that we share our future, then at least through this box, we can share our past.

Be happy and well, my child. Know that whatever your future holds, you are loved unconditionally.

Affectueusement, Mére

Daniel stared at the stationery in Liz's hands. It was hard to sit still when a part of him wanted to get up and run. Run where, he didn't know, but it was difficult to tamp down the fight or flight response. How was he supposed to react? How would this change his life? How would it change who he was?

A vast array of emotions clashed around the words he attempted to process. He was used to reading letters from John Patrick to Annie but knowing this one was meant specifically for him only twisted everything in his mind.

It was difficult to imagine himself as an infant in Paris, lying in a crib, not being old enough to comprehend that when his mother kissed him goodbye almost forty-eight years ago, that they would never see each other again. Or, just trying to imagine that he even *had* a mother there blew his mind.

His only memories were a handful of sepia-toned

photos of him in a crib here in *this* house, with *this* mother. How did someone retrain their brain to accept that they had been someone else?

Daniel unclasped his hands and took the letter, reading it all again. Neither Liz nor Maggie spoke, but instead waited patiently for him to take it all in. He was aware of the clock ticking its rhythm above the table, punctuating that time marches on whether we're aware of it or not. Now, time was the only thing not standing still, because decades of his life seemed to be rushing past him, like a movie on fast forward.

Liz finally broke the thick silence.

"I know this is shocking, Dan." She laid her fingers on his wrist. "I'm just as shocked by all of this as you, but if there's any solace here, it's that you can tell she loved you and your unc - unc —" Liz stammered — "she loved you and your *father* so much. You were her world, Danny. The two of you kept her going when she thought there was nothing to live for."

He nodded acknowledgement, his mind in a haze.

Maggie wrapped her hands around the cup and leaned forward. "There is wisdom in her words."

Without moving his head, Daniel shifted his eyes in her direction. "Did *you* know she was Jewish?"

She tapped her fingers against the hard enamel of the cup. "Aye. The reason she refused John Patrick's proposal at first was because of it. After ye were born, she wanted ta do what was right by ye, so she told J.P. and let him decide if the religious differences changed how he felt about her. Timothy learned it when he stood up as a witness when they married in Paris."

Liz squeezed her warm fingers around his wrist. "By

being a serviceman in Europe, John Patrick had the perfect excuse and opportunity to walk away. But, he didn't. He chose love and acceptance." She lowered her voice. "Danny, he chose *you*."

He stared at Liz, considering her words. She was right. John Patrick had made the choice to stick by Annie despite their differences. He turned his attention to his mother.

"This is the healing between Liam and me that you were referring to, isn't it?"

Maggie nodded. "John Patrick never questioned what his heart told him ta do."

"You think if Uncle —" Like Liz, he stumbled over how to refer to the man he'd called his uncle his whole life. At this point, he wasn't ready to refer to him as his father. "It doesn't change the challenges that Liam and Mora might face, but I need to be more open-minded. I acknowledge that, but I can't just snap my fingers and be a different person with different beliefs."

"'Tis called learnin', Daniel. Ye have the rest of yer life to gain understanding. I can't take back the years when I had ye ta myself and we didn't tell ye the circumstances of yer birth, but I don't regret a single decision we made. Ye were raised a Coughlin."

His attention was drawn to Liz's hands as she refolded the letter from Annie, put it in the envelope, then set it next to the wooden box.

The box. He'd been so distracted by the shocking discovery with the letter that he'd ignored the box.

"So, is this all I have from that time in my life?" he asked.

Maggie nodded. "Yer mother had few possessions. I

have ta guess these are what she thought were most important." She drew in a deep breath, then looked at him with pain in her eyes. "I'm sorry we held this from ye, Daniel. Fear had a powerful hold over us, and yer father —" she balked — "Timothy and I were afraid of how ye'd be if ye learned the truth. Ye were everything ta us, Daniel." Her voice cracked. "Everything." He couldn't miss the way her lips quivered. "'Twas easier ta pretend ye was ours from the beginnin'. I'm sorry."

Daniel's throat tightened. He launched from his chair and knelt in front of her, pulling her against him. In his wildest dreams he could have never imagined being the center of such a complicated situation. As hard as the truth was on him, he could see now it was equally hard on his mother.

"Don't apologize. I can't honestly say how I feel right now, but I do know I never knew anything but love. You, and Dad, gave me the best possible life."

He took her by the shoulders and leaned her back in her chair. "You know, when I became a parent, I remember thinking I owed you so much. Now, I know that I owe you more than I could have ever imagined."

Maggie shrugged off his compliment by diverting the attention. She tapped the box from Annie. "Maybe ye should see what yer mother left ye."

Daniel stared at her for a moment. Her comment rolled off her tongue as if it were the most natural thing to refer to Annie as his mother. He wasn't there and wasn't sure if he ever would be.

He took hold of the box's lid with trepidation. Would lifting it open a Pandora's box? He raised it to reveal a burgundy cloth that he removed and set aside. Under that was a worn, dark leather journal Annie had mentioned in the letter. He opened it to the first page, dated July 27, 1938. The page was full of writing, but it wasn't in English.

He tipped the journal toward Liz. "I wonder if this is German."

She studied a few lines. "I don't know the language, but some of those words look German, so you're probably right."

"Makes sense," he said, setting it aside.

Next, he withdrew several photographs of varying sizes, most of them no bigger than a wallet-size picture. A few he recognized as Annie, John Patrick, and apparently himself as an infant. One was of the three of them on a blanket on the grass in a park. Everything looked so normal. So family like.

There were several of Annie. He flipped through them slowly, staring at her face and trying to connect himself to this woman who had brought him into the world. Her dark, wavy hair reminded him of his daughter's. He passed the photo to Liz.

"I guess this explains the mystery behind the gene Cathleen inherited."

Liz smiled and nodded. "And all this time you blamed it on my side of the family, even though everyone in my family has perfectly straight hair." Then, she looked closer. "Wow!" she said, almost inaudibly. "Cathleen looks a lot like Annie." She handed the photo to Maggie who, with a nod, silently agreed with the assessment.

Daniel reached for a larger photo that was turned face down. It was a family photo — Daniel guessed it was Annie's family. *His* family. He assumed the adults were her parents, and in front of them were a boy and three girls. Even though she was younger, he recognized Annie. He could see the edges of Jewish yarmulkes on her father's and brother's heads.

His mind drifted to the atrocities committed against the Jews by Nazi soldiers. Before, those were stories about people with whom he had no connection. Now, he knew the horrendous crimes were perpetrated against *his* ancestors. This man and woman in the picture were murdered in the street by Nazi soldiers. His grandparents.

The horrors of the past weighted his shoulders. His mouth went dry as he flipped through the rest of the photos, realizing what was lost to him, but more importantly, also realizing that if fate hadn't intervened, he never would have been born.

Daniel's chair scraped against the linoleum as he pushed away from the table. He took a tall glass from the cupboard and drew water from the sink. His mouth was dry, but he wasn't thirsty; he just needed something to do. He downed half of the contents, then leaned back against the sink, staring at the ceiling, grappling with his emotions.

"This is just all so much to take in," he said, looking back at Maggie and Liz. "I wonder if I'd be a different person now if you had told me all of this when I was a kid."

"I told ye, I was afraid ye wouldn't understand. I was afraid ye might tell others. It was selfish, but because I raised ye from a wee babe, in me mind, ye were mine as sure as if I birthed ye."

She stopped and rubbed her hands on her apron as if

her palms were sweaty. He wondered if she was afraid now.

"No one could replace me wee Martin, but I was happy to take ye to love. We loved yer father. Ye were a part of him." Her eyes glistened. "'Twas a fight for us at first. Timothy's parents didn't want to acknowledge ye and fought us bringin' ye here. They thought ye should stay there and be adopted. But to Timothy and me, ye were a Coughlin with Coughlin blood."

She stared off as if taking herself back to another world, another time.

"Yer Grandfather Coughlin was a stubborn Irishman with blinders on his eyes. He was angry that his son had been taken in war, and I'm sorry to say, he was angry ye had been born. He couldn't accept a baby born out of wedlock, and especially one not baptized in the Catholic church.

"After Timothy and Father Michael brought ye home, there were some hard feelings between us and yer grandparents. We didn't see them for almost a year. 'Twas Father Michael and Sister Siobhan who finally pulled the family back together."

She smiled up at Daniel. "And it didn't take ye long to soften yer granddaddy to ye. Father Michael made him see that ye were a gift from God to help us heal from John Patrick's death and losing Martin." She shrugged. "'Twas the agreement with Timothy's father that we not speak of yer past and we only look forward."

Daniel set the glass on the counter. His stomach gurgled, protesting the unneeded water. He drew in a loud, long breath through his nose, then raised his shoulders and slowly exhaled.

"Well, that revelation leaves me feeling warm and fuzzy."

He ground his palms together, attempting to work out the tingling sensation. "So, where do I go from here?"

"Ye go to yer boy," Maggie responded. "I wanted ye to learn the truth so ye could heal the wound between ye and yer son. Liam loves Mora the same way yer father loved yer mother. It's not yer place to be the judge. Remember the meaning of yer name, Daniel — *He has judged*. Our love for God should not separate us, it should bind us."

Daniel crossed his arms. "You can't expect me to suddenly change. I don't even know who I am now. I don't know anything about being Jewish."

Liz rose from her chair and came to stand next to him. She rubbed circles on his back as she looked up at him. Her eyes were soft with obvious compassion, and his heart ached with the depth of his love for her.

"You're still the same person, Danny. You don't have to change, but now that your eyes have been opened, you should take this opportunity to learn." She tipped her head and smiled. "You can learn with Liam. Instead of this being something that divides you, this can be the thing that strengthens your relationship."

Daniel looked back at Maggie. Her face was tight with emotion. Tears shimmered on her eyelids. He moved away from Liz to kneel in front of Maggie, covering her small hand with his.

"Ma, is there something more?"

She used the end of her apron to wipe her eyes, then shook her head.

"I never knew if there would be a right time to let ye

know the truth." Her voice held a slight quiver. "I pray ye can forgive me for not telling ye before. I've always loved ye with my whole heart, Danny Boy, and never wanted to see ye hurt. I know I've hurt ye, though, but I love ye so."

She dropped her chin to her chest, and an errant hot tear splattered on the back of Daniel's hand. A shard of empathy sliced through his chest. God love her, she was as frightened of this as he was.

"Look, I know I was angry when I came in, and I said some awful things." He squeezed her hand and dipped down to look up into her downcast eyes. His own filled up, but he didn't fight it. "Like you so staunchly declared, you may not have given birth to me, but you will *always* be my mother. And, I couldn't have asked for a better one."

Even with her in the chair, he gathered her in his arms and felt her cheek press against his shoulder.

"I love you, Ma."

Her small body shook against his, and almost simultaneously, he felt Liz's arms come around them, wrapping them in her strength. Their fear, confusion, and anger melded into the one emotion Annie had written about: unconditional love.

It was Maggie who withdrew from his embrace first. As she had when he was a little boy, she used her apron to wipe away the tears that he knew streaked his face.

"Ye haven't finished lookin' at yer box."

He cleared his throat and again took his place at the table. Liz stood between them, a hand on each of their shoulders. Lord how he loved her. The last few weeks had been the most difficult and tense of their married lives, and he'd been the cause. But, still, she stuck by him. He turned and kissed her slender fingers, and in return, he was rewarded with a smile that told him how deeply he was loved.

Turning his attention to the box, he started to lift the first item, a small leather book with a foreign language on it, then stopped. Underneath it were items he didn't recognize, and he guessed were connected to his mother's Jewish faith. He picked up a little cloth pouch and peered inside. This was the only thing he recognized: a necklace with a Star of David on it. His ignorance blossomed into an idea, and he took the burgundy cloth and covered the interior of the box as he'd found it.

"No. This isn't what I should do," he said.

Liz frowned. "What do you mean?"

"I'd like Liam and Mora to be with us when I take out the rest of these things. After all, this is Liam's heritage, too." He sat back in his chair. "That is if he's not too angry with me. Our conversation this morning didn't exactly end on a positive note."

"Maybe because of someone's stubbornness?" Liz chided.

Fingers of heat streaked up Daniel's neck. "Apparently I inherited that trait from the Coughlin side of the family." Why was it he could suddenly see so clearly how wrong he'd been? "Liam and Mora might have some rough patches, but if they know we're all there for support, maybe it will be easier for them to work through them."

Maggie perked up. "If it's true love, they'll work through it just like yer mother and father did. Those are decisions they'll have ta make."

"A lot of decisions." He tried to picture John Patrick

and Annie navigating these tumultuous waters, when suddenly a thought came to him. "Wait a minute. Did Uncle Jo— my father convert?"

"We never knew," Maggie answered. "That decision was made between him, Annie, and God."

Daniel pondered that for a moment, then glanced at the wall clock. It was almost four o'clock. Liam would be getting off the extra shift soon.

He pointed at the small cupboard his father had made for his mother when they were first married. "Your phone book still in that drawer, Ma?"

"Aye."

Liz moved to the cupboard, found the book, and handed it to Daniel. "Whose number are you looking for?"

"The routine number at the precinct. I want to leave a message with dispatch for Liam and Mora to come by the house when they get out of work."

Liz lifted her brows, a hint of concern in her expression.

"I know what you're thinking. I'm hoping my son is a bigger man than I've been. All I can do now is offer the olive branch and hope he accepts it."

CHAPTER SIXTEEN

The sound of car doors slamming drew Daniel's attention toward the driveway. He hurried into the living room to pull back the curtain. When he saw Liam's car, he dropped the fabric and headed for the front door, his heart hammering.

"They're here," he called to Liz from the hallway.

He heard the oven door close and then a pan clink against the top of the stove. She'd started cooking as soon as they got home in case Liam and Mora did come and would stay for dinner.

Daniel stopped in front of the door, drew in a bolstering breath, and shook out his hands. This day topped the list of the most bizarre days of his life, for sure. Since asking Liam to come over, he'd rehearsed in his head dozens of times how he'd share what he'd learned. He was still trying to process the convoluted situation himself, but he hoped sharing it with Liam, given their current discord, might be the salve to heal the wound, just as his mother hoped.

When he heard their voices, he pulled open the door and stepped to the threshold. They walked hand-in-hand along the sidewalk, then looked up and stopped talking when they heard him. In the light of the porch, Daniel could see lines of tension creasing Liam's forehead. He understood the feeling. His muscles had practically been twitching since he and Liz had returned home.

"Thanks for coming," he said as they climbed the front stairs. He stepped aside and held the door open wide for them to enter.

"Hi, Mr. Coughlin," Mora said as she dropped Liam's hand and stepped onto the rug to wipe snow from the bottom of her boots.

"Mr. Coughlin?" Daniel said, attempting to sound light-hearted. "Come on, I've told you before, Daniel or Dan is fine."

She smiled. "Okay. Sorry."

"No need to apologize, Mora," he said. "I just don't want to be so formal."

Daniel met Liam's eyes. "Hello, son."

"Dad." There was no warmth in the acknowledgement, but it didn't matter. At least Liam and Mora had come. "Is Nana okay?" Liam asked.

Confused, Daniel answered, "She's fine. We just came from there. Why?"

Liam shrugged. "Because the message you left at dispatch sounded urgent, and when I tried calling here, you didn't answer, so I was concerned that something was wrong with Nana."

Liz came down the hall, wiping her hands on a small kitchen towel as she approached. "She'll outlive us all," she said, stopping to give Liam a hug.

"Hi, honey." She then turned to Mora and gave her a hug, as well. "Hi, sweetie. I'm so glad you both came. I hope you'll consider staying for dinner. I'm making chicken casserole."

Liam and Mora exchanged a quick, unreadable look, before Liam said, "Maybe."

There was a moment of awkward silence, punctuated by the chime of the grandfather clock, before Daniel spoke

"Why don't you hang your coats," he said, indicating the rack that had stood in the corner next to the door for Liam's entire life, "and then come into the den. There's something important I need to share with you."

Despite Daniel's attempt to behave like everything was normal between them, he couldn't ignore the palpable tension in the air. He watched Liam help Mora out of her coat, ever the gentleman, just as they'd raised him, then Liam shrugged out of his own and hung both on the rack.

Daniel led the way into the den, where he'd put the crate of letters in the middle of the floor between the chairs and love seat. He'd put the box from Annie on the floor next to his recliner. Liam and Mora took the loveseat, while Daniel and Liz sat in the chairs.

Steepling his fingers between his knees, Daniel stared at them while he gathered his racing thoughts. He didn't think this was going to be easy, but he didn't expect the sudden overwhelming feeling that he was a fraud and his life had been a sham — even though he'd been unaware until just a few hours ago.

Looking up at Liam and Mora, he said, "I appreciate

you coming, because what I have to tell you has to be done in person."

Taking hold of Mora's hand, Liam looked directly at Daniel. "If you brought us here to try to convince us to not get married, you're wasting your time, Dad."

Daniel raised his hand to stop Liam. "I can understand why that would be your first thought, but that's not it."

"Okay," Liam said, sliding a couple of more inches closer to Mora so their hips touched. Assuming a protective mode. Daniel understood and admired it.

"What I'm about to tell you is something that we'll share with Cathleen and Brendan, later, but considering your situation, your mom and I felt it was best to share with you, first. And, I'm going to be direct."

Concern flashed in Liam's eyes, and he glanced between Daniel and Liz. "Are one of you —"

"We're fine," Liz said. "Really. Put that worry out of your head."

Liam's shoulders relaxed, so Daniel continued.

"A few weeks ago, after you announced your engagement, I know I made it obvious that I had concerns."

Liam rolled his eyes, a behavior that typically drew a corrective reaction from Liz, but he knew she'd let it go in this situation. Daniel's bigger concern was the way Mora shifted her attention to stare at her and Liam's clasped hands, telling him exactly what he feared: Liam had shared the specifics of his father's concerns about her being Jewish. Considering that, he gave her credit for showing up today.

Daniel looked directly at Liam. "Your grandmother

was upset about the tension between us, and honestly, so was your mother. I won't belabor this, because we all know that I dug my heels in because my thinking is 'I'm the father and my kids are supposed to listen to me.' But, I asked you to come here, because I was wrong, and I owe you an apology."

"Why the sudden epiphany?" Liam asked, a bit of sarcasm in his tone.

Daniel winced. He deserved the skepticism, but it still cut him to the core. He pointed at the crate.

"So that crate has been in your grandmother's attic since 1946. It was nailed shut and shoved into a corner behind some old furniture, so I never knew it existed. It was full of letters written during World War II."

Mora looked up, and Liam straightened a bit, so Daniel knew he'd piqued their interest.

"Who wrote them?" Liam asked.

"Your grandparents wrote some to each other, then there were letters to Uncle John Patrick from his mother and your grandmother, and letters he wrote to them."

Liam interrupted and looked at Mora. "Uncle John Patrick is the one I told you about who was also a police officer back in the 30's and 40's. It's his picture hanging on the wall in my precinct."

"Oh, right," she said, nodding. "He's the one who inspired you to become a cop."

"Yeah," Liam said. "He's a legend." He looked back at his father. "Go on."

"There were other letters, too, from a woman in Paris, to Uncle John."

"A love interest?" Liam asked.

Daniel nodded. "Yeah. Her name was Annie. She left

Germany just before Hitler started rounding up the Jewish people and sending them to concentration and death camps."

Mora grimaced, and Daniel wondered if she was already putting some of the pieces together based on her own family history.

Daniel continued, attempting to give a condensed version of the story.

"Uncle John met her while his unit was in Paris shortly after the liberation. She had been taking care of German refugee children in a Catholic orphanage. It was a cover for Jewish children who had been sneaked out of Germany. Her own parents were instrumental in helping Jewish families escape, and somehow the government found out, and they were shot in the street by Nazi soldiers as examples. Annie's brother and sister disappeared at the same time."

Mora gasped, and Liam shifted to put his arm around her, so he could nestle her even closer under his protective arm. A renewed sense of pride washed over Daniel. His son was going to be a great husband.

Liam looked back at Daniel "So, the woman — what did you say her name was?"

"Annie."

"Annie. So, her siblings were killed, too?"

Daniel moved in his chair to rest his elbow on the arm rest. "She had reports from former neighbors that there was a good possibility that they were taken underground and sneaked to a place on the border with France, but she also couldn't be sure that they hadn't been captured by the Nazis and taken to a work camp or someplace else."

"A work camp?" Liam said, looking startled. "They were Jewish?"

Daniel nodded.

"So, Uncle John Patrick fell in love with a Jewish woman." Liam slanted a look at Mora and squeezed her shoulder. "He and I are more alike than I thought."

In his peripheral vision, Daniel saw Liz purse her lips as if trying to keep from speaking. He was sure he knew what she was thinking: it made perfect sense since now they knew John Patrick was his grandfather, not his great uncle. But, that would come.

Mora smiled at Liam. "I guess you are a lot like him." She looked back at Daniel. "Did Annie find her brother and sisters?"

"Once Hitler killed himself and Germany surrendered, she made plans to go to the place where the neighbors suggested they could be."

"And, she found them?"

"I don't know, but I don't think so. It was still dangerous to travel, because not all the Nazi soldiers had given up. We don't know if she and Uncle John were killed on the way to find them or on the way back."

"Wait!" Liam said. "Uncle John was killed while he was still in the service. He wasn't with his unit when he was killed?"

Daniel shook his head. "He got leave to go with Annie, and according to a letter from the government that was received after his death, they were run off the road and into a ravine by some outlying Nazi soldiers. The car and their bodies were found about a week later."

Liam whistled under his breath. "I didn't see that one coming."

"Yeah, neither did I," Daniel said. "Apparently there was a letter from the government with the details, but it was ripped up so no one would ever learn the truth."

Liam frowned. "Then, how do you know that?"

"Nana told us," Liz explained.

"Wow! That's crazy," Liam said, shaking his head. "They say there are skeletons in every family's closet. I guess I shouldn't have expected anything different in ours."

Suddenly needing a little extra support, Daniel reached over and took hold of Liz's hand. She graced him with an encouraging smile. This part was the hardest, because once he shared it with someone else, then the reality kicked up thousands of notches. He cleared his throat.

"That's nothing," Daniel said, focusing on Liam. "There's more, and believe me, it shoots way off the crazy chart."

Liam smirked. "And all these years I thought my family was dull and ordinary." It seemed Liam's anger had dissipated as the intrigue grew, and Daniel was at least thankful for that. "So, what else is there?"

"It turns out that John Patrick and Annie had another secret."

"Okay," Liam said. "I'll bite. What was it?"

Daniel hesitated for a moment. This all sounded like someone else's story, not his.

"They had a baby together."

Liam laughed. "No sh—" He stopped himself mid-word and glanced at his mother. "Sorry, Mom, but you have to admit, Dad's right. This *is* crazy stuff."

Mora spoke up this time, her eyes registering sadness. "Was the baby also killed in the accident?"

Daniel shook his head. "No, the baby wasn't with them."

"So, their baby's alive?" Liam asked. "Do you know where it is?"

"Yeah, we do." Daniel answered, realizing they had no idea where this conversation was leading.

"This is nuts!" Liam exclaimed. "So, you have a cousin you never knew about?"

Shaking his head, Daniel leaned forward. "No, there's no cousin."

"How do you figure? If it was your uncle's baby —"

"Liam," Daniel said, his attention locking onto Liam's eyes. "*I'm* that baby."

Liam's Adams apple visibly slid up and down his throat as he glanced between his parents. A slight, uneasy smile crossed his face.

"Sorry, I'm not following."

"It's a long story, but I just learned today that John Patrick and Annie are my parents," Daniel explained.

Liam frowned, reminding Daniel of what an inquisitive boy Liam had been. "But what about Nana and Grandad?"

"They're really my aunt and uncle. Your great aunt and uncle. They adopted me."

Liam shifted, looking uncomfortable. He glanced at Mora then back at Daniel and Liz. "Is this some kind of joke?"

Stifling a snort, Daniel said, "Oh, how I wish, but believe me, I was as shocked as you."

"How did you figure this out?" Liam asked.

Daniel gave him a condensed version of the day, including the highlights from the letters, his visit to Father Michael, and the stunning visit with his mother.

He turned and took the small wooden box from the stand next to him.

"Nana also gave me this box." He rested his palm on the smooth wooden lid, suddenly feeling a connection to the woman who'd given him life. No doubt, she had probably also laid her palm on it.

"I started to look at the contents when Nana first gave it to me, but when I saw what was inside, I decided it would be more meaningful to go through it with the two of you." He turned to Liz. "How long before dinner will be ready?"

Liz glanced at the wall clock. "At least half an hour."

"Let's go into the kitchen where we can lay things out on the table," Daniel suggested, rising from the chair and tucking the box under his arm.

Liam and Mora, both still looking stunned, stood as well, and followed Daniel, with Liz bringing up the rear.

When they entered the kitchen, the aroma of the baking chicken casserole and heat from the oven created a homey atmosphere. To Daniel, it was something comfortable and familiar in the midst of mental chaos.

"Here, have a seat." Daniel pulled out a chair and indicated for her to sit, then he went around the table and pulled one out for Liz, too, before sitting across from Liam.

"I guess this is my heritage," he said, smoothing his hand across the top, "and yours," he added, nodding at Liam. Then Daniel looked at Mora.

"I'm embarrassed to say that I've never taken the time

to get to know anything about your faith." He hesitated, then continued. "You love our son, and you make him happy. That's what I should have been focused on, not our differences."

He looked away as his chin began to quiver. So many thoughts rioted in his mind that he had to stop to collect himself. Even his stomach was uneasy hours after learning the truth. Would he ever feel normal again?

Finally, he cleared the emotion from his throat and continued.

"I'm not going to pretend that suddenly I'm a different person because of what I've learned. To be honest, I'm confused, I'm shocked, and, even angry as hell. We all have a lot to process, but I thought I'd start here, with the three of you." He focused his attention on Mora again. "I don't understand anything about these things Annie —"

He stopped and stared at the box. What did he call her? His mother? That mysterious woman from the letters? Maybe biologically Annie was his mother, but she wasn't the one who mothered him.

Was this how adopted people who found their birth mothers felt? Not sure who to call their mother? Was calling someone else "mother" after almost fifty years a betrayal of the woman who raised you?

Liz touched his hand and leaned down to look into his eyes. "Danny, are you okay?"

He mentally shook himself and looked up. "Yeah, sorry. It's just so much."

She patted his hand. "Maybe the box should wait until another day."

"No," he said, shaking his head. "I'm counting on

Mora to help me understand these things in here. They're obviously important."

He glanced at Mora, saw the warm look in her eyes, and realized how lucky they all were to have her in their lives. Damn his Irish Catholic pride! He'd come close to making the biggest mistake of his life.

"Let's look." He lifted the lid and decided to pull the items out one at a time.

Laying on top was the little cloth pouch he'd looked in earlier. He picked it up and shook the contents into his hand.

"This, I know," he said. He held up the necklace, then noticed a small piece of paper stuck out of the envelope, so he pulled it out the rest of the way and read it silently before looking up.

"This belonged to my grandfather Irving Goodman," Daniel shared. "Wow!" he whispered, setting aside the slip of paper.

He laid the pendant in his palm and stared at it, realizing this thing touching his skin now had also touched his grandfather's skin decades before. His grandfather who was shot in the street by Nazi soldiers for trying to save Jews. A true hero. A shiver skittered up his spine, and his throat constricted again.

"I wonder how Annie got that?" Liz asked. It was a rhetorical question that none of them could answer, but it was a great question.

Daniel set aside the necklace, dug back into the box and pulled up the next thing. It was a leather-bound book a little bigger than a Gideon New Testament, but he was sure that wasn't what it was. Words in a different language, which given the circumstances he assumed was Hebrew, were stamped in gold on the cover.

"The Siddur," Mora said, smiling. "The Jewish prayer book. It's used at all holidays and celebrations."

Daniel flipped through the pages, unable to decipher any of the Hebrew writing. "Is it like the Bible?" he asked.

"It has verses from the Old Testament in it," Mora explained, "but it also has ritual prayers that have been passed down for centuries. They're always used at the Seder, the feast at the beginning of Passover."

Opening the book to a middle page, Daniel asked, "Can you read this?"

Mora laughed. "I had many years of Hebrew School, which is sort of like your Sunday School, except it's much more intense since we also have to learn the language."

Daniel looked at her in awe. "So, you speak French, Italian, and Hebrew?"

She nodded.

He whistled. "That's impressive."

"It's what I studied. And, hopefully someday, it will also give me the chance to work in international relations."

Daniel removed the next item, again something he recognized as the head covering worn by Jewish men. "A yarmulke," he said. "This, I get, too."

"Also called a kippah," Mora shared. "In my family, the men wear them to synagogue and during holiday celebrations at home. Some Jewish men wear them all the time."

As he was setting the yarmulke on the table, out of the corner of his eye, Daniel saw Liam squeeze Mora's hand. No doubt pride and love bundled together.

There were three or four things wrapped and laying side by side. He took the biggest one first and removed the cloth covering. It was a silver cup with a raised design of grapes, leaves, and vines. He held it up for the others to see.

"That's a Kiddush cup. The kiddush is a blessing recited over grape juice or wine to sanctify the Jewish and Shabbat holidays." Mora tipped her head to see the design better. "I'm sure that was a family piece, also."

Liz put her hand on his arm. "How lucky for you that you have these family heirlooms."

Daniel considered that. As the only child in his generation on the Coughlin side, he'd also inherited many family gems that had been passed down through the generations. But these were wholly different from any of those.

He set the cup down and took out the next wrapped piece, carefully unfolding the cloth. Something long and round with ornate carvings almost rolled out.

"A mini rolling pin for dolls?" he joked. That's all he could think of when he looked at the shape as he held it up.

"It's a mezuzah. In Hebrew it means 'doorpost.' According to tradition, the mezuzah is hung on the doorpost at the entrance to a Jewish home as well as the entrance to each of the interior rooms except for bathrooms. My family only puts one at the front door. Take off one end," Mora instructed.

Daniel removed one end. Inside was a tiny piece of parchment. "Should I pull it out?" he asked.

Mora shook her head. "I wouldn't. They have to be put in a certain way, but there are two Bible verses written on it. The first one is Deuteronomy 6:4–9 and the second is Deuteronomy 11:13–21."

"From the Old Testament," Daniel said. "I'll look them up later."

"See, Dad," Liam said, "the two religions aren't as far apart as you thought."

Daniel glanced at his son. "Right now, they're colliding."

"Given what you now know about your heritage, will you hang that on the door?" Liam asked.

Daniel replaced the end of the mezuzah. "I don't know what I'll do, but I'm not suddenly going to not be Catholic."

"But your mother was Jewish. Judaism is matrilineal," Liam pressed. "So, now that you know the truth, under Judaic law, you can claim that heritage."

Sitting back in his chair and setting the mezuzah aside, Daniel looked at Liam. "Have you studied Jewish law or something?"

"Kind of. I love Mora, and I care about learning everything about her. And, that means understanding how she was raised in her faith and how that will affect us if we have kids someday." Liam leaned forward, his features tight with conviction. "It doesn't mean I can't still be Catholic, but the Jewish religion is just as rich in history as Catholicism. I want our kids to know both."

Daniel considered that. Why had he never listened to what Liam was saying before?

He knew why. Stubborn Irish pride closed off his mind. It was something he'd need to say to himself repeatedly to get it through his own head that his son was a better man than he had been. And, he had to credit Liz for her role and influence in raising kids who saw the worldview.

"You're right," Daniel conceded. "I've reacted to something I know nothing about. Thank you, Mora, for jump-starting my education."

Liz peered around the side of the small box. "What about the other things in there?"

Daniel reached in and removed two pieces of embroidered cloth. He held up the first one. It was white with Hebrew symbols embroidered in the middle and gold fringe encircling it.

"Most likely a challah cover," Mora said. "Challah is the braided bread used on Shabbat, our Sabbath. It must be covered before the prayers begin."

Daniel laid that one down and picked up the other. This was a heavier maroon cloth. "Is this another one?"

Mora took it and shook her head. "No, you see these three pockets?" She lifted each one to demonstrate. "This is for the matzo."

"The unleavened bread," Liz supplied.

Daniel jerked around to look at her. "You know about that?"

"I know they have it at Passover, and that there's no yeast in it. I've never had it."

Mora continued. "Right. When the Israelites fled Egypt, they didn't have time to wait for the bread to rise, so they partially baked it, and of course, it came out flat. Unleavened. It's the only bread we eat during Passover to commemorate that event in Jewish history, and the bread is put into these pockets."

She handed the cloth back to Daniel and he set those aside, as well. He picked up the last three cloth-covered items in the box. He set two aside and kept the one with a piece of leather tied around it. It was wrapped into a cylindrical shape. He pulled one end to undo the bow and opened the fabric.

Inside were candles. He rolled his hand over them to lay them out next to each other on the cloth. Eight were white, one blue, and all had been partially burned.

"Huh! Candles," Daniel said. "I hadn't thought about it, but I wonder if she didn't have electricity."

Mora smiled and pointed at the larger of the two items left. "Check the big one. I'm going to guess they go together, and then it will make sense."

He followed her suggestion and removed the covering of the larger one, surprised by its weight. It had barely fit in the box, and even through the cloth, he could tell this was metal. As soon as he peeled back the first fold to reveal one side, Liz gasped.

"A menorah. It's beautiful."

Daniel removed the last flap and set the menorah in the middle of the table. The gold was partly tarnished. Ornately-crafted scrolls connected each of the candle holders in it. "I do know this is a menorah," he said. "But, I'll be honest, I know nothing about its significance."

"Over two thousand years ago, there was always a menorah burning in the Temple," Mora explained. "The Greeks took over the Jews, and then their Temple, and tried to force them to believe in their gods. The Maccabees, the Jews under oppression, revolted and liberated Jerusalem. They went back to their Temple and found the Greeks had destroyed it. They found enough olive oil to light the menorah for one day, but it ended up burning for eight days, instead. It was the miracle from

God. So, a candle is lit for each of the eight days of Hanukkah."

Daniel quickly counted the candle holders in the menorah.

"But there are nine."

"The taller one is Shamash, the helper candle that's used to light the others."

"The blue one?" he asked.

Mora nodded.

"When is Hanukkah?" Daniel asked. "Isn't it the same time as Christmas?"

"No, it changes every year, but it's always around November and December. Today is the final day. Our family just lit the remaining candle last night," she said.

The timer on the stove buzzed, and Liz got up to check the casserole. She pulled it from the oven, and steam rose from the top.

"There's a lot here," she said, placing it on a hot pad on the counter. She looked over her shoulder at Liam and Mora. "I hope you'll stay and help us eat it."

Liam and Mora exchanged a quick glance before Liam answered. "Sure, Mom, it smells delicious."

She stepped behind Daniel and laid a hand on his shoulder. "It has to cool and set for a few minutes. Let's see what that last thing is."

Daniel removed it, and like the others, folded the cloth back to reveal its contents. There was a piece of stationery wrapped around it. He pulled the paper off revealing a wooden top, and turned the note over, reading it to himself. A lump filled his throat as he read.

"A dreidel," Liz said.

He picked it up by the stem and held it for the others to see.

"This note says it was carved by Annie's grandfather and given to her just before he died. He made one for each of his grandchildren to eventually give to their own children as a family heirloom." He twirled it, looking at the Hebrew symbols painstakingly carved into each side. "He made this for me."

"Do you know what the message is in the symbols?" Mora asked.

Daniel's mind was overwhelmed by the fact that he was holding a gift from a great grandfather he'd never know. He barely acknowledged Mora's question with a small movement of his head.

"It's nun, gimel, hay and shin. Translated it means 'a great miracle happened there.' It references the oil burning in the menorah for the eight days. When the Greeks took over they forbade the children from studying the Torah, so the dreidels were made as a cover. Being caught with the Torah was punishable by death. They'd quickly put it away and start playing the game. When a soldier approached, the children hid their books and took out the dreidel to make it look like they were gathered to play a game."

Daniel stared at the dreidel for a minute before he spun it on the table. There was silence until it wobbled and finally tumbled to one side. He flipped it to reveal the symbol on each side, then glanced at each of the things from the box before pushing his chair away from the table.

"Liz, is there enough for one more for dinner? And, will it hold for twenty minutes?"

She raised her eyebrows. "Sure," she said, drawing the word out as if it had three syllables.

"Okay, I'll be right back."

He hurried to the door, snatching his coat from the rack on his way by. He had something to say to his mother, and he didn't want to wait.

CHAPTER SEVENTEEN

When Daniel pulled in front of his mother's house, there was a light on in the living room, and through the sheer curtain he could see the silhouette of her on the couch. Using the key he'd had since childhood, he let himself in the front door. Even after he'd married, she'd insisted that he walk in and never knock.

"This will always be yer home, Danny Boy. I don't care how old ye are."

And there'd never been a moment of his life when it hadn't felt like home, either.

"Ma, it's me," he called, knowing the tinkling of the bells had alerted her to someone coming in.

He shut the door but didn't bother to take off his coat since he wasn't planning on staying long. When he stepped around the corner into the living room, she looked up. His heart lurched when he saw her red, puffy eyes.

"Ma!" He hurried to the couch and sat next to her. "What's wrong?"

She pulled a flowered handkerchief from her apron pocket and wiped her eyes.

"I was lookin' at pictures." She held a few in her hands, but there were also several stacks on the coffee table in front of her.

Daniel sat on the couch next to her and scanned them, realizing immediately that even though some were of more than one person, the common denominator in every one of them was him. Dozens of photos of him as a baby and a tow-headed toddler. In each picture, he was clearly the center of attention.

His mother sniffled. "I beg ye to forgive me for keeping the secret for so long. I wanted to always believe that ye were mine, so if I didn't share the secret, ye were."

She stacked the photos in one hand and turned the top one for Daniel to see. He recognized her as a young woman cradling an infant, and she was staring into the infant's eyes. The tears streaking down her cheeks and her wide smile revealed the raw emotions of the moment.

"Is that me?" Daniel asked, taking the photo from her to look closer.

"Aye," she responded, her voice choked. "'Twas the first time we ever looked in ta each other's eyes." Her face crumpled as she began to cry. "Oh, Danny, I loved ye from the very second I took ye in me arms and looked upon yer angelic face."

Daniel put his arm around her, emotion welling inside him.

"I was sure ye were a gift from heaven to help heal me broken heart." She pressed her hand to her chest as if illustrating. "Mebbe I didn't birth ye, but ye were mine and Timothy's from that moment, and I vowed I would be the best mother ta ye that I could."

She wrung her hands around the handkerchief. "No one except yer grandma and grandda even knew ye weren't the baby I birthed. I was so full of grief when Martin was born without breath that I didn't leave the house. I was in the worst depression of me life. Me husband was gone. Our baby was gone."

She lifted her face to look at him. "Then a sad twist of fate put ye in me arms, and I thought 'twould be me and Timothy's secret." More tears sprung to her eyes. "Then one day I was in the grocery with ye in the carriage and a woman came up to me and asked who the baby was. And, when I told her 'twas my son, she asked me where ye came from because she knew me baby had died."

His mother started to shake, so he held her closer.

"Who was she?" Daniel asked.

"'Twas the doctor's nurse. I gave birth at home, but he was called in when I started having trouble. And, after, she recorded his notes. I didn't have time ta explain before she hurried away saying she would tell the doctor and he would report me to the authorities."

"For what? Did she think you had kidnapped me?"

"Because the blues were so bad, she thought I was confused and believed someone else's baby was mine. The doctor came ta see me right away when I got home."

"So, then that was the end," Daniel said, as if reassuring her five decades later mattered.

"Every time I saw her after that, she gave me a look almost ta remind me that I was living a lie. My biggest fear yer whole life was that ye would find out the truth and I'd lose ye. And, now, that time is here."

He pulled her closer to him. "Look, I'm going to be honest with you. There's a part of me that's angry that I didn't know this long ago. After all these years of feeling confident in life, suddenly I'm struggling to wrap my head around who I really am. I'm not the same Daniel Coughlin who got out of bed in the middle of the night last night. I don't know when the shock of all of this will wear off, but I came over here because there was something I needed to say to you."

He leaned back and looked at her straight on. The fear and uncertainty etched on her face tugged at his gut. Almost fifty years ago, even though he wasn't aware of it, he'd healed her broken heart; and today, he was the source of her heartbreak all over again.

"I understand your fear, Ma, and I hope you can understand mine." He took her hands in his and held them on his knees. "But one thing will not change. You might not have brought me into this world, but you're the one who has seen me through it. Motherhood isn't defined by giving birth. Motherhood is defined by the nurturing, the educating, and the loving you give a child."

As tears streamed down her face, Daniel felt the heat in his own eyes.

"You —" Emotion sucked the breath from his lungs, making it difficult to speak. He gave himself a few seconds for the air to return, then continued.

"You *are* my mother," he said emphatically, tightening his grip on her hands. "Those letters in the crate may hold the secrets of love and war, but our hearts, Ma," he said taking one of her hands and splaying her palm on his chest, "our hearts hold no secrets. You've always loved me, and I'll always love you. No matter what else I may learn, there's a part of my heart that will always be grateful for you."

He kissed her forehead, then hugged her while she sobbed against his shoulder. He allowed her a few minutes of emotional release, then drew back.

"I'd like to take you back to the house for dinner with Liz, Liam, Mora, and me," he said. "There's something I'd like to do, and I want you there to help me through it."

She nodded. "Give me a minute to splash some water on me face."

"Why? You don't want to look as bad as I do right now?" he joked.

She smiled, but Daniel could tell it was forced. Her shoulders sagged, and she looked emotionally and physically spent as she left the room. He guessed harboring a secret this big for all these years would take its toll.

He picked up the photos she'd been looking at. Most of them he'd seen many times before, but now he looked at them with new understanding. Now he knew the heartbreak and fear behind those smiles. He knew there was more to this baby than what people could see on the surface. And, he wondered if someday he'd get the chance to find the family members Annie and John Patrick had been seeking when they died.

"I'm ready," his mother said from the doorway, her coat already on.

He set down the pictures and joined her, walking her to his car.

A few blocks later, Daniel pulled into his driveway. They hadn't spoken for minutes, both lost in their own thoughts.

Liam came out the door and was at the passenger side of the car before Daniel had even gotten out of his side.

"Nana," Liam said as he opened her door, "let me help you so you don't slip on the snow." He assisted her from the seat and into the house, with Daniel close behind.

After Liz and Mora greeted her, Daniel and his mother removed their coats.

"There's something I'd like us all to do before dinner," Daniel said, putting one hand on Liz's back and the other on his mother's to guide them. "Is the box still in the kitchen?"

"Yes," Liz said. "We left everything there. Mora and Liam set the dining room table, instead."

"Good. You four go in the dining room, and I'll be right in."

They veered to the right as he continued into the kitchen. He went to the cupboard above the stove and took a box of matches from the top shelf. Then he retrieved the menorah and candles from the kitchen table and carried them into the dining room.

He held them out to Mora. "Just because I was raised Catholic, it doesn't mean I can't learn about the other part of my heritage. I hope you'll teach me."

"What would you like me to do?" she asked, taking the menorah and setting it on the table.

"Teach us how this is done. Let's light the candles together," he said. "Can we do that?"

"Um, okay," she said, setting them in the holders right to left. "Like I said earlier, today is the eighth day of Hanukkah, so the last candle would have been lit last night, but I guess these are special circumstances, so we can break tradition this one time."

Tradition. Daniel smiled. The word reminded him of the musical *Fiddler on the Roof*. The theme was about tradition. It's what unified families. In this time of uncertainty, he desperately wanted something to unify them. He didn't understand this tradition that he now knew was part of his roots, and even if he made the choice of not practicing it, understanding it was just as important.

"The candles will be lit left to right," she explained. "Who would you like to do the lighting?"

"All of us," Daniel responded. "I want each of you to light two candles with me, starting with Ma, then Liz, then you, Mora, and I'd like to light the final two with Liam."

His mother stepped to him. "Okay, what next?"

"I'd like to recite the blessings, first," Mora said. "At home we do it in Hebrew, but I can do it in English tonight."

Not knowing what else to do, Daniel bowed his head, and the others followed suit. When Mora finished, she picked up the blue candle from where she'd placed it in the center, and highest spot, of the menorah.

Daniel removed a match from the box and lit the candle, then took it from Mora. He held it toward his mother.

"Put your hand around mine, Ma," he said.

She did as he requested, then Mora guided them to the left, to the first candle. They lit it and moved on to the second one. With those two lit, Liz took his mother's place next to him, and the two of them lit the next two.

Mora continued the sequence with him, then he turned to Liam.

"Your turn, Son," Daniel said.

Liam stepped next to Daniel, and after a moment's hesitation, also took hold of the candle. The flame flickered a little higher with the movement, and Daniel glanced to Liam to see if he had also noticed. Their eyes met, then both shifted their attention to the candle. They tipped the Shamash candle toward the unlit candles, then once they were lit, Daniel replaced the blue candle in the middle holder.

Daniel looked at Mora. "What did you say about the meaning of the symbols on the dreidel?"

"It means a great miracle happened there," she repeated.

"Miracle," Daniel mumbled. He continued staring at the menorah as he put one arm around Liz and the other around his mother. A moment later, he felt Liam's arm cross Liz's back so his hand could settle on Daniel's shoulder.

Relief cascaded through Daniel's body. Through some miracle his family would survive this uncertainty. From his vantage point, he could see the crate of letters in the den. It was appropriate that they had referred to the letters as the secrets of love and war.

Those were the past. How to navigate his family's blended future had been put into his hands. He was determined that the miracle of love would win.

ABOUT THE AUTHOR

Laurie Gifford Adams was born and raised in the Finger Lakes of western NY, lived in Connecticut for 28 years, and then moved back to the Finger Lakes in 2011. She and her husband, Jim, live in their dream home on a small farm with their canine "child", Mollie, and two horses, Sasha and Lacey.

Laurie and Jim have two adult children, Carrie Beth and Nick, and a daughter-in-law, Amy.

Laurie taught middle school English and directed musicals in Glastonbury, CT for 26 years. Now, she works in alumni relations at her first college alma mater, Keuka College.

In addition to writing, Laurie loves to do anything outdoors: horseback riding, kayaking, gardening, playing sports, and soaking up nature. She also loves photography, and particularly enjoys nature photography.

facebook.com/lauriegiffordadamsauthor

twitter.com/LaurieGAdams

amazon.com/author/adamslaurie

Made in the USA
Middletown, DE
10 July 2019